The Columbarium

Emily Gallo

The Columbarium is a real place, a designated landmark at One Lorraine Court in San Francisco. A man named Emmitt Watson helped bring it back from a state of disrepair in the 1980's. He works there still and calls himself a caretaker/historian. Reports of his accomplishments and the beauty and history of the building are what inspired me, but Jed and all of the characters in this novel, living or dead, and their personal stories, as well as the businesses and events depicted, are entirely fictitious and imagined. Any resemblance to actual events, locales, or persons, living or dead, is entirely coincidental and unintentional.

Cover photographs by Andy Beetley-Hagler and Emily Gallo.

The author may be reached at ecegallo@gmail.com
http://emilygallo.blogspot.com/

ISBN-13: 978-1507591154
The Columbarium Copyright 2015 © by Emily Gallo

With much appreciation to my dear friend Tommy Sherwood for introducing me to the San Francisco Columbarium

To my husband David for helping me pull this story together and then watching me change it a million times

And my son Chris and daughter Eva just because

Also by Emily Gallo

Venice Beach – a novel

PROLOGUE

"White Night! White Night! Everyone to the pavilion right away! Your lives are in danger!" Was this the real thing or another one of his cruel jokes, the ones he called rehearsals? We had been on our best behavior for the congressman and his entourage last night. We sang and danced and told them how much we loved being here and how wonderful father was. I asked my mother why she believed all this crap. She looked at me with vacant, fearful eyes but didn't answer. She just held my baby sister tight to her chest. When his voice came over the loudspeaker, we knew we had to go. She took my hand and we walked to the pavilion.

When we got there, it was obvious that this was not a rehearsal. Armed guards stood along the perimeter and people were running and shouting and crying. I let go of my mother's hand and told her I'd be back. I ran outside to see what was going on. I heard people saying the congressman and others were dead. People had tried to leave. The guards were rounding people up and pushing them inside the pavilion. I could hear words coming over the loudspeaker. "They took us and put us in chains. They robbed us of our land. We tried to find a new beginning but it's too late. Don't lay down with tears and agony. We must die with some dignity. Mother, mother, mother, mother, please. Mother, please, please, please. Don't do this. Lay down your life with your child, but don't do this." A boy screamed, "No!" and staggered out. He foamed at the mouth; his eyes popped out of his head. He fell face down and shook uncontrollably until his body shuddered one last time.

I had to find my mother and my sister. I ran inside to look for them. People screamed and sobbed while father's slurred words pleaded over the loudspeaker. My throat burned and I couldn't take a deep breath. It felt like the wind had been knocked out of me. I finally saw my mother. She was pounding on a nurse who was pulling my sister out of her arms. I watched the nurse open my baby sister's mouth and empty a syringe into it. I heard my mother scream "Noooo!" Then the nurse plunged the needle into my mother's arm. My chest was pounding. I felt like I would explode. I knew that I had to run or I, too, would be poisoned.

I was quick and small enough to dart through the line of guards without being noticed. Their eyes were focused on the adults. Once I got past them, I ran toward the jungle. The bushes scratched my arms and legs. My heart beat so fast I thought it would jump out of my body. I could barely swallow. Even my teeth throbbed. I gasped for breath but I didn't stop. I ran and hid, too scared to think about what was happening. I didn't know where to go. I just knew I had to get out

6

of there. I ran past the tarmac where the plane was parked. It was supposed to have taken off with the congressman and the defectors. There were people lying on the ground surrounding the plane. I saw someone with a gun and I kept running. The pounding in my chest got stronger and stronger. I thought I was having a heart attack.

I don't know how much time had passed or how far I had gone. When I couldn't hear the sounds of screaming and gunshots anymore, I slowed down. I was still having trouble breathing and my chest and back still hurt, but I was too scared to stop. Then I stumbled upon three others who had escaped and together we ran until night fell and we couldn't go another step.

1

IT HAD BEEN DUSK WHEN JED LEFT
LOS ANGELES. By the time he got to Ventura
where the 101 hugged the coast, all he could see
of the Pacific were the sudden bursts of white
foam as the waves tumbled toward the shore. It
didn't matter, though. He had spent the last few
years living on the boardwalk in Venice Beach
and he needed sleep more than he needed
picturesque scenery. He crumpled his jacket
into a ball and put it against the window of the
bus. He leaned his head into it and shut his
eyes. It did its job: a warm soft barrier between
him and the cold glass. He closed his eyes and
started practicing his breathing techniques.
Sleep never came easily. He had spent too many
nighttime hours having to be vigilant and had
learned to function on very little sleep. But it
also meant that sleep evaded him on those few

occasions when he felt safe and secure in his bedtime circumstances.

He had learned these breathing techniques when one of the boardwalk denizens had steered him to the Venice Buddhist Temple. They taught techniques called Pranayama as a vehicle for meditation, but Jed wasn't interested in that. He didn't care much for the spiritual benefits of the Buddhist religion, or any religion for that matter. He used the exercises purely to release tension. He didn't care much for the yoga part either. He just liked to walk.

The bus pulled into San Francisco just as the sun rose. It felt good to stand up and stretch his legs. He wasn't used to sitting for long periods of time. Most of his days had been spent walking on the beach or in the Santa Monica Mountains. He made his way through the throng of passengers standing by the bus, waiting for their suitcases. All he had was his well-worn yellow backpack. Clean clothing was easy enough to come by in thrift shops or the free stores at the homeless resource centers.

Jed was a tall, thin, muscular African-American. He was pushing fifty but easily looked fifteen years younger. His hair, cut short, was barely graying at the temples and his skin was smooth. He was one of those people who turned heads but not because of his physical attractiveness, although he was quite handsome. It was his air of mystery and aloofness that drew them in.

He had the stamina of a long-distance runner with a gait and demeanor that were slow and deliberate. He had anger issues, but he was never physically aggressive unless someone threw the first punch. When he did lose his temper he would walk for miles. That helped some to calm him. He didn't like to lose control, but it could happen a little too easily.

He hadn't been back to the Bay area for a number of years. He thought it would be a good place to hide and get the proverbial fresh start. He had already had several fresh starts, but this one was different. This one was imperative. This time he was running from the law.

It was typical San Francisco weather, foggy and cool. He walked through the skyscrapers of the financial district toward the Tenderloin. Watching the people in their Armani suits, rushing to get their next dollar, was a source of amusement at first, but he soon tired of the incessant car horns and cell phone conversations. He decided to go the rest of the way on Market Street where at least high-end clothing shops intermingled with Mini-marts generating a little more diversity in the pedestrians. When he reached the Tenderloin, the attire of the pedestrians changed to sweatshirts and polyester and the noise to drunken, solitary rants. The shop windows were boarded up and the doorways were littered with sleeping bodies and their belongings.

He got to Glide Memorial Church just before they locked the cafeteria doors. The inside of the building was typical of institutions: old, rundown and painted that dull light green. But it was also clean, warm and familiar. Breakfast had ended but they gave him a cup of coffee and some cold pancakes while they finished mopping the floor. He was glad that most of the others had finished eating. He wasn't big on making small talk. It always surprised him how pompous many of these derelicts could be.

He finished his meal, stopped off at the Free Store to get some clean clothes and got in line to use the showers. He had chosen a pair of clean khakis and a button down shirt so he was ready for a job interview should one materialize. It had been a while since he'd had a shower. He stood there a long time, hoping the warm water would wash away the fear and anguish of the last, several weeks, and tried to ignore the relentless knocking and yelling of the impatient men on line.

After his shower, he dressed and went upstairs. He passed a room where babies and toddlers played while their mothers were in the room next door marked "Parenting Classes." He turned a corner and came upon another room with a long row of computers and bookshelves. It was occupied by a group of teenagers who were surprisingly hard at work. Music filled the halls as he descended the stairs to the sanctuary where he saw a band and a choir rehearsing. The music was closer to rock and roll and blues, than to spiritual and gospel. It was far superior to the church choirs he remembered from his childhood.

He found the resource room and entered tentatively, not sure if he was ready for this new turn of events. He hadn't had a real job for several years. He had been living on the streets and washing dishes in a restaurant, getting paid under the table. But now he wanted something more reliable, something that gave his life some structure and purpose. It would still need to be somewhat under the radar, though.

A tall, stunning, multiracial woman approached him. She was impeccably dressed in understated business attire, totally out of place in this refuge for the homeless and destitute. She looked to be in her mid-forties because of her smooth coffee-colored skin, but her eyes had the look of an older weary soul, one that had seen its own share of anguish and sorrow.

"Can I help you?"

"I'm looking for housing and a job."

She smiled and motioned him to her desk that was piled high with papers and folders.

"Please . . . sit down. Would you like a cup of coffee?"

He gazed at her curiously. How many hundreds or thousands of people must walk in with the same request, yet she made the office seem like a regular employment agency, not a homeless shelter. "Yes. Black. No sugar."

She came back to the desk with two cups of coffee and handed one to Jed. "My name is Monica and I'm a social worker here at Glide. And you are?"

"Jed. Jed Gibbons."

"You're new here. I haven't seen you before."

"A lot of people must come through these doors. How do you remember?"

"I remember all of them." She smiled again. "Maybe not by name, but I remember their faces."

"That's impressive."

"I try. So, Jed, did you just arrive in San Francisco?"

"Just got off the bus."

"Where from?"

"South."

"The South like from Mississippi or from southern California?"

"Both."

"That must have been a long trip."

"This last trip was just from Los Angeles."

"Well as far as housing goes, the policy for getting a bed here ——"

Jed interrupted her. "No. I don't need a bed. I need a room. I have money."

"Oh, okay. I'm sorry. I didn't mean anything ——"

He interrupted again. "Do you know of an SRO hotel; a good, clean, sober one?"

She wrote some names down on a piece of paper and handed it to him. "Here are some places. I think they're what you are looking for."

"Thanks." He put the list in his pocket. "What about a job?"

"What kind of job?"

"Anything. I'm smart and capable and a hard worker."

Monica sat back in her chair and grinned at him. "And modest."

Jed smiled back and also relaxed into the back of his chair. "I've done a lot of different jobs in a lot of different places. I'm experienced in just about anything in construction or agriculture. I've worked in restaurants, on fishing boats, in manufacturing plants."

"And I bet you're very good at all of them." She winked at him and started to shuffle through some papers on her desk. "Actually, I think I have a perfect job for you. I just need to find his number. I'm afraid the information is buried at the bottom of the pile. The job has been open for quite awhile. Mr. Henshaw has had a hard time filling the position."

"Why?"

She intentionally ignored his question and continued pushing papers around. "Ah, here it is." She looked at the paper and then looked back up at Jed.

"Do you know what a columbarium is?"

"No, I don't believe I do."

She handed him the paper. "Call Mr. Henshaw. He needs a handyman."

Jed stared at her for a minute, a little perplexed. He finally spoke. "Okay, but are you going to tell me what a columbarium is?"

"I'll let Mr. Henshaw tell you, but I think this job will suit you."

He downed the remainder of his coffee, glanced down at the paper and rose, grabbing his backpack. "Thanks." He started to leave.

"You know, there's a lot going on here at Glide Church and we can always use volunteers."

"I am not a religious man."

"You don't have to be religious to volunteer." Monica handed him a pamphlet. "We are affiliated with the United Methodist Church but that's not what we're about. Our mission is ——"

Jed interrupted her, reading from the pamphlet: " *To create a radically, inclusive, just and loving community mobilized to alleviate suffering and break the cycles of poverty and marginalization.*" He looked up at her. "Nice sentiment."

"Our Sunday services are called celebrations. We have a terrific band and it's all about the music. Our pastor's sermons are nondenominational and our members and volunteers are too."

"I'll see after I get settled with a job and a place to live."

"Let me know how things turn out," she called after him as he walked out the door.

Jed walked around a ten-block radius of Glide but his search for a pay phone was fruitless. He went into a small grocery/liquor store and approached the counter. "Do you know where I can find a pay phone?"

A young man sat on a stool, his eyes glued to his cell phone while his fingers whizzed back and forth on the screen. "Nope," he said without looking up.

Jed hesitated a moment, hoping the young man would offer his phone. Not only did he not offer it, he seemed oblivious to the fact that Jed was standing there. Jed turned around and left, resigned to the fact that he would probably have to go back to Glide to use their phone. He was reluctant to face Monica again. He felt that she had more than a professional interest in him. That made him uncomfortable, although she was certainly an attractive woman.

Maybe he should go to the hotel first. He was sure there wouldn't be a phone in the room. It wouldn't be that kind of place. But maybe there would be one at the front desk and perhaps they would be a little more accommodating than the store clerk. He felt ridiculous at his immature reaction to a woman's attention. He went back to the church.

He knocked on the window of Monica's cubicle. She beamed when she saw him. "Did you talk to Mr. Henshaw?"

Jed shrugged his shoulders and smiled. "I couldn't find a pay phone."

"Pay phones are definitely few and far between these days."

"Do you have a phone that clients can use?"

"Yes, but why don't you use mine." She pushed the phone across the desk. "I have some copies to make. I can leave you alone to make the call." She gathered a file folder and left.

Jed took the paper out of his pocket and dialed the number. "Hello? Is this Mr. Henshaw? I understand you're looking for a handyman. Yes, I can do all that. Tomorrow? Sure. What's the address? Just a minute, I need to get a pen." He rummaged around the surface of Monica's desk and then opened the center drawer. He found a pen and wrote. "Got it. One Lorraine Court. Nine o'clock." He hung up and placed the pen back in the drawer. As he did, he noticed a pill container divided into the days of the week as well as morning, noon and night. Monica walked in just as he was closing the drawer. "I'm sorry. I needed a pen." He stood to give her the chair.

She sat down. "Did you reach him?"

"Yes I did. I have an appointment tomorrow." He glanced at the address. "Do you know where One Lorraine Court is?"

"It's off of Geary between Stanyan and Arguello in the Richmond District. I can look up how to get there on the muni system map for you."

"I like to walk. I'll find it."

She sat back in her chair and took a sip of coffee. "So what brings you to San Francisco?"

"I was born in Oakland, lived there until I was ten. I thought it might be time to return to my roots."

She smiled coyly. "Why do I think you're pulling my leg?"

He smiled back. "Okay. Maybe it's more like I needed to leave Los Angeles and this was where the bus was going."

"Somehow that sounds more like the truth." There was something about this man that fascinated her. He just didn't fit the usual profile of the people who needed Glide's services: addiction, mental illness, physical disabilities, just released from prison. He even seemed to have some money. She was curious why he needed to leave L.A., though. It didn't sound like it was a choice.

Jed wondered why he spoke so candidly to her. It wasn't like him to share any piece of himself, especially with a stranger. He liked her, though. And he trusted her. For most of his life he hadn't trusted anyone, not until he had met Finn in Venice. He had been a true friend. But then, it all fell apart. He started to leave. "Thanks for your help."

"It was nice meeting you, Jed. I hope you'll come back and volunteer. Will you let me know how it works out with the interview?"

"Uh, sure," he answered hesitantly.

She watched him leave and opened the drawer. She saw the pill container and stiffened. "Damn." She had forgotten to put it back in her purse after taking her morning dose. How could she be so careless? She had managed to keep it from everyone at work all this time, but not from a man she hoped to get to know better. This was the first time she had allowed herself to think about dating since the diagnosis. What was she thinking? A client? This was crazy. She tried to put Jed out of her mind by busying herself with routine paperwork, but she wasn't very successful.

Jed took the list of hotels out of his pocket as he walked down Taylor Street. He took a left on Eddy and threw the list into the trashcan on the corner. He didn't need a list. This part of San Francisco, the Tenderloin, had plenty of SRO hotels to choose from. He didn't care about how it looked. He just had some basic criteria: his own bathroom and a place where you paid by the week, not by the day or the hour.

He passed a couple of hotels where addicts shooting up occupied the doorways. He kept walking. He went inside another and before he got to the desk, he was accosted by a lady of the night asking if he wanted a quickie. He turned around without answering and continued his trek. He dismissed the next two because they only had shared bathrooms. When he walked into The Windsor, he saw a room off to the left that had an old RCA television and a couple of worn couches. Two elderly men were watching a quiz show. Maybe not exactly watching it, as they were both fast asleep, but they looked harmless. Jed went up to the desk where another elderly man sat watching his own personal TV. He had it turned to a baseball game.

"Do you have rooms with their own bath?"

"Yes, but you know we don't rent by the night."

"That's good. And I assume you don't rent by the hour either."

"Absolutely not sir!" the old man said emphatically. "This is not that kind of place!"

"Perfect. How much?"

"Two fifty a week."

Jed took out two hundred-dollar bills and a fifty and offered it to the man. "Is there tax?"

"It's included." The man put a piece of paper on the counter. "Write your name and next of kin."

"What if you don't have any next of kin?"

21

"You gotta write someone down cuz I need someone to call in case something happens to you."

Jed was silent. Who could he put down? It had been a long time since he'd had to fill out any kind of paperwork. Maybe he should write down Monica's name and Glide Church's phone number. He decided to write down Finn's name. He had left his cat with Finn and Mother was probably the closest he had to a next of kin. And anyway, at least he knew Finn's phone number. "You're not going to call him for anything unless I die or something. Right?"

The clerk narrowed his eyes and stared hard at Jed. "Why? Are you hiding something?"

"No, I would just prefer he doesn't know I'm here."

"Yeah, only if you're dead." Jed wrote down the information and handed the paper to the clerk who gave him a key in return. "Third floor on the right. Number 303."

Jed climbed the stairs and found the room at the end of the hall. It was sparse, of course: a single bed, a dresser, a table with one chair, a microwave and a tiny refrigerator. It was perfect.

He opened his backpack and took out his few belongings. He put two framed pictures on the dresser and draped a locket over one of them. That was the one of the woman with a young boy on her lap. They sat under a sign that said, "Those who do not remember the past are condemned to repeat it." The other picture was of a baby. It was the first time in a long time that he'd had a place to display the pictures, but he always carried them in his backpack. His clothes fit easily into one drawer of the dresser. He figured he'd buy more with his first paycheck. As for now, he had enough to wash one set while wearing the other.

He worried that he would have to fill out an application with his social security number and whether he would have to be fingerprinted for the job. But he was ahead of himself. He hadn't even had the interview yet. And if Monica was right and this job was so hard to fill, maybe he could get away with not doing all the usual stuff. Maybe he could get paid under the table.

He lay down and closed his eyes and thought about the last time he had slept on a real bed. He was exhausted and hungry, but he thought he'd just rest a bit before venturing out for some dinner. His mind went into overdrive, trying to piece together all that had happened in the last few months. But before he could get too wrapped up in his memories, he fell fast asleep.

2

JED AWOKE AND FIGURED THAT HE
HAD DOZED FOR A COUPLE OF HOURS
AND IT WAS PROBABLY DINNERTIME.
He would look for a McDonald's or some sort
of fast food place on Market Street. He needed
to buy an alarm clock or a watch so he wouldn't
be late for his appointment in the morning. It
had been ages since he had to be anywhere at a
specific time. He was used to being in public
places where there were clocks or people to ask.
Maybe there was a thrift shop nearby that was
still open.

He got out of bed and pulled up the
window shade. He was shocked to see that it
was actually starting to get light, not starting to
get dark. He must have been asleep for close to
twenty hours straight! Probably because it was
the first real bed he had slept in for a long time.
He showered, dressed in his one set of clean
clothes, and set off to find One Lorraine Court.

When he got downstairs, he saw the
same old man at the desk that had been there

when he checked in. The clerk had probably gone home for dinner and a few beers, watched television, slept, eaten breakfast and was now back on his stool. He looked up at the clock over the door and sure enough, it was seven-thirty. He didn't know how far it was to the columbarium, but he hoped the clerk could give him directions.

"Do you know where One Lorraine Court is?" Jed asked as he approached the desk.

The clerk didn't take his eyes off the small black and white television as he shook his head. "Nope."

"It's supposed to be off Geary and Anza between Stanyan and Arguello."

"Well then just go up Geary."

"And Geary is?"

"Walk up Mason to Geary. You can catch a bus there."

"Do you know how far it would be to walk?"

The old man finally looked up, annoyed. "Three, four miles - a long walk."

"Left or right on Geary."

"Left. Then left on Stanyan."

Jed figured it would take him about an hour to get there. He would skip breakfast until after the appointment. "Thanks." The old man nodded and went back to his television.

Jed had forgotten how chilly it was in San Francisco, especially in the morning. It had been many years since he'd been here, more like decades, and his memories were mixed. He had lived in Oakland in his early childhood years, but his mother had often taken him into the city after she had become active in The People's Temple. Those days had been happy and carefree. He had enjoyed accompanying her on the recruitment bus trips up and down the state. It was only after that, after the move to Guyana, that things got ugly and his life became a nightmare. He had managed to suppress it all for many years until the awful moment in the motel with Antoinette that brought up all those heinous memories.

The area was starting to look vaguely familiar. And then it dawned on him. The building was no longer there, but there was enough left of the rest of buildings on the block for him to remember. 1859 Geary Boulevard was now an empty lot, but it had once been the headquarters for The People's Temple. He felt his chest tighten and his throat burn so he picked up his pace. Walking hard and fast helped. He wished he was near the ocean or in the mountains, but it was easy to be invisible in the city. Soon his breathing calmed and stabilized and he started to look for a thrift shop. He couldn't take the time now, but maybe

26

on his way home. A bank sign blinked its neon numbers: first 8:05 and then 53°. He had plenty of time to buy a cup of coffee to drink while he walked.

When he got to Stanyan, he turned left and found himself in a residential neighborhood. The lawns were mowed and edged, the houses were neat and well cared for, the cars in the driveways were all late models. This was a middle-class area, which in San Francisco real estate prices meant the houses were in the million-dollar range. Since Jed didn't know what a columbarium was, he didn't know exactly what he was looking for. He did find a street sign that said Anza and then there was a sign with an arrow that said Columbarium.

Lorraine Court was on the right, off Anza, and when he made the turn, his mouth dropped. Looming straight ahead at the end of that short cul-de-sac stood a magnificent building behind a wrought iron fence. It looked like a planetarium or a coliseum. The walls were curved rather than set at right angles. Its domed roof was copper and most of the windows were stained glass.

The building and the grounds surrounding it, however, seemed to need more than just a handyman. They needed a gardener, a landscape designer, a painter, a carpenter, a stonemason and God only knows what else. No wonder they had had a hard time finding someone who fit the bill. He walked up to the gate and saw the sign: "Neptune Society Columbarium of San Francisco" and then it became totally clear to him why they couldn't fill the position. If the Neptune Society was involved, it had to do with cremation and ashes and death.

He went through the gate and explored the environs. The plants were dying with no hope of recovery. Around them grew what couldn't really be called grass. It was more like a few weeds sticking out of the dirt. It looked like a garbage dump. There were liquor bottles and soda cans, hypodermic needles and plastic bags: the litter of people just passing through. Then there were condom wrappers and tampon tubes, sleeping bags and eating utensils: the items left by people who had made the grounds of the columbarium their temporary home. There were also lumber scraps and broken glass, broken pipe and metal shards: the residue of construction that had long been abandoned.

But beyond all this debris, standing proudly in its midst, was an intricately adorned Victorian architectural masterpiece. Its stone walls were dirty and chipped, its windows were cracked and grimy, but there was no denying its exquisiteness. He heard footsteps behind him and a voice bellowed out, "Are you Jed?"

Jed turned around. "Yes."

A portly, bald-headed, kindly looking man in his fifties stood smiling in front of him. He looked like an accountant or a low level manager by his rumpled brown suit. He put his hand out to shake Jed's. "Nice to meet you. I'm Carl Henshaw. I guess you can see how much work there is to be done."

"Yes, I see."

"Most of our applicants were put off either by the amount of work to be done or by the idea of working in a columbarium. You have a problem with either of those?"

"No. But what is a columbarium?"

"You'll see. Are you capable of doing the work that's needed?"

"Yes."

"Good. Let's go inside and I'll show you around."

Mr. Henshaw unlocked the door and they entered the building. The inside was as Jed expected . . . stunning! The dome and several of the upper crescent-shaped stained glass windows were still intact. They were too high up to be damaged by the thugs who got a kick out of throwing rocks. The lower windows, however, were another story. Most of them were either broken or cracked.

The tile floor was covered with dirt, dust, broken glass and the droppings from the birds that had flown through the broken windows and the rats that had come through the broken tiles and floorboards. But when you looked through the spider webs and mold growing on the walls, it was still possible to admire the carvings and mosaics.

It was three stories high and built as a rotunda. The walls of all the floors were filled both horizontally and vertically with glass-door indentations of different sizes. They stood in the center of the main room and were surrounded by thousands of these niches. Jed noticed there were small rooms off the circle and the walls of these rooms were also covered from floor to ceiling with niches.

"It's quite an incredible place, eh?" Henshaw commented.

Jed was speechless. He walked up to one of the walls and peered inside the niches. There were many ordinary metal urns of brass or copper and there were some ceramic ones and wooden boxes. There were also glass and bronze urns, and some of the bigger ones had marble or quartz. It was quite an array. Some of the niches were stark with just the urns and perhaps a picture inside. Others, however, were ornately decorated with items that were obviously meaningful to those who knew the dead person as well as to the ones whose ashes were inside. There were war medals, or ribbons and prizes won in sports and other competitions. There were membership cards for various organizations and pictures of people, places and things.

But this was San Francisco. The city was synonymous with art, music, design, style, gays, beatniks, hippies, and carnival-like merriment and lunacy. Many niches, therefore, were decorated to reflect that San Francisco spirit. He read a few of the plaques underneath the niches and was quite impressed: Henry Haight, Harvey Milk, Chet Helms.

"Yes, it's quite something, " Jed finally said.

"When can you start?"

"Now."

"Great. I can give you my account number at the hardware store and then you go order whatever you need."

"Don't you want me to fill out some paperwork?"

"Nope. There's something about you, Jed. You're trustworthy. I can tell you're a good man."

Jed smiled. "And I'm willing to work here. And I can start right away."

Mr. Henshaw smiled back. "That too. There's an office in the back. There ought to be a pencil and paper in there and an extra set of keys."

Jed followed him out the back door. A short distance from the main rotunda was another building with just one story and two rooms. It was a grey cement rectangle, the size and shape of a singlewide mobile home. The office inside had its standard, institutional, metal desk. The cracked, Naugahyde swivel chair leaned back too far and had long ago lost its ability to go up and down. But more than that, there was a layer of dust over everything. It took him a few tries, but Mr. Henshaw finally got one of the desk drawers to open. He found a piece of paper and a pencil with a point and took a small notebook out of his pocket. He copied down an account number and gave the paper to Jed along with his business card.

"I should get some information about you." He stood silently, poised to write in the notebook and looked up at Jed inquisitively.

"What do you want to know?"

"Name, address, phone number, social security number so I can pay you."

"By the way, what is the pay?"

"What do you want?"

Jed was surprised there wasn't a set salary. "I don't know." He calculated in his head. The room was two hundred fifty a week. He added in some money for food and incidentals. "How's four hundred a week?"

"What? That's all?"

32

"I don't need much."

"I'll give you five hundred a week. Have some fun once in awhile."

Jed smiled to himself. It had been a long time since he'd had anything he could characterize as fun. "Okay. Five hundred will be fine. The name's Jed Gibbons. That's short for Jedidiah. I'm staying at The Windsor Hotel. I'm sorry but I don't know the phone number there, but you can look it up and then leave me a message if you need to talk to me."

He reached in his pocket and took out an old leather wallet. It was cracked and ripped but still usable. He handed Henshaw his social security card but felt a little uneasy about it. He feared being found, but he also knew that he had no choice if he was ever to do any kind of legitimate work.

Mr. Henshaw wrote the information in his book and put it back in his pocket. "There's a hardware store on Clement and Fourth. Give them the account number and my name and just tell them you're working on the columbarium. They'll fix you up with everything you'll need to get started."

"I don't have a truck. Or even a car."

"They'll deliver." Mr. Henshaw said as he handed over a ring of keys. "There's something about you, Jed." He shook his head.

"I can't explain it. Call it intuition. I think this is going to work well for both of us."

"Thanks for your vote of confidence." They shook hands and Mr. Henshaw left the office.

Jed took a handkerchief out of his pocket, brushed off the chair and sat down. Where and how should he begin? He thought about Mother, and smiled. She would have fit in well here. There was much to explore and many places to sleep. But he knew he had done the right thing leaving her in Los Angeles with Finn and quickly put her out of his mind. He went back to contemplating the immensity of the task ahead of him.

3

JED TRIED SEVERAL KEYS AND FOUND
THE ONE THAT LOCKED THE OFFICE.
He walked outside and made sure all the doors
of the columbarium were locked before
venturing out to Clement Street and the
hardware store. He hoped there'd be a thrift
shop on the way. He wanted that watch or
alarm clock, even though his hours would be his
own and no one else but him would notice or
even care what time he showed up or how long
he stayed. He picked up a trashcan that was
lying on its side and he placed it upright. A rat
scurried out of it and he jumped back, startled.
But then he had to laugh. It wasn't like he
hadn't been around rats and garbage before. He
had spent many nights dumpster-diving in
Venice Beach.

He crossed Geary at Arguello and went
the one block to Clement. He had made a short
list of immediate needs: cleaning supplies, a
ladder, a rake. But then he realized he should
have looked first. Those items might be there

already, hidden in some closet. He started to turn around and go back, but he was awfully hungry. He hadn't eaten anything for two days. He didn't have to be so careful with the remaining money from Finn's book. He had a job and a paycheck now. He looked up and down Clement but all he saw were restaurants with signs written in some Asian language: Thai, Japanese, Vietnamese and Korean. Finally he saw one that advertised food he recognized: won ton soup, chow mein, fried rice. He entered the restaurant, figuring he'd bring his lunch back to the columbarium to eat. Then he could take inventory and make a more complete list for the hardware store.

There were several elderly men sitting at tables. They slurped their food and spoke rapidly in Chinese. One man waited in line ahead of him while a tiny Chinese woman about eighty years old stood at the counter. She wore a San Francisco Giants warm-up jacket and a Giants baseball cap. On the counter in front of her was a metal *I Love Lucy* lunchbox and under her arm was a clipboard. She opened the lunchbox and took out an empty plastic container. She handed the container to the counterman who took it into the back kitchen.

Meanwhile, the man in front of Jed tapped his foot while his eyes darted nervously around the restaurant. He was clearly impatient and annoyed. He was White, about sixty, tall and thin, and obviously not a stranger to the gym. He seemed irritated with life in general, rather than just the fact that he had to wait for his lunch.

The counterman returned with the plastic container, now filled with noodles, and handed it to her. "Here, Rose." She put it in her *I Love Lucy* lunchbox along with a napkin and a pair of chopsticks wrapped in paper. It was one of those vintage metal lunchboxes and she struggled to close the clasp. It might have been because the latch was so old that it wouldn't line up correctly anymore, or perhaps she had arthritis in her fingers.

Jed stepped up to the counter. "Can I help you with that?"

Rose looked at him without smiling, but took her hands off the clasp to allow him to fasten it for her. "Thanks," she mumbled as she turned to leave.

Jed went back to his place in line. The impatient man approached the counter. "I need an empty cardboard take-out carton."

The counterman stared at him like he was crazy. "Huh?"

"I said I need an empty cardboard take-out carton!" His voice sounded loud and harsh.

"I heard you." The counterman glared back at him.

"I'll buy it."

"You can't do that," the counterman answered.

"Why not? I said I'd pay for it."

"Ten dollar."

"What? I could buy chow mein for half that and then the carton would be free!"

"Then buy chow mein."

"But I want the carton clean and empty!" He was yelling at this point, getting more and more agitated.

"Then pay ten dollar for clean carton!" The rest of the restaurant patrons had stopped trying to talk above the shouting match.

"Okay, chicken chow mein to go, hold the chow mein! Here's five dollars!"

"Five nineteen with tax." The counterman took a carton off a tall pile on a shelf behind him.

The man slapped a five-dollar bill and a quarter on the counter as he grabbed the carton and walked out in a huff. The patrons went back to their conversation as Jed stepped up for his turn.

"Five dollars is a pretty hefty price for an empty carton," Jed commented. The counterman was stone-faced; he didn't find it amusing. Jed gave up trying to make light of the situation. "Uh, okay, I'll take a number seven to go."

He sat down at one of the tables to wait for his food, contemplating the scene he had just witnessed. He wasn't sure which conversation had been more entertaining. Rose, with her heavy Chinese accent, using an antique lunchbox straight out of the pop culture of 1950's Americana or the silliness of the debate over a take out carton. He didn't blame the customer for being exasperated. It must have cost the restaurant owner a nickel, maybe a quarter. Was it because the guy was obviously gay? Was that why the counterman had been so stubborn and cantankerous?

"Number seven! Eight dollar twenty-two cent."

Jed was jolted out of his musings and went back to the counter. He gave the man a ten. "Keep the change."

The counterman looked at Jed warily. He wasn't used to a tip. This was not the kind of place that had a jar by the cash register. Jed smiled at him as he took the bag and left the restaurant.

When he got back to the columbarium office, he realized that it would have been a lot more sanitary to eat at the restaurant, but he had certainly dined in worse places than this grimy office. He cleaned the desk with his handkerchief and set out his meal. It was ridiculous that these three take-out cartons would be added to the garbage when he was finished and all that poor man wanted was one.

He finished his meal, threw out the containers, and started exploring. He searched every room and closet in both buildings for cleaning supplies. He decided to concentrate on the needs of the inside of the building. There wasn't much there. A couple of brooms and mops, a rake, a shovel: all of them old and falling apart. He should probably just get all new stuff. After all, this was a new beginning in many ways.

It took about an hour to inventory the place. It was getting late so he set out right away for Clement Street, glancing through the window of the Chinese restaurant as he passed. He saw the same old men sitting at the tables, but now they were playing mahjong instead of eating. He walked on a couple more blocks until he saw some old metal garbage cans on the sidewalk. There were brooms and mops sticking out, all of them withered and dirty from having sat in the San Francisco rain and fog for decades. The hardware store had a faded sign that said it was established in 1924 and when Jed entered the store, he felt like he had time-traveled back to that very year.

A young Black man sat at the counter cleaning his fingernails with a large rusty nail, oblivious to the group of elderly Black men standing around with cups of coffee. These men didn't look like they bought much; it seemed they just stood around talking about the good old days. Apparently this hardware store was a meeting place, much like a cafe in a hip urban area might be, or like a bar in a blue-collar ghetto or in a rural town. This neighborhood was none of those. It was pure middle class . . . an ordinary, nondescript, residential enclave.

As Jed approached the clerk, he heard the bell ring over the door and noticed the same agitated man who had been in the Chinese restaurant. He went straight to the back corner of the store, not acknowledging anyone and not greeted by the distracted clerk. Jed watched as he stood under an old, faded sign advertising Dutch Boy Pure White Lead Paint. Was this store so behind the times that they still sold lead paint? Hopefully it was just an old sign. The take-out carton man came back to the clerk with a dusty, dented can of acrylic spray paint and stood behind Jed.

"Why don't you go ahead of me. I have a long list," Jed motioned to him.

"Thanks," he said, taken aback by Jed's graciousness. He was used to being on the defensive and prepared to argue or confront. He shook the paint can as he approached the clerk. "So is this stuff still good?"

"And why wouldn't it be?" The clerk answered without raising his eyes.

"Isn't there an expiration date? It's probably been on the shelf for twenty years."

The clerk finally looked up and stared at him. "Do you want it or not?"

"Only if it's still good."

The clerk glared at him. "I'm sure it's still good."

"It better be." He reached into his pocket and took out a five-dollar bill. "Here!" He slapped the bill loudly on the counter.

"That will be $7.49," the clerk said.

"The price on the can says $4.49."

"That's the wrong price. It's gone up."

"But you have to sell it to me for the price on the label. That's the law." He was shouting now and the group of older men stopped talking. Jed suppressed a smile. This poor guy had the worst luck with retail clerks.

"There's no law that says I have to sell it to you at all," the clerk retorted. "Do you want it or not?"

"No! I'll get it somewhere else!" The man stormed out but immediately turned around and came back, threw another three dollars on the counter and grabbed the can. "Keep the damn change!"

The clerk took the money, put it in the cash register and went back to cleaning his nails.

"It's probably not a good idea to use that rusty nail," Jed said as he put the list on the counter. The clerk looked up at him disdainfully, but didn't answer. He just took the list and looked at it. "Mr. Henshaw said to put it on his account," Jed added and handed him the card with the account number.

"It'll take me awhile to get all this stuff together."

"That's okay. I'll put it together now if you can deliver it tomorrow morning."

"Where's it going?"

"The address is on the bottom."

The clerk glanced at the paper and then looked back at Jed suspiciously. "The columbarium?"

"Yes. Is that a problem?"

"No."

"I'll be there at nine. You can deliver it then." Jed went to the back of the store and started gathering together some cleaning and painting implements. He wondered if the clerk's resistance had been about having to make a delivery at all or about where the delivery was going. He brought a couple of loads of tools and equipment to the front of the store. There would be plenty of additions to the list later on. After he started working he would have a better idea of what he needed. The job was somewhat daunting, but he was eager to get started. It had

43

been awhile since he had worked at a full time job. And even longer since he'd had a job where he was his own boss and where he could actually utilize his talent and skills.

"Is this everything?" the clerk asked.

"It is for now. I need to talk to Mr. Henshaw about color before getting the paint. I'll get back to you on that. Did you copy down the account number? I need the card back."

The clerk put his rusty nail down and wrote down the account number, then handed the card back to Jed. The clerk started to transfer Jed's stuff to the back of the store. "Hey Willie, you want to make a few bucks?"

One of the older men looked up. "Sure. What'cha need?"

"Your brother still got a pick up?"

"Yeah."

"Bring it here tomorrow morning."

"What time?"

The clerk glanced at Jed. "Ten."

"I said nine." Jed turned to Willie. "Can you come earlier?"

"No, he'll be here at ten and deliver after that," the clerk answered.

A year ago, Jed would have had one of his fits and left, yelling at anyone standing near him. He felt his chest tighten and his muscles tense, but he took some deep breaths and used the guided imagery that had worked well for

44

him at the Buddhist Temple. He imagined himself walking along the beach and in the mountains. His body started to relax. He thought about the hours he spent in the rocking chair with the babies and how it had served as a calming influence. He missed it. He thought about Monica and smiled. He felt good. It had been a long time since he'd thought about being with a woman. "Okay. See you just after ten."

It was almost dark when he got back to the columbarium. There wasn't much to do until the delivery arrived so he locked up and started walking back to his hotel. He passed a Jewish deli on his route and decided to pick up a sandwich for dinner.

A group of elderly Jewish men played cards at a table. One of them got up and went behind the counter when Jed entered. "What can I get you?"

Jed studied the sandwich menu written on a chalkboard and turned around when the door opened. There was that same man who had been so agitated in both the Chinese restaurant and the hardware store. "Why don't you help him while I decide." Jed wanted to diffuse any possible altercation that might arise. So far, every store clerk had been less than helpful and this man had very little patience. He smiled at him, wondering if he should make a comment on how much they were running into each other. But he decided against it when the man barely acknowledged his smile.

"I need a jar of gefilte fish."

"What kind?"

"I don't care. Whatever's the cheapest, I guess."

"Jellied broth?"

"Fine!"

"Kosher?"

"I don't care! Just give me the first fucking jar you see!"

"No need to get so upset." The clerk took a jar off the shelf and placed it on the counter. The man threw down a five-dollar bill and grabbed the jar. "Do you want your change?" the deli owner yelled after him as he walked out. There was no answer as the door slammed shut. The deli owner shook his head at his cohorts at the table and they chuckled back. He turned to Jed. "Have you decided yet?"

"Pastrami on rye, lots of mustard." Jed sat down to wait for his sandwich.

The door to the deli opened and in shuffled a short, stout man, smoking a cigar. He had to be at least eighty-five. He wore a rumpled suit and a tie that looked like it had been stained by many cups of coffee. He had a fedora hat on his head and the top of a white handkerchief was visible sticking out of the upper pocket of his jacket. His outfit looked straight out of the 1940's. "Who's on first?" he announced as he walked in.

"What are you asking me for?" the deli owner answered.

"What's on second?"

"I don't know."

"No, I don't know's on third."

"I don't give a darn."

"No, that's the shortstop."

They both laughed. "Sam!" The men at the table welcomed the old man in unison. Jed listened as they spoke Yiddish to each other, captivated by their warm camaraderie. These men had probably been friends for fifty years and exchanged that same Abbott and Costello routine hundreds of times.

"Your sandwich is ready. You want a drink?"

"No thanks." Jed got up and went to the counter. "How much?"

"That'll be eight dollars and fifty-five cents." Jed gave him a ten-dollar bill and started to leave. "Here's your change."

"Keep it." Jed waved and left. He walked back to his room, stopping first at a liquor store to buy a beer. He wasn't much of a drinker, but he felt like there was reason to celebrate. He was actually lighthearted, not a familiar feeling for him.

4

JED WOKE UP AFTER ANOTHER LONG, DEEP SLEEP AND NOTICED BRIGHT SUN PEEKING THROUGH THE WINDOW SHADE. He jumped out of bed. He had probably passed two or three thrift shops on his way home, but had totally forgotten to buy an alarm clock. He showered and dressed quickly and ran down the stairs to the lobby. The clerk was half asleep, watching cartoons on his personal television. The lobby denizens, meanwhile, were fully asleep while the weather report blared out of the lobby television. Jed found it amusing that people who were probably not going to step outside today had the weather on.

"Can you tell me the time?" he asked the clerk who raised an eyelid just enough to glance at a clock on the wall. Jed got the message and looked across the room. It was eight o'clock, enough time to buy breakfast and still get there before the delivery. He walked out and made a mental note to buy the alarm clock on his way home. He picked up a couple of donuts and a large coffee and got to the columbarium before nine.

He unlocked the gate and the door to the office. He had already decided to start cleaning in there first. The main building was a wreck. It would be an overwhelming job and he wanted time to consider how he would attack it. The office was just a matter of elbow grease and a lot of perseverance. Cleaning and painting was all that was required. Any repairs would be minor ones. He winced at the amount of rat turds and spider webs he uncovered and coughed at the swirls of dust. He took out the old, beat-up broom and used it to fight through the webs. He soon heard the roar of a muffler-less, diesel engine and went outside to greet Willie and the delivery.

Willie had parked the truck at the gate and was looking in a window of the rotunda when Jed got to him. "What is this place anyway?" he asked.

"It's like an indoor cemetery for ashes rather than bodies," Jed answered.

"Really? No kidding. That's weird." Willie shuddered and shook his head.

"Would you mind driving the truck to the back building? We'll unload everything there."

"What's in the back building?" Willie asked with apprehension.

Jed smiled. "The office."

"Oh okay. Sure." He lumbered back to the truck and got in slowly. Everything Jed did he did quickly and efficiently. It was difficult for him to adjust to the slower timetables of others. That was why he liked working alone. Unfortunately, there were some jobs that took two people. He didn't know anyone else in San Francisco and he figured Willie could use the funds. He decided to ask him for his number, just in case.

They unloaded the truck or rather Jed unloaded the truck. Willie looked around the outside, exclaiming over and over about what a grueling job it was going to be. Jed had second thoughts about asking Willie for help. Then he remembered how Mr. Henshaw had said that it was hard to get people to work here. He would at least get the phone number. "Hey Willie, would you like to earn a few extra bucks?"

"Doing what?"

"Just helping me out sometimes; nothing hard."

"I don't know." Willie frowned as his eyes followed the perimeter of the grounds.

"Think about it. Give me your phone number and I'll call you when I need you. You can always say no when I call."

"Okay. But best to call the hardware store and leave me a message there."

He handed Willie a ten. "Thanks."

Willie's eyes lit up. He hadn't expected a tip. "Thanks. I guess I could handle working here." He shuffled back to his truck and tried to turn on the engine. It struggled as it let out puffs of smelly exhaust. After several tries it finally turned over and Willie drove off slowly. Jed decided to lock the gate behind him. There was definitely something eerie about working here and he wasn't sure why locking the gate made him feel better, but it did.

He went back into the office and immediately got to work moving furniture out of the way so he could scrub and paint. Before he moved the desk, he searched through the drawers and found a stained, yellowed pad and a stub of a pencil. He knew he'd be discovering things he needed as he went along. He also needed to find out what was expected of him. He wondered if Mr. Henshaw was in charge or just the go-between. He wasn't sure of his own role, either. And who owned this building? Was it private? Did it belong to the city or the county? Did he need some kind of building permits for renovation? He was sure it must be listed as an historical structure in San Francisco archives.

He started to feel a little dejected. Maybe this was going to be way too much for him to handle. He opened a file cabinet, hoping to find some information that would help. He took out a bunch of well-worn pamphlets from the Neptune Society and opened one. He had heard of them. He knew they had to do with cremation. Maybe they owned the building? Now he was getting a little paranoid. Should they be contacted? Would he do a bunch of work and then find out he needed to do it to their specifications? His anxiety level was rising rapidly. He wasn't cut out for jobs that required dealing with bureaucrats or working under other people's rules. He'd better give Mr. Henshaw a call before getting started.

He searched through his pockets and found Mr. Henshaw's phone number. Then he remembered all the trouble he'd had finding a pay phone. He knew there wouldn't be one here. Maybe he could go back to the hardware store and the clerk would let him use the phone. He could just see him saying no, though, just to be contrary. The Chinese restaurant was closer, but he didn't have high hopes that the clerk there would be any more accommodating. The Jewish deli was probably his best bet. At least the counterman had been pleasant. He was getting hungry anyway. Maybe if he bought a sandwich, the owner would let him use his phone. He locked up and started walking. He was aggravated that he had gotten so little done. He hated wasting time, but he knew he was doing the right thing calling Mr. Henshaw.

He got to the deli about half past eleven. The lunch rush hadn't started, if there was one. He walked inside and found the same group of old men playing pinochle. Sam looked up as he walked in and welcomed him as if he was one of the regulars. "Look who's back today. Shalom. Come. Sit down and schmooze." Jed looked behind him. Was he talking to him? "Yes, you, young fella."

Just then the deli owner came out from the back. "Well, hello again. Another pastrami sandwich?"

Jed was surprised that he remembered the sandwich he had ordered. Maybe they didn't get much business. "Uh, sure. Pastrami and a cup of coffee."

"For here or to go?"

Jed looked over at Sam and his buddies. Sam patted the chair next to him. Jed smiled and sat down. "I'll eat here."

"I'm Sam Cohen. This is Milton Kramer and that's Irving Eisenberg and that handsome guy behind the counter is Abe Levy."

"Nice to meet you all. I'm Jedidiah Gibbons."

"Well isn't that mashugana. Another nice biblical name."

"Mashugana?" Jed asked.

"You know . . . crazy."

The deli owner, Abe, put Jed's sandwich and coffee in front of him and went back to get the coffee pot to refill the others' cups. He placed the pot on the table after pouring and joined the group. "You new to the neighborhood or just passing through?" he asked Jed.

"I'm working here."

"Yeah? Where at?"

Jed took a bite of his sandwich to give himself time before answering. Should he tell them the truth? He swallowed and decided these guys would be a good group to try out his new job title on.

"The columbarium."

"They opened that place up again?" Sam asked.

"I'm cleaning it up; painting, fixing the windows, getting it ready to reopen I guess."

"How could they have closed it? There are people buried in there. They didn't let people come in and visit their relatives?" Milton asked.

"People could make appointments I think," said Sam. "But they weren't letting anybody new sign up for a niche."

"I doubt too many people want to go in there anyway. Oy vey, what a mess it became," Irving added.

"They probably ran out of money to keep it going," Milton said.

"Who owns it?" Abe asked.

"The Neptune Society," Jed answered.

Sam sat back in his chair, while the others bantered back and forth. They glanced at each other when it became apparent that Sam had stopped joining in the conversation. Jed studied their faces, trying to figure out what was going on.

Without Sam's input, the conversation stalled and the men seemed eager to get back to their pinochle game. Jed finished his sandwich quickly and turned to Abe. "Could I use your phone? It's a local call."

Abe stood up and took Jed's plate. "Follow me." They went behind the counter, through the swinging kitchen doors, into a tiny room. There was a desk piled high with papers in disarray. Abe found the phone after pushing the papers around, not even caring that half of them fell to the floor. "Here you go." He left the room.

Jed looked at the note and dialed Mr. Henshaw's phone number. He waited through several rings, picking up all the papers that had been knocked to the floor. He piled them neatly and was about to hang up when Mr. Henshaw finally answered. "Hello, this is Jed Gibbons. I have a few questions before I get started."

"Hello Jed. What's the problem?"

"No problem. I just need to know the parameters. You know, do I need permits before I do any work? Are there historical preservation rules that need to be followed? Who owns the building? Should I be talking to them?"

Mr. Henshaw chuckled. "Nobody's touched that building in years. Why don't you just do whatever you think and we'll worry about the rest later."

"I don't know, Mr. Henshaw. It doesn't seem ——"

Mr. Henshaw interrupted. "Really, Jed. As long as you don't change the original structure, that's all that matters. Painting and repairing won't be a problem."

"If you say so."

"And by the way, call me Carl, please. I have a feeling we're going to have a good, long relationship."

"Okay. Bye." Jed hung up and went back out to the dining area. "Thanks for the use of your phone."

Abe, Irving and Milton all mumbled good-bye, engrossed in their cards. Sam looked up at Jed. "So, do you go to the columbarium every day?"

"Every day, all day."

Sam nodded and smiled wanly. Jed left the deli and walked back to the columbarium with new tenacity and resolve. He even remembered to stop at the thrift shop. He opted for a watch instead of the alarm clock.

It was strange that time was now a factor in his life. Seldom in the past few years had he needed to be anyplace at any specific time. Actually, he didn't mind. He kind of liked it. Structure, routine, and purpose were not so bad.

Jed worked long hours for the next two days. He dusted and scrubbed the office and then painted it. He raked and cleaned up the outside creating piles that were divided into garden waste and garbage.

At the end of the second day, he decided to go back to the hardware store and look for Willie. He hoped he could get him to borrow his brother's truck again and remove the piles. His funds from Finn for the book interviews was running low, but he had enough to give Willie some money, pay for another week at the hotel, and eat frugally.

He had not formalized anything with Mr. Henshaw about how and when he would get paid so he decided to give him a call from the hardware store when he got there. Maybe the clerk would be more willing to let him use the phone, if he bought more. He had a much better idea, now, of what would be needed for the main building. If Willie could get the truck, it would be a good time to get another delivery.

He hadn't started on the main building yet because he wasn't sure that Mr. Henshaw knew what he was talking about. Could he really do whatever he wanted? He would just get some basic tools.

When he got to the hardware store, Willie and the clerk were both friendly and happy to be of help. Jed figured they didn't get much business. Anyone who had access to a vehicle would be shopping at the nearest Home Depot, rather than an overpriced store with outdated merchandise.

He called Mr. Henshaw who said he would stop by in a couple of days with his first paycheck. Jed realized he would probably have to open a bank account, something else he hadn't had in years. He worried about being in the system and being found, but he couldn't run forever. He hadn't done anything wrong and he had nothing to hide, but he didn't want to have to prove that to the Los Angeles police.

It was getting dark so he figured he'd just go back to his room. Willie said he would be there with the truck in the morning. Since he was going to be starting on the inside of the main building, it would be good to start fresh tomorrow. It was only about four thirty. What would he do all evening in his room after he ate dinner? He definitely couldn't see himself joining the men sitting in the lobby watching television. Maybe he'd get a book from the thrift store. The only books he had with him were the two that Finn had written. He'd read them both more than once and he didn't really want to think about Finn.

He thought about Monica and Glide Church. Maybe he would like to volunteer there after all. If not, maybe Monica could get him into a situation like he'd had in Venice rocking the babies. And then he got sad. There go those damn memories. He stopped himself before he went any further back than that, but he was already starting to get that feeling in his chest: the anxiety, the rage.

He made an abrupt U-turn and started walking west instead of east on Geary, remembering that Geary Blvd was a street that ended at the beach. He decided to take a left on Arguello and walk through Golden Gate Park. By the time he got to Ocean Beach and breathed in the salt air, he had pushed all those memories out of his mind and felt hopeful.

5

JED WOKE UP VERY EARLY THE NEXT MORNING. He hadn't needed the alarm on his new watch, but it was nice to know what time it was. He paid for another week at the hotel and stopped at a diner for breakfast. He knew that once he opened up the main building and started planning how to attack the job, he wouldn't stop for lunch. He ate a hearty eggs, bacon and home fries breakfast. He took another cup of coffee to go and got to the columbarium by nine.

He grabbed a broom from the office closet, admiring how clean and orderly the office looked, and then went outside. First he walked around the circumference of the building and appreciated the bareness of the outside grounds. He had filled the garbage bins with the trash and litter and all the dead plants were in piles waiting for Willie and his brother's pick-up. The landscaping could wait until he had done something with the main building.

He unlocked the door and walked inside cautiously. In many ways he was fearless, but rats and snakes still put him on edge. It was cold, damp, and dusty and he had to fight his way through the maze of spider webs, stepping over shards of broken glass and piles of animal excrement. There were birds flying in and out of the broken windows and rodents scurrying about the chipped tile floor. He set the ladder down and used the broom as a weapon, tearing away the webs as he walked throughout the building. Other than the windows and floor, it wasn't as bad as he'd originally thought. Elbow grease would take care of a lot of it. Repairing the windows and tiles would take skill and patience, but he had both.

By the time he got to the top floor of the rotunda, he had noticed that the niches varied in size as well as contents. Some of the larger ones were the sparsest with just a brass or copper urn inside. The smaller ones were more creative and extensive with their adornment. He glanced at his watch and saw that he'd wasted an hour enjoying his exploration of the niches. He needed to get going with the major cleaning. Willie was an hour late, but it didn't matter, as long as he got there some time today. He was only needed to get rid of the debris and deliver the next collection of tools.

By noon the spider webs were gone, the floors on each level were swept, and Jed had started dusting the outside of the niches. He hadn't been able to reach the top couple of rows, but Willie would be bringing a ladder in the next delivery. Where was he anyway? He went outside to see if Willie had arrived and saw him knocking on the office door.

"Hey Willie, over here."

Willie turned around and nodded to Jed. "Sorry I'm late. My brother needed his truck this morning."

"Let's unload it into the main building and then we need to get these piles out here into the truck bed."

"You know you're gonna need to pay for the dumping fee?"

"Do you know how much it will cost?"

"Nope."

"I don't suppose you could pay it and then let me know how much and I'll pay you back." Willie narrowed his eyes and looked at him long and hard. Jed got it. Willie was not about to front the money. "Well, do you have any idea?"

"Fifty bucks should cover it," Willie answered.

"Seems a bit steep. It's a pretty light load." Willie didn't answer and Jed just smiled and shook his head. He wasn't going to get anywhere arguing with him. "Fine. Let's get to work."

They dumped the branches and leaves into the truck bed and covered it with a tarp. Willie was breathing heavily after they were done and Jed wondered whether he would be much help if the work got more strenuous. At least he had a truck and he was somewhat reliable and he was definitely appreciative. That was obvious by the size of his grin when Jed handed him a hundred dollars. It only left him twenty bucks for meals until Mr. Henshaw got there with his paycheck. That wasn't much spending money in one of the most expensive cities in America.

After Willie left, Jed decided to finish what he started. He took the ladder and a couple of rags to the third story and started working on the top row of the niches. He wondered how much his paycheck would be and started fantasizing on what he might buy. A radio would be nice. He could listen to music while he worked. By the time he got down to the first floor, it was the middle of the afternoon. He was hungry but he wanted to finish before getting something to eat. It was easier to just pick up something on his way home. Anyway, the restaurants near his hotel were a lot cheaper than the ones near the columbarium.

He was halfway around the first level when he heard the front door open. It was Sam from the deli, shuffling in with his cane. "Hello? Anybody home?"

"I'm up here." Sam looked around, bewildered. "On the ladder," Jed added.

"Oh there you are, young man. Oy vey! Be careful! Don't fall! "

Jed got down to greet Sam. "What are you doing here?"

"Looking for the caretaker."

"There is no caretaker. I'm the only one here."

"Then you must be the caretaker."

"I'm just painting and cleaning."

"Doesn't that mean you're taking care of the place?"

Jed smiled. "I guess it does."

"So, Mr. Caretaker, I'd like to get some information."

"About what?"

"What do you mean about what? About this place."

"You mean what this place is?"

"No, I know what this place is. About renting or buying or whatever you do to get one of these . . . these what do you call them?"

"Niches. You'll have to call the Neptune Society."

"Can't you help me, Mr. Caretaker?"

64

Jed took Sam's arm. "Let's go to the office and see if we can find out some information."

"Thank you, Mr. Caretaker. You're a good man."

"Name's Jed."

Sam smiled. "I remember."

They started to walk together to the office, Sam hobbling with his cane and Jed walking ahead. He was a bit peeved at having to stop his work. He was used to a much faster pace and he wasn't used to walking with or waiting for other people. He unlocked the office and went inside to find those pamphlets about the Neptune Society. Sam was huffing and puffing when he got there. Jed pulled out a chair for him and he dropped into it. "Are you okay?" Jed asked.

"I used to be like you, always in a hurry, always rushing around. I hated getting old and having all these aches and pains. But then, I said to myself, this is mashugana. Why shouldn't I just appreciate the scenery; enjoy the gentle pace."

Jed sat down and smiled at him. "You're a wise man."

"No. I'm an old man. Wise comes with the territory."

Jed handed him the Neptune Society pamphlet. "There's a phone number you can call."

Sam opened the pamphlet and squinted at it. He handed it back to Jed. "I don't have my glasses. What does it say? When was it built and is it neo-classical architecture?"

"It was built in 1898," Jed read. "And yes, it is neo-classical. It says the architect, Cahill, was inspired by the Columbian Exposition of 1893 in Chicago."

"I thought so. Have you ever been to Chicago?"

"Several years ago."

"Nice city. We enjoyed visiting that Field Museum. That's all that's left of the Exposition, you know." Sam got lost in his thoughts for a moment. "So how much for one of these?"

"You'll have to ask the Neptune Society. Is the niche for yourself?"

"It's for both Sadie and me. Sadie's my wife of fifty-eight years. She's dying. Stage four cancer."

"I'm sorry, Sam."

Sam shook his head and sighed. "We've had a good life. Someone had to go first."

"Do you have children?"

"No children. Sadie had her garden. I had my job."

66

"Is she in the hospital?"

"No. She's home, thank God. There's a nurse with her, now. I try to get out every day for a couple of hours. Go play pinochle with the fellas."

Jed was quiet. His mind drifted into thoughts of Finn. It must be hard to watch your wife die, especially one that you've been married to for so long. At least Finn had his health and his daughter. He hoped Sam had a nurse he could trust, unlike Finn. He felt his chest tighten. He took long, deep, rhythmic breaths. Stay in the moment, learn to let go, clear the mind, be here now. And then he looked at Sam and remembered his advice: appreciate the scenery and enjoy the gentle pace.

Sam pulled himself up, leaning on his cane. "Well, I'd better get going. I need to water Sadie's tomatoes before it gets dark. She was a magician in her garden. Me? I'm not so good at it. But I want to keep it going as long as I can until . . ." His voice trailed off.

"Can I get you a cab?" Jed asked.

"No. I'll walk. It's strenuous but I need to do it."

"I certainly understand that. I need to walk too."

"I'll call this place – what did you call it? Neptune?"

"Yes. The Neptune Society."

"Okay. Thank you, Jed. You're a real mensch."

"I hope a mensch is a good word."

"It's an admirable person."

"Then thanks."

"You take care, Mr. Caretaker." Sam laughed at his own joke.

"You too, Sam."

Jed walked him out to the gate. This time he went slowly, staying next to Sam, enjoying the conversation. He watched him hobble down the street and then went back inside the main building to finish his dusting. He wanted to look forward, not backward. The title of Finn's book was wrong. Best to forget the past when you have one you want to forget.

6

IT WAS ONE OF THOSE CRISP CLEAR EVENINGS IN SAN FRANCISCO. The Giants had a home game and the downtown was crowded with their fans, as well as the usual business people and tourists. The weather at the stadium was a thousand times better than at Candlestick Park. It had always been so cold and windy there and the fog sometimes made it impossible to watch the game. Now that the stadium had moved downtown, Rose could be in the bleachers in an hour. She had to walk through Golden Gate Park to catch the MUNI, but she was a dynamo who walked quickly and she enjoyed it. When a game ran really late, she would even splurge for a cab. She could never do that from Candlestick. It would have cost a fortune. Of course, she was younger then and she had been fearless.

Tonight her beloved Giants were playing the Dodgers, their archrival from the early days when both teams played in New York. She left her flat about five o'clock so she'd have time to pick up dinner before settling into her seat. She wore her Giants warm up jacket and hat. She carried her *I Love Lucy* lunchbox in her hand and her Giants blanket under her arm. She stopped at the Chinese restaurant and got her regular take-out: chow mein and coca cola. The ushers never questioned her about bringing her lunchbox. Maybe they thought it was some new stylish handbag fad. They never even asked her to open it. An eighty-year-old Chinese lady was not about to blow up the stadium or shoot someone. Anyway, they knew her well and most of the ushers even knew her by name.

She arrived at the stadium before seven, got to her seat high up in the bleachers, and spread out her blanket. She opened her lunchbox and took out the food and drink, setting it on the bench beside her. Then she took out her chopsticks and napkin and began to eat dinner. She liked to finish before the game started so she could devote all her attention to working in the scorebook. She kept meticulous records and she had kept every scorebook since her first game in 1958, the year the Giants moved west from New York.

After she finished eating, she closed her lunchbox and took out an old transistor radio from her jacket pocket. She unraveled the earphones and put them in her ears. She tinkered with the dial until she found KNBR 680, and listened carefully so she could copy down the first lineups for each team. She wrote in perfect block letters and when she finished, she settled into her seat. She was ready for the first pitch.

She recorded every hit, RBI, strikeout, fielder's choice and error, just like she had for the past fifty-five years. She was up and down out of her seat throughout the game, cheering for her beloved Giants and also booing every time the Dodgers got a hit. She stayed seated when the game was over to finish filling out her scorebook. When everyone had left and the ushers had started cleaning up, she packed up her stuff and left. She liked to take her time. She had nothing special to get up for in the morning and she had always been a night owl. MUNI had a good night schedule from the stadium so she wasn't worried.

She walked quickly through the park after getting off the bus and got to the front door of her tenement building about midnight. She took out the key, fumbling a little in the dark. After climbing those famous San Francisco hills in the cold air that blanketed the city at night, and then the three flights to her apartment, she was glad to be home.

Rose's apartment was dark and tiny. The living room was sparsely furnished with an old, tattered, upholstered couch facing an ancient, twenty-six inch console television on legs. On the floor under the television was a VCR. The kitchen was barely big enough for one person to stand in, so the small Formica table and its two vinyl chairs were in the living room. Off of that was a closet-sized bedroom just big enough for a twin bed. It had a clothesline strung across with all her clothes hanging on it and a night table with two drawers.

One full wall of floor-to-ceiling bookcases dominated the living room, but there were no books in it. Instead it was filled with homemade videotapes with handwritten labels. There were a couple of shelves of Giants games and a couple of boxes marked "Scorebooks," but most of the tapes were old TV comedies. The labels were organized in alphabetical order by the name of the show. Besides *I Love Lucy* there were shelves for *The Honeymooners, Ozzie and Harriet, George Burns and Gracie Allen, Leave it to Beaver, Father Knows Best,* and an assortment of other shows from the fifties. It was as if this apartment was in a time warp.

Rose had worked for more than fifty years with many Chinese immigrants in a Mission District garment factory. She had worked long hours and was finally forced to retire when the factory closed. She never married, had few friends, and had outlived all the family members who had immigrated with her. She was a loner, though, who never complained as long as she had her beloved giants and her cherished television families.

7

JED WAS ON THE 3RD FLOOR WHEN
THE COLUMBARIUM DOOR OPENED
AND MR. HENSHAW ENTERED.

"Jed?"

"Up here. I'll be right down."

"I can't believe how great this place
looks!" Mr. Henshaw shouted. "You've done all
this in just the last few days? It's amazing!"

Jed came down the last flight of stairs,
wiping his hands on a rag. He even looked the
part, having found a pair of denim overalls and
a carpenter's apron at the thrift store. "There
really wasn't that much damage after cleaning
and removing the spider webs, just some
broken windows and a few floor tiles. I should
be done with the painting in a few days. Then
there are some small repairs and the outside
landscaping."

"You've done an incredible job! Can we
reopen for business hours soon?"

Jed wasn't sure how to react. Did that
mean he was out of a job after he did the

outside landscaping? He hadn't really thought about that: what would happen when they reopened for visitors every day? Was he just going to be on call for repairs? "Uh, I guess so."

Mr. Henshaw noticed the uncertainty in Jed's voice. "You'll still have a job here. I hope that's what you want."

Jed relaxed. "Absolutely."

"I don't think it would require too much. Just open and close and be available for questions. But most of these visitors want to be alone with their thoughts. They only come for a few minutes. You can just refer them to the Neptune Society if they want to get a niche. What do you say?"

"Okay. And I've already referred someone to the Neptune Society."

"Then you already know what to do." He handed Jed a check and asked, "Do you have a bank account?"

"Not yet."

"Will that be a problem?"

"I don't really know," Jed answered honestly.

"Do you want cash?"

"Might be best."

"I'll be back later with the cash. Thanks, Jed. Hours will be nine to five. Shall we open next week?"

"I guess that would work."

"Take time for lunch and close the place. Just post the hours somewhere. I can't wait to show the Neptune Society board what you've done. They'll probably come out to see it next week."

"Thanks, Mr. Henshaw."

"Carl."

Jed smiled and shook his hand. Mr. Henshaw left and Jed went back upstairs to finish the job. He was hungry but had run out of money so he'd have to wait until later when Carl came back with the cash. He certainly had gone much longer than this without money or food. He had barely started his painting when the door opened again. "Yoo Hoo Mr. Caretaker?" It was Sam.

"Just a minute. I'll be right there." Jed came off the ladder and down the stairs. "How's my man, Sam, doing today?"

"Oy vey iz mir. I've had better days."

"Is it Sadie?"

Sam smiled at Jed. "You remembered her name."

"Sure I did."

Sam shook his head. "Sadie's about the same. She just sleeps. All I can do is sit and wait and hope she feels no pain."

"Is she on medication?"

"Oh yes. Morphine. The nurse gives it to her." He sighed. "But I'm here to get my niche. I called the Neptune Society. They said I should come and pick one out. I should see what size I want. Then I should pay them."

"Okay. Let's go pick one out." Jed and Sam wandered around the building, checking out the empty ones. They decided on a larger size so Sam could join her when his time came. He wanted to be on the first floor. It was too difficult for him to climb the stairs. They found one next to a cowboy with a western themed niche. It had a belt buckle, a pair of spurs, a picture of a man on a horse, a 45rpm record of Gene Autry singing "Back in the Saddle Again," and a ceramic cowboy boot that was presumably the container for the ashes. On the other side there was a more conventional one with a metal urn and a few family pictures.

"This one." Sam pointed.

"I'll be right back." Jed went back to the office and returned with a post-it note pad and a pen. He wrote SADIE COHEN on the note and pasted it on the front glass door of the chosen niche.

"Okay. Now let's get some lunch. It's on me."

"Oh no, you don't need to —"

Sam interrupted. "Yes I do. I want to thank you for taking care of me. You're a good caretaker."

Jed started to protest again but he was awfully hungry. "Okay. Let me wash up."

"Go ahead." Sam glanced around and saw a chair. "I'll just sit here and wait for you." He hobbled over and sat down while Jed went back to the office. Jed returned, having changed out of his paint-spattered overalls into a clean shirt and jeans. "Okay with you if we go to the deli?" Sam asked.

"Of course." Jed took Sam's arm to help him out of the chair and they walked out arm in arm.

All the regulars were at the deli and they treated Jed as one of their own. They schooled Jed in familiar Yiddish expressions and Jewish customs. There was plenty of laughter at the Jewish jokes they shared with him as they ate.

After Abe cleared away the plates, the decks of cards came out. "All right, Jed," Milton said as he dealt the cards. "Now you need to learn how to play Pinochle."

"Wait a minute. There are only face cards here. Are you palming?" Jed asked, feigning suspicion.

"That's right. You better watch out for Milton. You can't trust him," Irving laughed.

"You only use nines, tens and the face cards. And there are only forty-eight cards instead of fifty-two. You play on Sam's team. He'll show you the ropes," Abe said.

"Do you know how to play bridge?" Sam asked.

"Not really."

"You ever play card games where you bid and take tricks?"

Jed laughed. "I think you may have your work cut out for you, trying to teach me how to play pinochle. I'd better just watch for now."

The games were fast and competitive and Jed was shocked when he saw that two hours had passed. "This was fun but I need to go. I have work to do." He was about to leave when the man who had bought the jar of gefilte fish walked in.

"Hello." Abe the owner greeted him. "More gefilte fish?"

"No. I still have the other one, but she wants a jar of kosher pickles too."

"Sounds like she has a bun in the oven," Abe joked as he took a jar of pickles off the shelf.

"Now that would be a kick!" the man laughed. "Goldie's sixty-five and very sick."

The deli got quiet. "I'm sorry young man," Sam said. "Is she your wife?"

"No. Just a friend . . . a good friend." He turned to Abe. "How much for the pickles?"

"Let's call it four bucks with the tax." He handed Abe the money and left.

"Why'd you ask if it was for his wife? Don't you know he's a faygala?" Milton asked.

"How can you possibly know that?" Sam responded.

"Oh come on, Sam. You can't tell?"

"What's a faygala?" Jed asked.

"A homosexual," Irving answered.

"Oh. Thanks for lunch, Sam, but I need to get back to work. And thank you all for teaching me pinochle."

"You come back and we'll beat the pants off your tuches," Irving teased.

"I'll try hard not to be too much of a schlemiel," Jed responded. They all laughed.

"Keep practicing those Yiddish words we taught you," Irving yelled after him.

"I will," Jed answered as he walked out the door. "Thanks for schmoozing with me."

Irving turned to Sam. "Nice boy."

"Man!" Sam snapped back. "He's a grown man, Irv! Don't be such a zhlub!"

Irving was taken aback. He had never seen Sam show annoyance or lose his patience. Sadie's impending death must be weighing on him. "I'm sorry, Sam," Irving said. He wasn't just apologizing for calling Jed "boy." It was more that he was sympathetic for Sam's sad predicament.

"Want some more coffee, Sam? Maybe a little rugalah?" Abe asked.

"No. I need to get home." Sam stood and teetered a minute on his cane.

"Let me call you a cab," Abe offered.

"I'm alright. I want to walk," he said as he hobbled out.

Jed hurried back to the columbarium. He didn't know what time Mr. Henshaw would be back with his money and he didn't want to miss him. Also, he wanted to finish the painting so he could get started on the outside. That was going to be a lot more difficult for him. He had never done landscaping before. He was usually the grunt worker, the lackey. He knew he'd be able to figure out how, though, as soon as he put his mind to it.

He changed back into his painting overalls and climbed back up the ladder. He had barely gotten started when he heard someone enter the building. "Hello?"

"I'll be right there," Jed answered. He was annoyed at being interrupted again, but he got down and walked down the stairs. He was taken aback when he saw who it was but then smiled broadly. "Well, hello."

It was the man from the deli who had bought the pickles and the gefilte fish. "You work here?"

"I do. I'm Jed."

"Small world. I'm Tony."

"We do seem to be running into each other quite a bit."

"So are you the guy who runs this place?"

"No. I'm the painter/handyman . . . uh caretaker I guess. But maybe I can help you."

"I need a niche."

Jed was surprised. Tony seemed to be a healthy man, about the same age as himself. It seemed a bit early to be worrying about such things. "For you?"

"No, it's for Goldie. That's why I bought all that stuff. She has explicit instructions on what she wants me to put in her niche."

"The pickles? The jar of fish?"

"Yes. And she wants her ashes in a take out carton, you know, like you get from a Chinese restaurant?"

"So that's why you wanted it without the chow mein?"

"You were there too?"

"Yes, and I was also at the hardware store when you bought the acrylic. Now I see. It was to spray the cardboard carton."

"That's right."

"You'll need to pick out a niche, but then you have to contact the Neptune Society to pay for it." Jed was getting to be an old hand at this.

82

"Okay. How do I choose one?"

"I'll show you ones that are still empty. Maybe you should pick one that's next to someone suitable. You know, someone Goldie would have appreciated."

"That sounds like as good a reason as any."

Jed led him around, pointing out the empty ones and showing Tony their neighbors. "Did Goldie like musicals?"

"Does," Tony corrected him. "She hasn't croaked yet."

"Oh, I'm sorry."

"No problem. But yes. She loves Broadway shows."

"I think I have just the place, then." Tony followed Jed up to the second floor and halfway around the rotunda. "This here is Frank La Rue."

Tony peered into Frank's niche. Inside was a picture of a man dressed in tails and a top hat, holding a wooden dummy on his lap, also dressed in a tuxedo, a miniature version of Frank. There was a faded newspaper headline taped to the picture that read *Frank LaRue and his Variety Show Light up San Francisco*. Also in the niche were a champagne glass, a New Years Eve noisemaker, and a kazoo.

"It looks like Frank was quite an entertainer," Tony said.

"Yes, I think so. These niches reflect the personalities and the history of the people inside. They tell their own story."

Tony smiled and nodded his head. "This is perfect. Goldie and Frank will get along well. It looks like he loved to party. Goldie did too before she became agoraphobic."

"Agoraphobic?"

"Goldie is afraid to leave her house and has been for many years."

"That must be difficult."

"I shop for her and take care of any business she has on the outside."

"That's very kind of you." Tony shrugged and looked away. "I'll be right back," Jed said as he walked to the staircase. He returned with a post-it note pad and a Neptune Society flyer. "What's Goldie's last name?"

"Klein."

Jed wrote GOLDIE KLEIN on the post-it and pasted it on the niche. "It's her apartment now."

"Apartment?"

"I think I'll call them apartments rather than niches. Niche is such a cold, impersonal word. These are people's homes, in a way. The smaller ones can be called "apartments" and the larger ones "condos." What do you think?"

"I think that's a nice idea."

Jed handed Tony the pamphlet. "This is who you have to call to make the arrangements for payment. When the time comes, I'll have it sparkling and I'll help you decorate."

"Thanks." Tony started to walk away and turned around to shake Jed's hand. "You've made this process very comfortable. I appreciate that."

Jed smiled. "Glad to help." Tony left and Jed went back to the third floor and climbed up the ladder to paint before it got too dark.

8

GOLDIE LIVED IN AN OLD, ORNATE
VICTORIAN IN THE MISSION. Much like
the columbarium, it had once been a beautiful
house but had long seen better days. Goldie had
bought it in the seventies when her income was
at its height. The late sixties and early seventies
had been like a dot-com boom for pot dealers.
At that time she didn't have the knowledge or
skill to maintain the house. By the time the
eighties rolled around, she didn't have the desire
or motivation. Some drug dealers never touch
what they sell. Goldie, however, was not one of
those. She liked to taste before she bought, and
she liked to "test" the high before she sold.
Potheads may not get violent or aggressive, but
they do tend toward laziness and apathy.

She had smoked cigarettes most of her
life and now had emphysema as well as heart
problems. Her agoraphobia had started about
fifteen years ago, even before she'd gotten too
sick to leave the house. And besides that, she
was morbidly obese. Smoking pot is hunger

inducing and since she never got any exercise, the pounds piled on.

She had grown up in a stereotypical New York Jewish family, but she was a child of the sixties and had moved to San Francisco after graduating from college in the heyday of the counterculture. She knew many of the musicians and artists of that era before they were famous and was their supplier as well as their friend. The Hells Angels were also part of that community in those days and they always kept a vigilant eye out.

She had lived in a commune for a while in the early sixties and it was there that she met her business partner. Together they had launched one of the largest marijuana dealing conglomerates of the times. They didn't want to compete with the dealers of mind-altering drugs like Owsley Stanley who was the king of manufacturing and selling LSD.

They stayed away from hard drugs like heroin so as not to compete with the large crime families like the mafia. They stuck to pot. They became a worldwide organization, picking up the weed in Mexico, Asia and South America and selling it all over the country. Goldie became very rich but she was also generous. She gave away lots of money to several "hippie" causes.

Tony had met her in the early seventies and became one of her couriers. After the arrest of her partner in the eighties, she scaled back quite a bit and chose Tony to be her right-hand man. She then became a "fag hag," hanging out almost exclusively with gay men. The term used to be thought of as an insult, but Goldie was way ahead of her time, and wore the title as a badge of honor. Her entourage and couriers were all gay men, as well as most of her customers. She felt they were more honest and trustworthy than women and straight men. Although she was a strong believer in the feminist movement, she never felt that she belonged with that group. And somehow, she had never been arrested after almost fifty years of dealing.

Tony had his own apartment, but he spent most of his time at Goldie's, especially now that she was sick. He didn't like to leave her alone, so whenever one of their regular buyers or sellers stopped by, he would ask them to stay with her so he could go out and run errands. He was not quite as trusting as Goldie and he always hid the merchandise when he left the house.

Tony had to make one more stop after leaving Jed and the columbarium. Jake had promised to keep Goldie company until he got back. She loved Chinese food and that was one of the things she still craved. He bought some egg drop soup and lo mein for Goldie because they would be easy to swallow. He just bought some spare ribs and eggrolls for himself. He knew he'd end up finishing what Goldie left. It was the total opposite of what their dinners used to be like. Goldie had been the one who ate everything in sight and Tony would be watching his weight almost to the point of anorexia. But those days were long gone, even for Tony. He had lost interest in going to the gym every day and trolling the bars and clubs.

It was dark by the time he climbed the stairs to Goldie's house. He heard the television blaring when he opened the front door with his key. She was sitting in her recliner watching the "Antiques Roadshow", wearing a red and yellow flowered Hawaiian muumuu. She was quite obese even though she was eating much less. Her frizzy hair was still red although it had started to go gray, and it had not been brushed or shampooed in several days.

There were several empty Chinese food cartons on the table next to her. Also on the table was an ashtray holding a smoldering cigarette as well as several old butts. An oxygen tank on wheels was next to her chair and she was holding the nosepiece in her hand as she puffed on the cigarette.

"Goldie! What are you doing! You can't smoke next to the oxygen tank! You'll blow up the house!" He dropped his bag of food and ran to take the cigarette out of her hand. He then rolled the oxygen tank into the next room. "I've told you that a million times! And where's Jake? He's supposed to be here with you," he called from the next room.

"Oh Tony, don't be such a nudge," Goldie answered as Tony re-entered the living room. "Jake went to get a friend of his who wants to buy some stuff."

"He was supposed to stay with you and make sure you didn't destroy yourself and your house!"

"He said he'd be right back."

"Where did you get this food? I bought you some."

"Jake got it for me earlier. He ended up eating most of it though so I'm ready for what you bought me."

Tony sighed loudly. "Damn Jake! I thought he'd –"

Goldie interrupted him. "I'm still here aren't I? And so is the house. So stop your kvetching and bring me my dinner. And by the way, did you get everything?"

"Yes, but it wasn't easy."

"Oh honey, nothing worth getting is ever easy." Goldie smiled.

Tony went into the kitchen and came back with plates, bowls, serving spoons and chopsticks. He cleared off the cartons that were on the table and set up the new ones. They ate in silence, Goldie watching her show and Tony looking around the room. It was an eclectic room, decorated with expensive antiques and art interspersed with psychedelic posters and kitschy knickknacks.

Now that he had taken care of the niche, rather the apartment, at the columbarium, he knew he had to bring up her will. She hadn't spoken to her family in many years. They were not too pleased with her choice of careers. But he knew that they needed to be notified and he wasn't sure if she wanted anything to go to them. He was about to bring it up when he glanced over and noticed that she was asleep in the chair. He cleared the table and picked up the magazines and newspapers piled up around her chair.

He was just finishing the dishes when Jake walked in with a young, attractive, muscular man. They were both dressed in tight jeans and white sleeveless muscle shirts. Jake was only about thirty, but the other man barely looked of legal age. "Where's that glamorous girl of mine," Jake called as he walked into the living room, gesturing effeminately and swishing as he walked. Tony figured he was performing for his teen-age "chicken." Jake was not usually such a queen.

"You were supposed to stay with Goldie! She almost blew up the house!" Tony exploded at Jake.

"Oh Tony dahling, calm down. You always get yourself into such a dither."

"You're back," Goldie said as she opened her eyes.

Jake turned to Goldie and air-kissed her on both sides of her face. "What do you have for my new twinkie here, Luke, to keep us elevated and firm?"

"It's in my bedroom, Tony. You know where."

Tony turned around in disgust and went to the bedroom. He returned with a brown paper bag and handed it to Goldie. She pushed herself slowly out of the recliner and hobbled over to a large, hand-carved, antique table on the other side of the room, hanging on to furniture as she went. Tony rushed over to help, but she pushed him away. It took several minutes but she finally got there and sat down on an old carved velvet side chair. "Come and sit," she said.

Jake and Luke sat down eagerly in two other velvet chairs while Tony sauntered over to the table. He stood next to Goldie's chair. She opened the paper bag and took out a saran-wrapped block of hashish about the size of a tennis ball. She placed the block on the table and unwrapped it. She reached into the pocket of her dress, took out a penknife, and carefully sliced off a small chunk from an edge. She then reached into her other pocket and took out a pipe and a lighter. She placed the small chunk into the bowl of the pipe, lit it, and took a long toke. She closed her eyes and leaned back in her chair, holding the pipe out in front of her.

Tony took the cue and removed the pipe from her hand. He sat down on the last remaining chair at the table and took his own long toke. He then passed it to Jake who took his own puff and then he handed it to Luke. After Luke finished, the three men passed it around again, coughing mildly after each toke. Tony finally placed it down on the table in front of Goldie. All this was done slowly, silently and ceremoniously and soon all four of them had retreated into their own separate worlds.

Jake finally broke the silence. "This stuff is heavenly. Where did you get it?"

Goldie opened her eyes. "Taye brought it back from the Caribbean."

Jake glanced at Luke and nodded to him. Luke reached in his pocket and took out a wad of bills. He handed it to Jake while Goldie cut off a larger piece of hash. Tony went to the kitchen while Jake presented the wad to Goldie who put it in her cleavage. Tony returned with a digital scale the size of a cell phone, a piece of aluminum foil, and a zip-lock sandwich bag. He weighed the chunk of hash, wrapped it in the foil and put it in the plastic bag. He rewrapped the large block before putting it back in the paper bag. This was obviously a ritual they were all used to. Jake and Luke stood up to leave and Tony brought the large block back to the bedroom.

"Well, tell Taye he needs to take more vacations," Jake said as he and Luke left.

Tony came out of the bedroom with a ledger book. He handed it to Goldie with a pen and she wrote in the book slowly and methodically. When she was done, Tony took the book and pen, brought it back to the bedroom and returned to the table. He sat down across from Goldie and they continued smoking the rest of the hash in silence, lost in their own thoughts.

Suddenly Goldie had a coughing fit and Tony jumped up to get the oxygen canister. He wheeled it to the table and removed all the smoking paraphernalia. He unraveled the plastic tubing and handed it to her. She placed the nosepiece into her nostrils and he sat down next to her. He took her hand and held it until she calmed down and her breathing became steady and regular. Throughout this process, she looked deeply into his eyes, first with fear and then with gratitude.

9

JED WOKE UP WAY BEFORE THE ALARM WENT OFF. He was eager to make his list of gardening tools and plants and then be at the hardware store when it opened. He didn't know what time Willie got there but he wanted him to deliver everything as soon as possible. He was anxious to get started on the landscaping now that the columbarium was open regular hours.

He had some new ideas for the inside of the building, but first impressions were important and the outside was still bare and bleak. People should feel a sense of serenity before entering the building. Flowers and shrubbery would generate that calming effect. He also wanted to place more benches, tiles, and artwork around the outside to make a kind of peace garden.

He'd learned about agriculture during his years at Jonestown, but he had never planned the gardens. He just did what he was told. He never lacked confidence, though; he could learn anything he wanted to attempt. His mother had shown him that. All those clichéd adages she had taught him stuck with him. Some were religious ones, but many were just old folk tales. The basic lesson was always the same. You can do anything if you put your mind to it. You just have to work hard and persevere.

He stopped and bought coffee and an egg sandwich to go and ate and drank as he walked. The sun was shining brightly by the time he got to the columbarium. It was still early, only about seven thirty

He had an hour and a half before the doors opened to the public. He went to the office for his clipboard and a pen and then started inspecting the outside.

He didn't know much about specific flowers and plants, but he had found a book at the thrift shop. It was an old edition of The Sunset Western Garden Book. They came out with a new one every couple of years so there were plenty of old editions lying around the dusty shelves of thrift shops and used bookstores. He had taken notes on what grew well in the climate and what kind of care they needed. He wasn't sure about the decorative part. That wasn't his strongpoint. He wanted to get a few things in, though, and then he could worry about beautification.

Rose had also gotten up very early. She had a frozen waffle and a coke for breakfast, as she did every day. It was always takeout from the Chinese restaurant for dinner. Lunch was leftovers from the previous night's dinner. She didn't cook anymore. She didn't want to pay for the gas. Electricity was part of the rent so she could use the toaster as much as she wanted.

She watched a couple of her favorite *I Love Lucy* reruns: the grape stomping and the candy making. She laughed as much as if she was watching them for the first time. She washed her plate and threw away the coke can, grabbed her Giants warm-up jacket and her TV Guide, and went downstairs to catch the bus. After a half-hour bus ride, she power-walked up the hill and got to the columbarium just as Jed was coming around the corner to unlock the gate. He had cleaned one of the benches so at least there was a place to sit outside.

Rose watched him unlock the gate silently, noticing the sign that had the hours posted. "Can I help you?" Jed asked her.

She looked at her watch. "It only eight thirty. I wait til nine when door open." She walked to the bench, sat down, and opened her TV Guide.

"You can go in now, if you like. I'll let you in."

"You in charge?"

"Not exactly. But I'm the only one here right now."

"Then you in charge."

"I guess I am then. Do you want to come in?"

"No. I wait til nine when it open."

"Suit yourself." He went inside and made sure the niches were all dusted and the floor was swept.

Rose continued to read her TV Guide and was checking her watch when Sam hobbled over and sat down next to her. "Do you have the time?" he asked.

"Eight forty-five. Fifteen minute til open."

Sam looked at the front door and noticed it was ajar. "But the door is open."

"I know but sign say nine."

"Is the caretaker inside?"

"Yeah."

"Then why don't you go in?"

"I wait til nine when it open."

Sam shrugged his shoulders. "Okay. I'll wait too."

"No matter to me," Rose replied.

"So, you're a Giants fan, I see?"

"Fifty-six years. Since they move here."

"Ah, I have you beat, young lady. I was at the New York Polo Grounds in 1954 for the greatest catch of all time by Willie Mays. Now that was baseball."

"It great catch. He great center fielder."

"I don't think anyone has ever been able to duplicate that over the shoulder catch."

"Nope," Rose agreed.

"And the Polo Grounds was one of the longest fields with that crazy little alcove. Did you ever go there?"

"No. Never been to New York. Always here in San Francisco. But see it on TV."

"He was quite a player."

"Yeah. But Willie Mays not bring championship to San Francisco."

"I don't blame Mays. You do?" Sam asked.

"Not only his fault."

"I don't blame McCovey for losing the '62 series either. Baseball's not a one-man sport. It's teamwork."

"There plenty of teamwork that game. Giants hit more than Yankees – more doubles, more triples, more homers."

"Yep. They had a higher team batting average and a lower earned run average. But they still lost the series to the Yankees."

"If only McCovey hit ball a little higher." Rose shook her head.

"Richardson would just have had to jump a little and he still probably would have caught it."

"McCovey say that pitch by Ralph Terry hardest ball he ever hit."

"Ralph Terry wasn't that great a pitcher."

"He off his game. Series take too long. Too much rain."

"I think that series lasted thirteen days. Rained in both cities. It took the Giants twenty-eight more years to win the National League pennant."

"Yep. 1989. Earthquake make them lose that series."

Sam laughed. "You think it's the weather and natural disasters that caused them to lose? What about the other teams? How come the weather didn't affect the Yankees in 1962 or Oakland in 1989?"

Rose checked her watch and stood abruptly. She'd had enough of Sam bashing her beloved Giants. "It time." She walked quickly into the Columbarium while Sam stood slowly and plodded after her.

She marveled at the inside of the building. Her jaw dropped as she looked up at the domed ceiling and the tiers of niches. She walked around the first floor, touching the ornate carvings on the walls, peering into the stained glass windows, stepping gingerly on the symmetrical mosaic tile designs on the floor. She was so taken with the building interior that she didn't even look inside any of the niches.

"Quite a place, isn't it?" Jed said. Rose gasped, jolted out of her trance. "I'm sorry. I didn't mean to startle you."

"I never go inside here before. Only seen outside."

"Well, the outside of the building is quite spectacular too. And I'm just starting to work on the landscaping so the grounds will soon reflect the beauty of the building."

"You fix this up?"

"Well, I cleaned and painted and did some repairs."

"You do good job."

"Thanks. Are you here visiting someone or looking to get an apartment?"

"Apartment? I no need apartment. I have apartment where I live."

"Apartments are what I call the niches. I think it's more fitting. I call the bigger ones condos."

"Oh. Well, I looking for apartment for me. Someone told me this good place to be. Don't want to go into cold ground."

"Your friend steered you well. You can put whatever you want into your apartment with your ashes. I can show you around some of the other ones so you can see what they've done to decorate theirs, if you'd like."

"That be nice." Jed led her around the building, showing her some of the more interesting and ornate ones. He showed her Phil's, the outdoorsman, with his miniature snowshoes and rabbit pelt, his ashes inside a Boy Scout canteen. He showed her Joanne's with the old-fashioned antique wooden wall phone and the ceramic rabbit that held her ashes. There was Margie's with her Beatles memorabilia, her ashes inside a guitar, and Matthew and Ben's with their dual painted Elvis jars. He showed her the famous ones: Harvey Milk's and Chet Helms' and even Mr. Haight's and Mr. Ashbury's. He also showed her the more sedate ones with just a photograph or two and a common brass urn.

"Why this one have lights?" Rose asked pointing to one bordered by a string of colored Christmas lights.

"This here is Charlie. His wife said he loved to decorate their house for Christmas. She said they had the prettiest one in the neighborhood."

"I like this place. It cheerful."

"Thank you. I'm glad you feel that way. Would you like the phone number for the Neptune Society so you can reserve one for yourself?"

"No. I not ready yet." She started to exit through the front door and turned around sharply. "What your name?"

"Jed. And yours?"

"Rose."

"Nice to meet you, Rose."

Meanwhile Sam had been sitting patiently, waiting for Jed to finish with Rose. His eyes were closed, trying to visualize what he wanted to put in Sadie's niche, and he soon dozed off. Jed saw him as he walked by with a ladder and long handled Webmaster. He set up the ladder quietly and climbed up to remove the spider webs. Sam opened his eyes and noticed Jed up on the ladder. "Why are you always so high up, Mr. Caretaker? Are you a luftmensh? You should get your head out of the clouds."

"How ya doin', Sam?" He climbed down the ladder and they shook hands. "What's a luftmensh?"

"A dreamer."

Jed nodded his head. "Maybe so. Did you get the information from the Neptune Society yet?"

"Not yet, but Sadie and I have been talking."

"Talking? Did she wake up?"

"No. But I still pretend we're talking." Jed didn't know how to answer. "You know,

Jews aren't supposed to be cremated, but my bubbala thinks that's bupkes," Sam went on.

"Bupkes?"

"Crap."

"Why is it that Jews aren't supposed to be cremated?"

"They say the soul needs time to separate from the body. It's also the memory of the holocaust . . . all those burning bodies, you know. So, that's why I'm here. My bubbala wanted to be cremated, though."

"Did you decide on what size?"

"I guess the bigger one so we can be together. Didn't you call that a condo?"

"Yes, a condo. She's a smart girl, that Sadie, choosing a condo."

"Such a salesman, you are."

Jed became alarmed. "I didn't mean to steer you into the more expensive one."

"I'm just kidding. I know you don't get a commission. So how do I sign up for this?"

"Wasn't there a form to fill out in the information you got?"

"I guess there was one. I don't know. Sadie always used to take care of this kind of stuff."

"Bring the papers in and I'll help you."

"Thank you, Mr. Big Shot Jed the Caretaker. I'll be back with the papers."

"You take care, Sam." Sam left and Jed went back to removing spider webs. He had enjoyed his time showing Rose around. He liked that he knew the people in the niches and he wanted to learn more about them. People seemed to enjoy sharing stories about their departed loved ones. That surprised him because he had never been one to reminisce. It had never brought him comfort.

But he thought about Finn and the book they had written together. Finn had actually written it, but he had interviewed and paid him for his help. Thoughts of Finn turned to thoughts of Mother and all that had happened in Venice. Mother was his cat but because of the murder investigation, he had to leave Venice hurriedly. He didn't know what would happen, so he left her with Finn and Finn's daughter, Kate. They loved her too, and he knew they would give her a better home.

His chest tightened and his teeth clenched and he knew that this line of thought was going to result in some emotions that he didn't want to feel. It was time to walk.

10

GOLDIE WAS LYING ON THE COUCH, HOOKED UP TO THE OXYGEN TANK. Her eyes were closed and she seemed to drift in and out of consciousness. Tony sat at the table with Jake and Luke. They had a bag of marijuana in front of them. Tony rolled a joint and they passed it around, each of them taking long, deep tokes.

Luke exhaled loudly and contentedly. "Wow. Goldie certainly comes through with the best stuff."

"Is this from Taye and his Caribbean friends?" Jake asked.

"I'm not sure. It might be from her East L.A. connection," Tony replied.

"Well, we'll take it, wherever it came from." Jake handed Tony the money and took the bag. Tony brought the money into the bedroom and returned with a framed picture of two naked men, their bodies entwined.

"Goldie wanted me to give her best customers something special. She said you always liked this painting."

Jake was truly surprised. "I can't believe she remembered that."

"She gave me the list awhile ago, before she got this sick."

Jake took the painting. "Did the doctors say how long she has?"

"She's already lasted longer than they thought she would."

Jake hugged Tony and then leaned over Goldie and gave her a kiss on her lips. "Thanks, darling." He took Luke's hand and they left.

Tony went to the bedroom and returned with the ledger book. He sat at the table and entered the sale of the weed to Jake.

"Tony?" Goldie asked in a raspy voice.

"I'm right here, Goldie. I'm recording a transaction in the book. Jake was here with that new squeeze of his. They bought an ounce."

"I need to get to the bathroom." Tony helped Goldie up and walked her to the bathroom. When they got inside, he lowered her down on the toilet and left the room. He shut the door and stood quietly just outside.

"Tony, I didn't make it. I'm sorry," she called from behind the door, starting to cry. "This is awful for you. You have to clean me up like a baby."

Tony went in and took a washcloth off the shelf. "It's okay. Don't worry about it." He cleaned her up and brought her back to the couch. The walk to and from the bathroom wore her out and she gasped for breath. He hooked her up to the oxygen machine and held her hand until she could breathe more easily. He had gotten to be quite adept at his nursing duties. He didn't even bat an eyelash at the clean up job. She was his family. And he was hers. Her family had pretty much disowned her after they stumbled upon her career choice. As for Tony, he had never really had a family.

He had plenty of practice in the eighties and nineties when almost all his friends were lost to AIDS. He had done a lot of caregiving then. In those days many gay men had never come out to their families until they got sick. And heartbreakingly, many of these families rejected their children so the gay community took over. He himself had been diagnosed HIV positive, but it had never turned into full-blown AIDS. In those days, it was considered miraculous that anyone could be HIV positive and not get AIDS. Doctors had interviewed him and examined him and written articles about him. But now it wasn't as much of a rarity and the epidemic itself had been controlled by the introduction of AZT and other drugs.

He glanced over at Goldie and saw that she had fallen back to sleep. He closed his eyes and curled up on the couch to take a nap. He was almost asleep when the front door opened.

"Honey, I'm home," a lilting voice sang out. An extremely handsome, willowy, Black man entered carrying a large suitcase in one hand and a tote bag strapped to his shoulder. He was supple and graceful, light on his feet, dancing noiselessly into the room. He was dressed in a black silk shirt open to the waist and tight designer jeans and his hair was braided in tight cornrows that emphasized his high cheekbones and the beautiful structure of his face. He was one of those people you couldn't take your eyes off of, men and women alike, gay or straight. He oozed sexuality and allure. And it was impossible to guess his age.

Tony opened his eyes and sat up. "Hi Taye. Where are you coming from now?"

"I've been trotting the globe, my friend. I have found me a very wealthy sugar daddy who is quite addicted to cocaine and even more so to me. Couldn't ask for a better deal." He set down his bags and took Goldie's hand. "Hey, love. How's my favorite fruit fly doing?"

She opened her eyes and smiled. "Taye, darling. Did you bring me the stuff?"

"Of course I did. Would I let you down?"

"I knew you wouldn't. You and Tony never let me down."

"Now don't start getting all mushy and sappy."

"Why not? If I can't be sentimental when I'm dying, then when the hell can I be?"

"Where's the stuff?" Tony asked.

"Keep your shorts on. It's in my bag." Taye unzipped the suitcase and took out a large teddy bear, the size of a toddler. It took up the whole inside of the bag.

"Cute touch."

"It works every time. It was Goldie's idea. Everyone appreciates a good daddy bringing a gift home to the kiddo."

"Somehow I don't think you could fool anyone that you have a missus and a bunch of kids waiting for you at home," Tony laughed. "How do you open it up? Just with a knife?"

"Yes, unless you want to keep the teddy bear for some reason," Taye teased.

Tony got a knife from the kitchen and took the teddy bear from Taye. He sat down at the table and cut the bear open along the seam. Out fell a vacuum-sealed, plastic bag. "Is it the same stuff you got last time from the Grenadines?"

"One and the same. It should sell for top dollar. Just tell people is comes from the Lesser Antilles Islands. It sounds exotic."

Tony shrugged and looked over at Goldie, but her eyes were closed. "Did you get it from the usual St. Vincent connection?"

"Yes. He adores me. He even threw in some extra just for me."

Tony wrote in the ledger. "I'll ask Goldie what she wants to charge when she wakes up."

"You know, that book's worth a lot more than anything else in this house."

Tony glared at Taye as if to say "Don't you dare think like that" but said nothing. The look was enough to shut Taye up and Tony changed the subject. "I got her signed up for an apartment today."

"Say what?"

"It's what they call the niches at the columbarium."

Taye laughs. "That's crazy."

"I thought it was kind of sweet."

"You would. You and Goldie are such sentimental saps."

"You should see how some of them are decorated."

"Oh yeah? Decorated how? Diamond-studded urns? Jewelry?"

"There are probably some like that, I guess. I just noticed a few of them near her on the second floor."

"Well I'll have to go size up Goldie's final resting place. We certainly don't want her apartment to bring down property values."

Tony rolled his eyes. "No, Taye, we certainly wouldn't want to do that."

Taye grinned smugly at Tony. "Well, my sugar daddy is waiting downstairs in his limo. Call me when Goldie wakes up and we can discuss the terms." Taye danced out and Tony curled back up on the sofa.

11

THE DISTANCE BETWEEN THE HOME THAT SAM AND SADIE HAD SHARED FOR MORE THAN FIFTY YEARS AND THE COLUMBARIUM WAS ABOUT TEN CITY BLOCKS. For most people the half-mile walk would take about fifteen or twenty minutes. For Jed or Tony or Rose, who were always in a hurry and impatient to get where they were going, it would take half that. For Sam, however, it would be more like forty-five minutes to an hour. He would usually stop on the way home for groceries. He needed to buy them every day because he couldn't carry too much at a time. If he needed large or heavy items, he had to ask the nurse to pick them up on her way to work.

There was a neighborhood grocery just a few doors down from the deli and they were both on the way home from the columbarium. Sam's world that had once included trips to other countries for his import business had narrowed to that ten- block radius. He stopped at the deli first for a bagel and a couple of games of pinochle, then went to the grocery store and got home in the middle of the afternoon.

Sam's house was compact; pink stucco, middle class box with a one-car garage and a small plot of land in front and back. His 1986 Pontiac Bonneville was still in the garage, although he hadn't driven in thirteen years. It took up the whole garage, making it impossible to get to anything else stored in there. But he refused to get rid of it. He still hoped to drive again. He didn't want to admit the loss of youth and freedom that selling the car would represent.

The walkway leading up to the front door was lined with purple impatiens and yellow roses. Sadie was the neighborhood guru when it came to gardening. In her backyard was her famous vegetable garden that she had nurtured and cherished. It had taken the place of the child she and Sam never had. Her crowning glory was her tomatoes, difficult to grow in San Francisco's cool, wet climate. Sadie's plants thrived and produced copiously every single year.

Sam was worn out by the time he got home. It had started to cloud up and the fog would be rolling in anytime. The nurse's hours were eight to five so she'd be leaving soon. He

115

didn't usually stay out this long but he needed a break from watching his beloved Sadie deteriorate. She was at the point where she could be woken up to eat, but she would barely open her mouth and didn't appear to recognize Sam. But she did seem to take comfort from his presence. He knew it wouldn't be long before she would slip into a coma.

He opened the front door and the sounds and smells of terminal illness permeated the house. The living room was packed tightly with dark, upholstered furniture, large heavy lamps and mahogany tables with intricate lace doilies. They held fifty years of knick-knacks and vases for Sadie's precious flowers. But now the vases were empty and the lamps were unlit. Sadie was bedridden and Sam spent little time in the living room.

He entered their bedroom where a hospital bed had replaced the double bed they had slept in for twenty-five years. Sam now slept in a narrow cot provided by the medical supply company free of charge. Bedrooms had to be stripped down to suit the needs of the elderly population and the companies used various methods to get business. The free cot worked for Sam. He could have slept in the other bedroom that had been his office before he retired, but he needed to be close at night in case she needed something. She no longer got

116

out of bed, though. The nurse took care of changing the diapers and she pretty much slept through the night, although fitfully.

"Has she been sleeping long?" Sam asked the nurse who sat on a chair next to the bed, reading a magazine. Her knitting was in a basket on the floor next to the chair.

"All day. The new medication makes her very tired."

"But no more pain, right?"

"I'm sure she's feeling no pain. I can wake her up now, if you like. It's almost time for her to try and eat something."

"No, no. Let her sleep. I'll go fix her something."

"I can do it, Sam. You stay with her."

"No, I'll do it. I'll heat up some matzo ball soup. Oh, how she loves that with sliced tomatoes from her own plants."

"I don't think she can handle the tomatoes or the matzo balls, Sam. Maybe just the broth."

"You know my Sadie grew the best tomatoes in San Francisco. Such a green thumb she had."

The nurse got up and put her hand on Sam's shoulder. "You stay here with her. I'll get some broth for Sadie and soup for us."

Sam nodded and sat gently on the bed. He took Sadie's hand and kissed it. "I'm watering the plants and trying to keep them going for you, my bubbala."

The nurse returned with a tray holding three bowls: two with matzo balls and carrots and one with just broth. She set the tray on the night table. "I should change her and clean her up before she eats."

Sam shook his head and padded out of the bedroom. He went into the kitchen and then out the back door to the garden. There wasn't much left but a couple of tomato plants and a withered vine with cucumbers that had long turned yellow. He found a fairly large tomato and gently picked it. He went back into the kitchen and put the tomato on a plate. He got a knife out of the drawer and cut the tomato into several thick slices and then brought the plate back into the bedroom. The back of the bed was more upright now and Sadie was sitting up, but her head drooped to the side.

The nurse handed Sam the spoon and bowl of plain broth and took the plate of sliced tomatoes. She knew he wanted to feed Sadie. It was one of very few things left that he could still do for her. "Sam, I'm going to talk to the hospice program about assigning a night nurse too."

"Why? I can handle the nights."

"We have to increase the medication so she will need to be monitored twenty-four hours a day. We want her to be comfortable."

Sam shook his head. "No. No night nurse." He bit his lip as he fed Sadie tiny spoonfuls of broth. It was as if she ate purely to allow Sam the feeling that he was being helpful. She knew him well, even in her semi comatose state.

The nurse took a bite of tomato and added, "These are by far the best tomatoes I've ever had."

Sam smiled but remained quiet and intent on feeding Sadie. After she had a few tastes of soup, though, she kept her mouth closed and looked into his eyes as if pleading with him to stop. He got it and put the bowl and spoon away. He dabbed at her mouth gently with a tissue and Sadie closed her eyes and settled back into her pillow. Meanwhile, Sam took his bowl of soup and he and the nurse ate in silence.

12

JED HAD GONE TO THE HARDWARE STORE AND HAD ASKED WILLIE IF HE COULD BORROW HIS BROTHER'S TRUCK AGAIN. He needed more supplies for the outside landscaping. The truck wasn't available until the following morning though, so Jed went back to work on the inside for the rest of the afternoon.

He was polishing the brass frames around the glass doors to the niches when Mr. Henshaw showed up. "You've really brought this place back to life," he said and then laughed. "Now that's an oxymoron."

Jed laughed with him. "Maybe that should be an advertising slogan."

"Yes! You can bury your loved ones at the columbarium and bring them back to life! I love it!"

"I'm glad to see you, Mr. Henshaw. I have a few questions."

"Call me Carl, please."

"Okay, Carl. I'm just not sure how much leeway I have. It seems that someone should be authorizing the work I'm doing. What if it goes against some law or rule or something?"

"Well, I'm here for two reasons, Jed. One is to give you your paycheck." He handed Jed a wad of cash. "The second is to tell you that members of the board of the Neptune Society would like to come tomorrow and see what you've done."

"But I haven't finished the outside. And there is still work to be done in here."

"They know you haven't finished yet. But the transformation is so remarkable! Believe me, they'll be beyond impressed. And you can ask them any questions when they're here."

"What time will they be here?"

"I told them ten o'clock. Is that okay?"

"That will be fine."

"Good. See you tomorrow, then." Carl left and Jed decided that any work he did tonight wouldn't make much difference. Anyway, he was tired and hungry and he wanted to get home. He had a long list of questions for the board and he wanted to write them down so he didn't forget. He hoped Willie would keep to his promise of delivering at eight thirty. He wanted to be finished with the unloading before the board members showed up.

121

He put the cleaning equipment away and locked up the main building. He went back to the office and changed into his street clothes. It was pitch black by then. He was outside the office door with his keys in his hand when he heard some footsteps behind him. He turned around to investigate and found himself facing the barrel of a gun. His eyes peered over the top of the gun and he saw a young man wearing a hooded sweatshirt sneering at him. Another man dressed similarly appeared next to him and grabbed the keys out of Jed's hand. "I'll take those."

"I'll get rid of him," the man with the gun said as he hit him on the side of the head and knocked him to the ground. Jed had not lost consciousness, but thought he ought to pretend that he had. Before he could decide whether to speak or to feign lifelessness, the man with the keys pulled him to his feet.

"What are you doing, you idiot!" the man with the keys said to the man with the gun. "How am I supposed to know which fucking key opens the door?" The key man turned to Jed. "Show me which one opens the big building over there."

The rage was building inside him and he had to work hard to resist the urge to explode. He knew he could easily beat up both these guys when he got that angry. But he figured he had better comply since they did have a gun. He didn't know what it was they would possibly want from the columbarium. There wasn't anything that valuable. Unless they knew something he didn't. He took the ring and selected the key to the front door of the columbarium and handed it back.

"Now can I hit him?" the gunman asked.

"Just hold the gun on him. If he moves, then use it."

The key man disappeared around the building while the gunman fidgeted nervously. Jed was worried that the gun would go off by accident or by incompetence. They stood looking at each other for a minute until finally the gunman ordered Jed to sit down. Jed did what he was told and closed his eyes. He used Pranayama to get past the boiling emotions. The exercises worked well enough to keep him from doing anything stupid like try to grab the gun. In the past, he would have reacted with outrage at being the victim in any situation, but he had finally learned not to take everything so personally.

"How do you work in a place like this surrounded by dead people? It gives me the creeps." Jed opened his eyes but said nothing. "Hey, I'm talking to you!" He prodded Jed with the gun and held it to his temple. Jed still said nothing. He wasn't sure if that was the best thing to do, but he didn't know how to answer. He thought that it was better to say nothing than to say something that might upset the guy. Luckily, the key man came out of the building at that moment and both Jed and the gunman watched him approach with a large duffle bag.

"What a waste! I got a few things but there wasn't much. I don't think Taye knew what he was talking about. There ain't no diamonds! Let's go." He threw the key ring at Jed.

The gunman kept the gun pointed at Jed as he backed away. When they got to the gate, they both turned and ran. Jed exhaled in relief and stood up slowly. He felt the lump on the side of his head where he'd been hit. He walked to the front door, not sure what to expect inside.

The destruction was rather minor: broken glass from smashed niche doors, the contents strewn about. The key man hadn't been inside long enough to do much. Jed couldn't imagine what the guys had expected to find. Used urns wouldn't be a big seller on EBay and most people didn't have expensive jewelry or mementoes.

He got a broom and dustpan and swept up the glass as he walked around inspecting the damage. He left the ashes that had been dumped on the floor. He needed to find something to put them in before he let the families know that they would need to get new urns. Maybe he could go to the Chinese restaurant and get a bunch of empty cartons. That memory lightened his mood a little.

It was midnight by the time he finished sweeping up the glass and putting things back in their niches. He had catalogued which ones had been broken into. All but one had been full. They had also broken the door that had Goldie's name attached. There was nothing inside it yet which made it especially peculiar. He couldn't know for certain what had been taken out of each niche, as he had never catalogued that, but at least he knew which families to contact. Now all he had left to do was figure out what to put the dumped ashes in.

He searched the closets and office for something appropriate. He found nothing. He did have a box of garbage bags, but he hated what that would symbolize. It was midnight, however, and he was exhausted and starving. He would put them in their own bags and label them. He would deal with it tomorrow after the Neptune Society board members left. Then he started to worry about whether he should tell them and Mr. Henson . . . Carl . . . what had happened. He looked around the first floor, and went upstairs to check out the second and third.

To the eyes of people who had last been inside the building before Jed had started working, it was pristine. He doubted they would notice that a few urns were actually missing. It wasn't like they would examine the inside of every niche. It was probably best that he didn't say anything.

He locked up and walked home, stopping at a twenty-four hour fast food restaurant for sustenance. He slept fitfully. There was a lot to worry about and a lot he would have to do the next day. And then his mind wandered where he didn't want it to go.

The incident with the key man and the gun man had brought him back to Venice Beach and the thugs that beat him up and tried to kill his cat, Mother. And then he thought back to Jonestown and the fear and despair he had felt while living there. He turned on the light and looked at the picture of the woman with the young boy on her lap. His heart raced, his hands trembled, his body was soaked in sweat, and he had so much trouble catching his breath that it felt like he was smothering.

We were found by a couple of Amerindians who gave us a ride in their canoe and after several days I ended up in a hospital in Georgetown, Guyana. I was interviewed and given pictures to look through. I had asked about my mother. They thought somehow I would want to look through the pictures of the bodies lying face

126

down in straight lines, arms around their children, to see if I could find my mother. I threw the pictures back at them. I could not look. I would not look. All the fear that had fueled the adrenaline to keep me going was replaced by fury. It spread through my veins until my body was racked with it. I had traded the imprisonment of Jonestown for the imprisonment of rage.

He breathed deeply and tried to turn off his brain. He lay on his back, stared at the ceiling, and waited for the sun to come up.

13

JED STOPPED FOR A CUP OF COFFEE TO DRINK WHILE HE WALKED TO THE COLUMBARIUM. He was anxious to get there now that it was light. He wanted to make sure everything looked good for the Neptune Society board. He knew that once Willie got there with the gardening supplies, he would be doing most of the unloading himself. Willie wasn't exactly a strong, eager worker. Since Willie would probably be late, as usual, he wanted to be finished cleaning up the inside before the delivery arrived. He needed to order some more glass and put the ashes in something other than the trash bags before calling the families about replacing the urns.

His head hurt. There was no getting around it. There was a large swollen lump. He hoped it wouldn't be too noticeable because he didn't know how to explain it if anyone asked. He had definitely decided not to tell Carl about what had happened. If he or any of the board members asked about the niches with no doors, he would explain that he hadn't finished replacing all the cracked ones. When he walked inside, he saw that there was still quite a bit of cleaning up to do. It had been dark and he may have been in a bit of a fog after the incident because he thought more had been accomplished than actually had. Willie pulled up outside just as Jed checked his thrift store watch. It was nine o'clock. He hoped to have enough time to unload the truck and have everything neatly arranged before ten. He worked fast and Willie was surprisingly more helpful than usual.

You know, Jed," Willie said as he hefted some heavy plants, "I like what you've done with this place. You made a creepy place into a cheery one. I used to be afraid to come here when you first asked me. I didn't want to touch anything. Now, I don't mind."

"Thanks Willie, I appreciate that."

They finished at just before ten and Jed paid Willie, hoping he would leave quickly. But Jed could tell that Willie wanted to hang around and talk when he took a thermos out of the cab of the truck. Jed wasn't sure if it was coffee or something stronger, but it was definitely an indication that Willie wasn't in any hurry. "You need some help getting this stuff planted?" Willie was not being friendly or polite. He wanted to make some more money.

"Not today. But I'll let you know." Jed turned to go inside, hoping Willie would get the hint.

"I can help you inside too," Willie called after him.

"No thanks Willie." Jed decided he had to be rude if he was ever going to get rid of him. He turned his back and started to go inside the columbarium, but then he remembered. "Wait, Willie. I have a list of some replacement glass I need. Can you get this and have them charge it to Mr. Henshaw?" He handed Willie the piece of paper. "If you could do that and deliver later today, I'd really appreciate it."

"Sure thing, Jed. Uh, how much?"

Jed was puzzled. "I said to charge to Mr. Henshaw."

"I mean for me."

"Oh, sorry. Uh, fifty do it?"

"I guess." Willie got into the truck and drove off.

Jed went back inside to continue his work. A few minutes later Carl and the board entered.

"Jed?" Carl's voice resonated through the building.

"Be right down," Jed answered. As he descended the stairs he could hear the oohs and aahs from the board members. He wasn't used to hobnobbing with that particular segment of society and was a little uptight about it.

There were seven people he didn't know and they were all obviously of a higher income level than Carl. They radiated money and power. They were dressed in expensive and well-fitting suits, not in rumpled, off-the- rack ones like Carl's. Jed approached the group tentatively, but they welcomed him into their circle warmly with abundant praise and enthusiasm.

"Remarkable!" exclaimed one of the board members.

"Miraculous!" another one added.

"You are a magician!" a third one gushed.

"How did you do it?" a fourth one asked.

"With blood, sweat, and tears." Carl answered for him. "And intelligence, skill, and patience."

Jed just smiled. He thought it best to keep quiet. He would probably be able to get a lot of his own ideas put into place, if he just did them without their permission. "You had some questions for the board, Jed?"

"No," Jed answered a little too quickly. "I think I got them answered."

Carl winked at him knowingly. They were both on the same page. You can always claim ignorance after the fact. They asked a few questions, walked around the first floor, and to Jed's relief, left about fifteen minutes after they arrived. He was eager to get to work on the outside.

It had been a long time since he'd worked in soil and he'd missed it. He had worked at many jobs in his lifetime and one of his favorites had been on a farm. He had a green thumb and an affinity with plants, although he didn't have any formal training. He had learned a tremendous amount in Guyana when he was at Jonestown as a child and he remembered all of it. Working in the gardens was one of the only happy memories he'd had from those years. He had to give Jim Jones credit for that, at least. He had taught him many skills that proved to be useful later in life when he was on the road.

He worked all day, not even stopping for lunch. He had already decided to treat himself to a special dinner that night. He wanted to celebrate life for the living, not just for the dead. He might as well start with his own.

Willie came back with the glass delivery about three and again he was helpful and careful while stacking them inside the building. This time Willie left right after Jed paid him. He probably had to get the truck back to his brother.

Jed was counting the panes of glass when Carl returned. "Hello Jed, can we go to the office? We need to talk."

"Okay." Jed was surprised to see him but led him back to the office and unlocked the door. They both sat down and Carl fidgeted while Jed sat quietly waiting for him to speak.

"I got a, um, disturbing phone call this afternoon."

Jed still said nothing, always the best strategy.

"One of the board members who didn't come along this morning is a real stickler for rules and protocol. She was not happy with the informal way I hired you without checking references. I told her she should have come with us to see what a wonderful job you've done here, but she wouldn't budge."

Jed still stayed silent, but his stomach was churning and his chest was burning.

Carl continued. "All the other board members are on your side, but she took out some stupid state or county book of proper hiring practices, etc. etc. You see where I'm going, Jed?"

"Yes. I do."

Carl took a deep breath. "Well, I guess she took it upon herself to do her own investigating. Her son-in-law is some big muckety-muck in law enforcement." Jed felt the rage bubbling up, but he did his breathing and stayed passive and silent. Carl fidgeted and cleared his throat several times before speaking again. "Apparently you're on some wanted list by the Los Angeles Police. Is that true?"

"Yes," Jed answered quickly. He took the keys out of his pocket and offered them out to Carl.

"Hold on, Jed. We can work this out. There must be some explanation."

"There is an explanation. But you asked me if the LA police are looking for me and the answer is yes, they are."

"What did you do?"

"Nothing."

"Let me rephrase that. What are they accusing you of?"

"Murder." Jed wanted to answer the questions quickly and honestly. He felt sure that Carl wouldn't call the police and would just let him leave.

Carl was taken aback and his face showed it. "Murder?"

"I didn't murder anyone. I was there when a woman died. That's it."

Carl exhaled and pushed the keys away. "I don't want you to leave and neither does the rest of the board. But obviously we can't knowingly harbor someone wanted by the police."

"I am wanted for questioning. There's a difference."

"Would you be willing to meet with the woman from the board and perhaps you can charm her and win her over?" Jed shrugged his shoulders. "Would you be able to get some references?"

"I don't know, Carl. Maybe it's time for me to leave. You can hire someone just to be the caretaker. It won't be as hard to find someone now that the place looks much better."

"Absolutely not! I'll figure something out. Just keep doing what you're doing and don't worry. I'll be in touch."

Carl left quickly before Jed could argue with him and without taking the keys.

Jed was not thrilled about locking up after dark, still feeling a little nervous that the key man and his crony would come back. Hopefully they realized that there wasn't anything valuable to steal.

He walked home, stopping at a Mexican restaurant for dinner. Eating burritos kindled his memory of Luis' Mexican restaurant where he'd worked in Venice as a dishwasher. It also brought back a few sadder ones, especially of his cat. Luis used to save the leftovers for both him and Mother. He missed her, but he knew she was better off. She had a wonderful home now with Finn and Kate. Jed was learning how to find ways to turn the sad memories into happy ones, but there were still many that he hadn't been able to reconcile. He tried not to let his mind go there.

14

JED GOT TO THE HARDWARE STORE
WHEN IT OPENED AT EIGHT. He needed
a few more items before he could install the
glass that Willie had delivered. He wanted to get
the inside repairs finished so he hurried through
the purchasing. Also, he didn't feel like seeing
Willie. He didn't want to be pestered for a job.
The clerk was friendlier than he had been in the
past; finally realizing that Jed was giving him
more and more business. The over-priced,
1940s-era hardware store was not exactly a
bustling place. Jed stopped at the deli for coffee
and a bagel but again, after a cursory hello to
Abe, he bought his food to go and rushed out.

It didn't take him long to repair the
niche doors once he figured out how to do it.
He finished by noon, even though he had to
stop several times for visitors. He welcomed
everyone who came in and if they wanted to
talk about their loved one, he always stopped
what he was doing to listen. It wasn't just out of
kindness and compassion. He enjoyed hearing

the stories about these people. They were always fascinating, not sad at all. In fact, when people talked about their memories of the dead, they were usually joyful and happy times. Rarely did listening to them bring him down.

Two African American women in their forties arrived with several children of various ages. They wanted a niche for their father and said they would go to the Neptune Society right away to pay for it. They also wanted to know if they could have the funeral right there at the columbarium because their father hadn't wanted his service to be held at a church. He had been very explicit in his instructions. He wanted to be put in the columbarium and he wanted a nonreligious service. And besides, they didn't have a lot of money.

At first Jed was against the idea. He didn't want to disturb the other residents and their families and friends. "What kind of service would you have?" he asked them.

"It would be a celebration of his life with music and stories," they answered.

Frank LaRue would like that and there were many others who had artifacts that were entertainment related. Celebrating people and their lives instead of mourning their deaths, was exactly what this columbarium was all about. Why not have memorials and funerals here too. There was certainly enough room. He had seen a couple of stacks of folding chairs in one of the closets. He might be able to find more at thrift stores if they were needed.

"When would you want to have the memorial?"

"As soon as possible," one of the women said.

"The Neptune Society will assist with the arrangements for getting a niche, and I will help you decorate and plan the memorial. We can do it here, on the first floor. How many chairs do you think you'll need?"

"No idea. We have a large family and he had a lot of friends." She and her sister laughed. "He was a man who loved singing and dancing. I doubt people will be doing much sitting."

"Do you want to choose an apartment now or come back later after you've been to the Neptune Society?"

"Apartment?"

"That's what I call the niches. It seems more personal."

"Apartment. That's nice. I like that."

"I call the larger ones condos."

"I'm sure Dad will be happy in an apartment. He doesn't need a condo."

"So shall we go find one for him?" Jed asked.

"That's okay. You pick it out."

"Are you sure?"

"Absolutely. Dad was one of the most gregarious people you'd ever meet. He loved everyone and everyone loved him. He'll be happy anywhere; next to anyone."

Jed smiled. "I wish I'd known him."

"You will after the funeral and after we decorate his apartment."

"You're right. I'm sure I will."

"We'll be back this afternoon. Thank you. What's your name?"

"Jed."

"I'm Melody and this is my sister, Harmony." Melody watched Jed's reaction and winked. "I told you he loved music."

Jed walked around the second floor. He wanted to find a good place for the musical father of Melody and Harmony. He decided to choose one close to Chet Helms. Chet had been a musical promoter in the sixties and an icon of the San Francisco hippie culture. He had discovered and promoted some of the biggest bands of the era. Although Jed doubted the musical tastes of the two men were similar, he figured it was still a musical corner of the columbarium. He wrote "Melody's and Harmony's Dad" on the post-it note.

Melody and Harmony came back later with all their children in tow. Their hands were filled with shopping bags and boxes, an easel, a boom box, and a poster-sized picture of a

140

handsome, elderly, Black man. He was smiling broadly, wearing a brightly colored shirt and top hat. Shiny plastic beads hung around his neck. "He loved Mardi Gras in New Orleans. He used to go every year before he got sick," Harmony explained.

"We have everything for the apartment and the celebration. We were hoping we could decorate today and have the memorial tomorrow. Is that too soon?" Melody asked.

"Tomorrow?" Jed still wasn't sure whether he should be doing this at all. Maybe some people would be offended. And he wasn't exactly on great footing with every member of the board. But he really liked fostering the idea of the columbarium being a place to celebrate life, not a receptacle for death.

"Ten?"

"Okay. Let's get started." Jed led the entourage to the second floor. "Here's his niche. I put him next to Chet Helms. Do you know who he was?"

"Sure. He was big in the sixties. My father was a blues man, but he loved all music. I think he would have enjoyed knowing Chet. Anyway, much of that psychedelic stuff was based on blues," Melody added.

"Did he play music too?"

"He liked to play horns. He didn't play professionally or anything; he just played at home."

"What was his name?" Jed asked.

"His given name was Clarence King, but everyone called him Sunny, with a u."

"From what you've told me about him, I think I know why," Jed said. "Well, let's get to work."

Melody and Harmony knew exactly how they wanted Sunny's apartment to look. There was a toy trumpet, a strand of Mardi Gras beads, pictures of many children and grandchildren, a couple of Louis Armstrong album covers and a music box shaped like an old hi-fi. It played "When the Saints Go Marching In" when you lifted the lid. Painted on the top of the box was a yellow sun. "This is for his ashes when we get them from the crematorium," Harmony said as she placed the box inside. "He found it at a flea market a few years ago. Dad loved it because it played one of Louis Armstrong's signature songs, even though he wasn't a church-goer."

"It's a powerful song even if you're not religious," Jed said.

"The box didn't have the sun on it. We painted that on," Melody added.

"It's perfect." Jed was still impressed by all the care and thought that went into what people put in their niches.

"Now, we want to talk about the celebration." Melody took the poster-size picture from her daughter's hand. "Where can we put this? We brought an easel."

"Let's go downstairs and find a good place." They all trooped down to the first floor. "How about here where people can see it when they first come in." Jed pointed to a place by the front door.

"Where can we plug in the boom box?"

Jed found an outlet and moved a small table over to it. They busied themselves putting up pictures and artifacts depicting Sunny's life. The children decorated with crepe paper, feathers, beads and balloons. When they were done, it looked more like a birthday or retirement party than a memorial service. But every visitor that came in that day commented on how much they liked it and how they wished the funerals for their loved ones had been at the columbarium.

After Sunny's family left, Jed hoed and planted the outside. He had only gotten a few plants. He didn't know much about them, just their names. He thought he might go to a nursery and find out what would grow well. He could also check out some books from the

143

library. But at least now there were some colorful flowers around the front door. It helped make it look more welcoming.

He stopped at five and locked up. He didn't want to take the chance of being there after dark. He still worried some about key man and his crony and he didn't want anything to mess up the decorations that were up for Sunny's memorial. He picked up a pizza and some beer and got home about seven. The couch potatoes were snoring as he walked by the blaring television and the front desk clerk barely nodded a greeting. When he got to his room, he placed the pizza box and beer bottle on the dresser and took a quick shower.

He ate slowly and thought about what he could do for the rest of the evening. He hadn't been home this early in several days. He was still getting used to the luxury of not having to spend his evenings looking for safe shelter. The pizza was cold and the beer was warm but he looked around the sparse room and felt somewhat content. His musing didn't last long, though. He fell fast asleep before he even finished his dinner.

15

WHEN JED WOKE UP, IT WAS STILL DARK. He checked his watch and saw it was five o'clock. He still had a couple of pieces of pizza left. That would suffice for breakfast. He would just grab a cup of coffee on his way to work. He ate the pizza and took his time in the shower. He worried about what to wear. That was a first! He wasn't a guest at the funeral, but it seemed disrespectful to attend in his work clothes. Since he didn't have anything appropriate to wear he thought about stopping at the thrift store. It probably didn't open until nine so he decided to wear his work clothes. After all, he was still just the painter/handyman/caretaker.

Sunny's family arrived at half past nine, dressed in their Sunday best. Lots of children of assorted ages ran around the building while Melody and Harmony greeted the guests. Jed was nervous about the kids breaking something or falling and getting hurt, but he didn't say anything. He knew he was taking a chance opening the columbarium up for this memorial celebration. It would be the responsibility of the Neptune Society if anything happened, but they must have insurance. He decided to go outside where he wouldn't have to watch the children running around. He did what he always did when he felt uncomfortable. He left.

When he went outside he noticed Rose standing off to the side. "Hi Rose, did you get the papers?"

"Hi Jed. Yeah." She handed them to him. "What going on here? Why all this people?"

"There's a funeral, well more like a celebration."

All of a sudden loud blues music started pouring out of the columbarium. Rose's eyes opened wide. "That not sound to me like funeral music."

"It's the music Sunny loved. Sunny's the man who died. I should probably go inside. We can find your apartment now if you like."

"I wait til funeral over."

"Okay but you can come in. You don't have to wait out here. It's chilly."

"It okay if I watch funeral?"

"Sure. His daughters said that Sunny loved everyone. He was a real friendly guy. He would have liked you to come to his memorial celebration."

"Okay." Rose and Jed went inside and stood together, watching. Music played, people sang and danced; it was truly like a party. Finally, an older man stopped the music to say a few words. Jed thought he looked a lot like Sunny so he figured it might be his brother. It was then that people shed some tears. Some other people said some eulogies, including Melody and Harmony. When they were done the music came back on and the dancing resumed. Jed sneaked a peek at Rose and saw her smiling and swaying ever so slightly to the music. You couldn't help it. The music was bright and joyful, not somber at all. It was definitely not typical funeral music.

When the celebration was over, Jed helped Sunny's family take down the decorations. After they all said good-byes that were both joyful and tearful, Jed found Rose sitting on a bench on the second floor. He had forgotten all about her. "Hi Rose, did you enjoy the celebration?"

"Yes. Good show."

"Shall we pick out your apartment now?"

"Okay."

They walked around the building, floor by floor. Jed pointed out certain niches that he

147

thought would be suitable, but she couldn't make up her mind. It was almost noon and he hadn't gotten any work done. "Maybe if you could tell me what you want to put inside your apartment, I could help you decide which one would be best," Jed proposed.

"I don't know what."

"Well, what do you like to do? How about family members? You could put in some photographs of your children or grandchildren? Maybe you had a dog or cat that meant a lot to you?"

"No family. No pets."

"Well, we don't have to decide today if you want to wait. There are still quite a few empty ones."

"You choose. Doesn't matter what one. I don't care. I be dead."

"Are you sure?"

"Yep."

"Okay. I'll pick one out for you. I'll think about it some more and find you one next to some real good people. Meanwhile, you think about what you want to put in it."

"Okay. Bye Jed."

"Good-bye Rose." He watched her powerwalk out of the building. She and Sam must be about the same age. What a difference in their gaits.

Jed thought he might go to a nursery to talk to them about plants and flowers. He was also getting hungry so maybe he'd stop at the deli but just then Sam hobbled in.

"There he is, my man Sam," Jed greeted him. "I was just thinking about you."

Sam raised his hand. "Gimmee five, Bro."

Jed slaps his hand in a high five. "Mazel tov."

"You've got shmutz on your face!" Sam teased.

"Don't be such a kvetch," Jed replied.

They laughed together, but then Sam's smile turned into a pained grimace. "Sadie sleeps all the time now. She can't eat." He started to cry. "It's just a matter of time. I'm losing my Sadie, Jed." He fell into Jed's arms. Jed held him uneasily, at first, but then more tightly. "Fifty-nine years of marriage. I don't remember one night spent without my Sadie sleeping near me." Jed patted him awkwardly on the back. After a minute or two, Sam straightened up and took out a handkerchief. He blew his nose loudly. "Let's check on the condo."

"It's all ready for her, Sam. We put the pictures in and I put up the two sconces to hold the tomatoes, one on either side of the door."

149

"I know. But I want to check on it anyway."

"Okay. Let's go look." Jed took Sam's arm and they shuffled slowly to Sadie's apartment. Jed got a chair for Sam and gently helped him sit down. "Do you want me to stay with you or do you want to be alone?" Jed asked.

"Do you mind staying? I feel better when you're near."

Jed put his hand on Sam's shoulder but didn't say anything. He had learned by now that in these circumstances, people wanted to talk, not listen. If Sam had asked, Jed could have offered plenty of his own experiences with loss and grief. He had had many. But Sam wanted to talk about Sadie, not hear about Jed's.

"See that picture of us by the lake? We used to go there every summer and rent a little cabin for a couple of weeks. How she loved it there! We would swim, go row boating, play shuffleboard. And you see that recipe box? Oh could she cook! She made the best cheesecake you ever ate. And her potato kugel was out of this world."

"What's in potato kugel, Sam?"

"Potatoes, Jed." Sam smiled at him.

"That much I figured." Jed smiled back.

"And eggs and onion and flour."

"Sounds good."

150

Sam shook his head and swallowed hard. "Abe has it at his deli, but it's not like my Sadie's."

"I guess I'll have to settle for Abe's."

Sam squeezed Jed's hand. "I'm done, Jed. Shall we get some kugel for lunch at Abe's?"

"I'd like that." Jed helped Sam up and put the chair away. "I have to lock up the office. I'll meet you at the gate."

"Gay ga zinta hate."

"Get lost? Good riddance?" Jed furrowed his brow.

"Something like that." Sam winked. "Not really. That would be gay avek. Gay ga zinte hate means go in good health."

"That's better," Jed replied, feigning relief.

"I'll meet you outside," Sam said as he started his trek.

It was a slow process, walking to the deli with Sam, but Jed enjoyed his company. They ate kugel and knishes and when they were finished, they played a couple of hands of pinochle.

"I'd better get back," Jed said as he stood to leave.

"Hold on there," Abe said as he went to his office. When he returned he handed Sam a small box. "They came yesterday afternoon."

Sam took the box and turned to Jed. "They're for you. Abe has a son-in-law who's a printer."

Jed took the box and gave them a quizzical look. He opened the box. Inside were five hundred business cards. He took one out and held it up. There was a picture of the columbarium and the words:

Jedidiah Gibbons
San Francisco Columbarium
Caretaker and Historian

"I don't know what to say."

"You don't have to say a thing," Abe said as he patted him on the back.

"Thank you. This means a lot to me."

"And you mean a lot to me," Sam replied.

16

THE NEXT COUPLE OF DAYS WERE SOMEWHAT UNEVENTFUL. Jed finished repairing all the glass doors and touching up any paint spots he had missed. He found one of those Sunset gardening books and looked up the best plants and flowers for Zone 17, the climate zone for the San Francisco Bay area. He bought plants from a nearby nursery and since it was a large order, they delivered them. He was glad not to have to pay Willie anything more out of his own pocket. He was finished with the landscaping by the end of the week, so he was finally just caretaking the building.

There had been some visitors, but no new people needing apartments or condos, and none of his newfound friends came in. It was the first time since he had gotten to San Francisco that he actually felt like he wasn't scrambling to finish his work. It was nice to feel relaxed, but it also gave him time to think and that was not always a good thing.

He thought about Finn, Kate, and Mother while he watered and weeded. Finn had fought through his own demons. He had gotten great acclaim for his book and that had helped. Kate had come to terms with having her father living with her, but only as long as he kept his drinking under control. That too had strengthened Finn's resolve.

Jed knew that Mother was better off with Finn and Kate. He wasn't sure how long cats lived, but she needed the warmth and comfort of a real home. She'd had enough years living on the streets, never knowing where her next meal would come from and what her next meal would be. She deserved to be spoiled and he knew that's what Kate and Finn were doing. They loved her. That's all he needed to know.

And then he thought of Monica. He liked her. It was such a strange stirring in his body, a sensation he hadn't allowed himself to have in years. And it was somehow a comfort to him that she was HIV positive. It meant that she was flawed like him. Just as he was appreciating the notion of calling her and contemplating a life that included a home and a job and a woman, Jed heard his name being called. "Jed? Where are you?"

He looked up and saw Sam standing in the parking lot. "What's wrong?"

Sam hobbled over to Jed and fell into his arms, sobbing. "She's gone . . . my Sadie's gone." He sobbed for several minutes and then finally straightened up.

"When, Sam?"

"Yesterday. They took her body and said the ashes will be ready later today. I'd like to do the funeral tomorrow."

"That will be fine, Sam, but so soon?"

"It's the custom. Jews bury their dead right away. I'll bring the ashes tomorrow. Today I brought the tomatoes. Can we put them up now?"

"Of course." Jed took Sam by the arm, helping him inside and up the stairs.

When they got to Sadie's condo, Sam took two tomatoes out of a shopping bag and placed them on the two sconces on either side of the glass door. He said a short prayer in Hebrew. "I'll bring fresh ones every few days. There are only a few left in her garden, but I'll buy them from the store after that. I don't want them to turn into dreck."

"What do you want to do at her funeral?"

"The rabbi will say a few prayers and then people can say what they wish. She was not one to like being in the limelight. She would want it short." He started to cry again and Jed hugged him.

155

"What else can I do to help, Sam?"

"Milton and Abe are taking care of calling people. I just need to get the urn and the ashes. Irving is driving me. He's picking me up here. He's probably outside now." He kissed Jed on the cheek. "You are such a special man. You are my haimisher mensch, a man with such rachmones, more like my mishpocha."

"You haven't taught me those words yet, Sam. I hope they're good."

"Haimisher mensch means someone you feel comfortable with. Rachmones means compassion, and mishpocha is family. Thank you Jed."

"You're welcome, Sam." He put his arm through Sam's and walked him outside where Irving was waiting in his car. " I'll have everything ready for you for the funeral tomorrow."

They drove off and Jed turned around to go back inside. He noticed a car in the parking lot with a young couple inside. The woman was in the passenger seat with her hands covering her face. The man in the driver's seat stared through the windshield, frozen. Jed approached the car to ask them if everything was all right. When he knocked on the window of the driver's side, the man shuddered back to reality and opened the window. Jed noticed there was a box in the back seat containing a teddy bear and a cookie jar in the shape of a pink heart. There was also a picture of a little girl about four years old sitting on the woman's lap with the man standing behind them. The woman sobbed loudly and uncontrollably, oblivious to Jed's presence.

"Yes?" the man asked.

"I just wanted to make sure you were okay. Are you coming inside?"

"Oh. I . . . we . . . I don't know."

The woman raised her head out of her hands and looked at Jed. "I'm sorry."

"No, no, don't be sorry. I can wait." Jed felt his body relax, his muscles release, and his heartbeat slow. "I'll be inside. Take your time." He turned and left as the man got out of the car and opened the passenger door.

"Come on, Heather. We have to do this," the man said.

Heather climbed out of the car while her husband got the box out of the back seat. He held her up as they crossed the parking lot. She was barely able to stand, let alone walk. Jed held the door open for them and they entered the columbarium. The man held out a piece of paper to Jed. "The Neptune Society said to give you this. We paid for a niche."

Jed took the paper. "Had you already chosen an apartment for — " Jed looked at the paper — "Chloe?"

157

"Apartment?" the man asked.

"That's what I call the smaller niches. The larger ones are condos."

"Oh. No. I didn't know we had a choice," the man said glumly.

"Would you like me to show you around and you can pick one out?"

The man looked at his wife and she spoke in a barely audible, broken whisper. "Any apartment will be fine. Let's just get this over with."

Jed led them to a niche near Sadie's. He knew that Sam and Sadie never had any children, but he thought she would have been a wonderful grandmother and would look after Chloe. He opened the apartment door and stepped aside so the husband and wife could put their daughter's ashes and teddy bear inside. Heather collapsed into her husband's arms and cried out to him, "Oh Eric! What kind of God takes a four year-old baby?" They both sobbed in each other's arms.

After a few minutes Eric turned to Jed. "I'm sorry. Thank you for being so patient. She had leukemia. It was only a few months ago that she was diagnosed. We are still in shock."

All of a sudden the ground shook and the niche doors rattled. The earthquake didn't last long and it wasn't that strong, but it jolted Heather out of weeping as she grabbed Eric's arm in fear. The teddy bear fell out of the niche onto the floor. Jed picked up the teddy bear and brushed it off carefully. He placed it gently back in the niche and then turned toward Eric and Heather. His own eyes brimmed with tears as he took both their hands. "My name is Jed Gibbons. I'm sorry for your loss and I know that there isn't much I can do. But I'm going to make you one promise. I promise you I'll take care of your daughter."

Heather and Eric were surprised at first, but then they hugged him. "Thank you," Heather said between sobs.

"She will never be alone," Jed added. "I will make sure of that. I will talk to her every day when you can't be here."

Heather smiled through her tears and then turned toward Eric. "I need to leave now."

Jed watched Eric take Heather out and then turned to the pink heart-shaped urn. "Hello Chloe. My name is Jed. Sadie will be here tomorrow and she'll be your neighbor. She'll watch over you and keep you company." He patted the urn, closed the door, and descended the stairs slowly.

17

ROSE STOPPED OFF AT THE CHINESE RESTAURANT TO GET FOOD TO FILL HER FAVORITE LUNCHBOX. She wore her Giants' jacket and hat and carried her scorebook. It was a night game in the middle of the week so she had to leave early. She would be traveling during rush hour and the stadium was right downtown. It was such a mess dealing with traffic between four and seven.

She got to the stadium by half past six so she had plenty of time to eat her dinner and write the lineups in her scorebook. They were playing the San Diego Padres. It was a clear, chilly night and the stands were only about half full. She liked the night games much better than the day ones. She never felt quite as claustrophobic as she did during day weekend games. She took out her headphones and radio and waited for the game to start.

Sam, meanwhile, had a long and difficult day. He and Irving had picked up the ashes at the crematorium and gotten a picture of Sadie blown up to poster size. Irving said he would bring an easel to place it on. He would pick up Sam at eight thirty the next morning because Sam wanted to be sure to be at the columbarium as soon as the doors opened. There wouldn't be that much to set up. Most of their friends had either died or moved. He didn't expect more than fifteen or twenty people. It would be a short service. They hadn't been to temple in years. In fact, the rabbi was new and young and hadn't even met Sadie. It didn't matter. She wouldn't have wanted much. He had thought he should write down something to say, but he couldn't bring himself to do it.

Sam tried to eat, but he wasn't hungry so he went to the living room and turned on the television. He turned the channel to the station with the Giants' game. He wasn't interested in watching something that required much attention. He just wanted the television on for company. In fact, he fell fast asleep in his chair right after the game started.

The Giants were up first. When the umpire said "Play ball," Rose was ready with her pencil to start marking the balls and strikes. After a little more than an hour, the score was tied. It was the fourth inning and the Giants

161

were up. The count was two and two. The San Diego pitcher threw a high inside fastball. The batter turned on the pitch and drove it high and deep to left field. It became obvious that the ball was going to clear the wall. The whole left field bleacher section stood, screaming. The ball sailed high into the air. When it reached its peak and started its descent, it gained even more velocity. The ball was going straight toward Rose's seating area. The fans surrounding her jostled each other as they vied for the ball. Some of them held out the baseball gloves they had brought, hoping for the moment when they might catch a souvenir.

Rose shoved them away, trying to get them out of her field of vision. She knew she couldn't catch the ball, but she was poised with pencil in hand to write in her book. She was focused on her scorekeeping and didn't want to be distracted by the group around her. Rose realized that the only way she was going to see where the ball was going was if she stood along with the other fans. Just as she stood, the ball grazed the glove of a man standing in the row behind her and dropped, striking her in the head.

No one knew what had happened, at first. Rose wasn't exactly a tall, formidable person and was hardly noticed in the melee. Everyone scrambled to find the ball and be the one to hold it victoriously in the air. Finally a woman saw Rose lying prone on the bench. The ball lay on the ground next to her scorebook.

"Lady, are you okay?" the woman shouted. "She's not moving! Is she dead?" The woman was frantic. A man picked up the ball and started to lift it up triumphantly, but realized it would probably be wiser just to put it in his pocket. A couple of fans had alerted the ushers and they arrived just as the man with the ball grabbed his ten year old son's hand and pulled him toward the exit.

"It's Rose! Give her air!" the ushers yelled as they tried to move people out of the way. It was pandemonium with people screaming and gasping. One of the ushers called 911 while Rose lay motionless with her eyes closed.

Sam woke with a start and focused his eyes on the television just as the medics arrived. The announcer shouted with alarm, "Someone's been hit by the ball! We don't know who it is or their condition. Okay . . . now our producer is hearing that it's a woman and she's been knocked unconscious." The players on the field were gathered in small groups, looking out toward the bleachers. The announcer added, "A spokesman from the Giants tells us that the umpires are conferring with both teams to determine if they should continue the game."

Finally they put Rose on a stretcher and carried her out. An usher retrieved the scorebook and lunchbox and gave them to the EMTs.

Sam didn't want to watch the rest of the game, even if they did resume play. He turned off the television and went to the kitchen. He knew he needed to eat but he had no appetite. He opened the refrigerator and shut it quickly when he saw the tomatoes that he was saving for the sconces. He decided to go to bed. He doubted he would sleep, but he didn't know what else to do.

Tony sat in Goldie's living room waiting for the ambulance. She had become bedridden and semi-comatose the last few days. He had set up hospice for her but when the nurse came to assess the situation, she noticed how labored her breathing was and insisted that she should be hospitalized. She needed to be on oxygen and a feeding tube continually and since Tony wasn't family, the nurse had to be the one to make the medical decision. Tony knew that Goldie wouldn't be happy spending her last days in a hospital, but he also knew that it had become more than he could handle. He had to admit that he felt a sense of relief. He called for an ambulance and sat in the living room to wait. The nurse was in the bedroom with Goldie and just as the doorbell rang and Tony got up to answer it, she came out of the bedroom. She patted Tony's arm gently and said, "She's gone. I'm sorry."

Tony stared back at the nurse and nodded his head. He answered the door and then, without a word, ushered the EMTs into the bedroom. He walked back into the living room and called the Neptune Society to ask them where her body needed to be taken for cremation.

18

IT WAS A BRIGHT SUNNY MORNING, NOT AT ALL WHAT ONE WOULD HAVE EXPECTED FOR THE DAY OF SADIE'S FUNERAL. Jed stopped at the deli for coffee and a bagel on his way to work. Abe was showing a young man, who looked to be about eighteen, how to run the cash register.

"I'll only be gone about an hour. Are you going to be able to handle it?" Abe said to the young man. He looked up when Jed entered. "Hi Jed. This is my nephew, Adam. He's going to watch the store for me while I attend Sadie's funeral." Jed and Adam nodded to each other.

"Should we bring some food to the service?" Jed asked. "I'd like to pay for it."

"I already asked Sam and he said no," Abe answered.

"How about after the service, at his house?"

"Sam was adamant that he did not want to sit Shiva, even though I told him I would take care of all the food."

"What's Shiva?"

"It's what Jews do, like Catholics have wakes. We sit at home and people come and pay their respects. It goes on for a week."

"Why wouldn't Sam want to do that?"

"You have to understand, Jed. Sam and Sadie were like one unit. They were never apart. He couldn't sit in his house and entertain people without her. Anyway, they had stopped being observant Jews years ago."

"I see," Jed said. "I guess I'll see you later then."

"I'll be there as soon as I finish with Adam here."

Jed left and got to the columbarium with plenty of time to set up the chairs before Sam would arrive. Sam, however, hadn't been able to sleep and was leaning against the gate, waiting for Jed. He had called Irving and told him he wanted to walk. Irving, however, would hear none of it. He rushed over to drive Sam to the columbarium and then went home to shower and dress for the memorial service.

"Shalom, Sam. Why are you here so early?"

"I couldn't sleep."

"Well let's go upstairs and finish setting up the condo. I made sure it was sparkling, the way Sadie would have made it."

Sam reached inside the shopping bag and took out a jewelry box. "I brought this for the ashes. And I have some fresh tomatoes for the sconces."

Jed took the box and opened it. He picked up the shopping bag with his other hand. "Hello Sadie. Come and see your new condo." It was slow going, but there was plenty of time before the memorial service.

Rose woke up frightened and bewildered. She looked around the hospital room, trying to comprehend where she was and why she was there. In all her eighty-plus years, she had never been to the hospital except to visit others. She lay motionless for several minutes, her eyes darting between the other two beds in the room. Finally a nurse entered the room. "Hello Rose. Do you know where you are?"

"How you know my name?" Rose asked testily.

"Your wallet. Do you remember what happened to you?"

"No. Why I here in hospital?"

"Do you remember being at the Giants' game?"

"Yes."

"You were hit in the head by a ball and knocked out."

Rose was silent. The nurse kept talking but Rose wasn't listening. She was trying to grasp what was happening. The nurse shook her shoulder gently. "What?" Rose asked.

"I asked you whether your head hurt."

"No."

"Okay. I just wanted to make sure the pain medication was working or whether I should increase the dosage."

"No medicine. I don't want any."

"I think you should, Rose. It would hurt a lot without it."

"No. No drug."

"The doctor will be in shortly. You can talk about it with him." The nurse took her temperature. "He wants to do some tests this morning so you can't have breakfast until after that."

"I not hungry. When I go home?"

"The doctor will talk to you."

The nurse was almost out the door when Rose called out to her, "Was it home run?"

The nurse paused and turned around, baffled. "Excuse me?"

"The ball that hit me. Was it home run?"

The nurse smiled. "I don't know. I'll see if I can find out." Rose nodded her head and lay back down.

Sadie's memorial was short, just as Sam wanted. Jed watched as the rabbi said a prayer and several of the fifteen or so guests said lovely things about her. It was a sedate service, a far cry from the dancing and music of Sunny's celebration. When the rabbi finished saying the final prayer, the mourners followed Sam upstairs to say goodbye to Sadie. It was an unusual Jewish service since there was no casket or burial at a cemetery and no gathering back at Sam's house. But Sam didn't care. He did what Sadie had wanted.

After the guests left, Irving took Sam's arm and tried to lead him out. Jed came over and hugged Sam. "Don't you worry. I'll watch over her."

"I'll be here every day, Jed."

Jed looked at Irving, asking him silently if he would be driving him. Irving understood and nodded his head. "I'll drive you, Sam, anytime you want to come."

"No. I'll walk. I have nothing else to do. See you tomorrow, Jed." Sam and Irving started to walk out when Tony rushed past them, almost knocking them both over. "Where's the fire, young man?" Sam asked Tony.

"I'm so sorry. Are you okay?"

"I'm fine. No worries."

Tony turned to Jed. "I can come back later if you're busy."

Sam patted Jed's arm and said, "You take care of this young man. He needs you now." Sam and Irving left.

"Goldie died," Tony said abruptly.

"I'm sorry, Tony. Are those things for Goldie's apartment?" Jed asked as he eyed the bag Tony was carrying.

"Yes."

"Then let's go upstairs and decorate her apartment." Tony and Jed walked upstairs. When they got to Goldie's niche, Jed removed the reserved sign. Tony took out the empty Chinese take-out carton, shiny from the spray-on acrylic, and placed it inside the niche. He put the gefilte fish jar next to it. He removed a mezuzah and a hammer and nail from the bag.

"I forgot to ask you if it was okay to hammer a nail into the wall."

"It's okay, but what is that?"

"It's a mezuzah. Jews put it outside their front door to bring them luck."

"Was she a religious person?"

"Not really, but she had this by the front door of her house and wanted it here."

171

"A lot of people seem to become religious when they know they are dying," Jed said.

"I guess we can't know how it feels until we're in their shoes," Tony replied.

"And what's the reason for the carton and jar?"

"I don't know why she wanted them exactly. She never told me. I guess just because she liked to eat Chinese food and gefilte fish. Is it okay to bring food?"

Jed thought about Sadie's tomatoes. "Sure."

"Goldie was quite unique."

"What did she do?"

Tony hesitated a minute but then decided that Jed wouldn't care. "She was a drug dealer. Well, just marijuana."

"That's a risky way to make a living."

"She was very careful."

"She never got caught?"

"Nope. She knew her clients well. And remember, she was agoraphobic. It's not like she was dealing it on street corners."

"Still, it must be hard never leaving your house. How did she manage a business without going out?"

"I did all her shopping and took care of her business. Her clients and suppliers came to the house. Anyway, neither of us have any family around. We just had each other."

"So you're the next of kin?" Jed thought about the question from the hotel clerk and how many people there were just like him.

"I guess you could say that. She left me her house."

"Oh, you lived together?"

"No. I have my own apartment."

"Are you going to move into her house?"

"No. I'm going to sell it."

"You'll be a rich man."

Tony laughed. "It's pretty rundown but it'll give me enough to live on while I decide what I'm going to do next."

"You're not going to keep her business going?"

"No!" Tony was quite emphatic. "I've had enough of that."

Jed heard the door open downstairs. A group entered laughing and chatting loudly. "I'd better get downstairs. Do you need any help putting up the mezuzah?"

"No, I can manage. Thanks, Jed."

Jed went downstairs to greet the new arrivals. He wondered why Sam hadn't put a mezuzah by Sadie's door. Before he got to the first floor he saw three elderly men walking up the stairs. Two of them walked slowly with canes, but one was as spry as a man twenty or thirty years younger. The spry one was dressed in a striped jacket, spats, and a straw hat. He looked straight out of a vaudeville revue. When he saw Jed he took off his hat and bowed. "Hello young man. We are here to see Frank La Rue. I believe he is on this floor."

"He is, right next to Goldie. You'll see a man hammering there."

"Thank you sir. My name is Ray. This is Harry and Andy. Together with Frank we were The Ragamuffins."

"Is that a musical group?"

"You betcha! We were pretty famous at one time."

"Very nice to meet you all. My name's Jed."

"We got together to say goodbye to Frank. Andy and Harry are moving in with their children and leaving San Francisco. It'll just be me coming to pay my respects to Frank from now on."

"He's lucky to have you, Ray. I'll show you where he is."

Ray did a little soft shoe dance and bowed again. The trio followed Jed upstairs and found Tony finishing up with his hammering. Jed and Tony watched and listened as the three men harmonized a barbershop tune, "Five foot two, eyes of blue, oh what those five feet can

174

do, has anybody seen my gal?" Ray danced while the others stood leaning on their canes. When the song was finished, the three took out toy horns resembling the one in Frank's niche. They blew them and said in unison, "Here's looking at you, Frank." They stood for a minute, staring at the floor, and then filed downstairs in silence. Jed and Tony glanced at each other and smiled. They both knew that Goldie was going to like her new apartment next to Frank.

19

TONY WENT STRAIGHT TO GOLDIE'S AFTER LEAVING THE COLUMBARIUM. He had given the leftover stash of drugs to Taye when the hospice nurse had started visiting regularly. Taye was supposed to sell the rest, but Tony was doubtful that he would ever see that money. As soon as Goldie had become semi-comatose, he deposited portions of cash into various bank accounts that he had opened. Goldie had always been very wary of banks and kept most of the cash hidden in her house. She was quite creative with her hiding places and Tony was the only person who knew where they were. When she got sick and slept most of the time, Tony decided to move the money. Even if the buyers didn't know she kept large amounts of cash in the house, they knew she probably had the best marijuana and hashish in San Francisco. He also knew, however, that the respect they had for Goldie didn't necessarily carry over to Tony.

He opened the bank accounts and got a safe deposit box for the ledger. That ledger was a goldmine for anyone in the drug-dealing business. Goldie had kept meticulous records. She had contact information for suppliers all over the world, as well as for her big-ticket clients. The San Francisco Police Department would also love to get their hands on that ledger. He wasn't going to take any chances by leaving it in her house or even his own car or apartment.

It was time for him to inventory her possessions and give away or sell the rest. Tony was quite good at this chore. Many of his friends had died of AIDS and he had been the one to pack up their stuff and send them to family members or charities. It was something he had to do way too many times.

He had stopped at a couple of grocery stores and picked up some boxes. He wanted to get all this over with as quickly as possible so he could put the house on the market. Goldie had already chosen the people who she wanted to have certain items. He had already contacted them. He had given them a taste of some high quality pot along with their keepsake. That had been Goldie's wish. He had done most of it while she was alive so they had been able to thank her in person.

It was dark by the time he finished packing up the house. He had divided up the boxes into antiques that were worth selling and items that would go to the thrift store. He worked fast and efficiently.

He had an appointment set up with the lawyer about the trust. Everything had been left to Tony. And the realtor was ready to list the house as soon as he emptied it out.

It was too late to get anyone to the house to pick up the boxes, so he sat on top of one of them and took out a joint. As he lit up and inhaled, he thought about his future. He would have money and time, but he would be alone and without purpose. And dear Goldie was gone. It had been a long time since he'd hit the bars. Maybe tonight would be a good time to do that. He could drink, dance, and forget.

It was fairly early when he arrived at The Cafe, but the place was hopping anyway. The Cafe was in the Castro on Market Street, and Tony used to be a regular customer. They had recently done a huge renovation and it had become more than Tony's senses could handle. The strobe lights were flashing, the music was thumping and the floor was crowded with gay men and women of a variety of ages, ethnicities and body types. They were dancing both erotically and mechanically, depending on their skill level. There was a sprinkling of men standing at the bar when Tony slid onto one of the stools.

The bartender's eyes opened wide. "Tony! Haven't seen you in a coon's age!"

Tony looked at this flaming queen skeptically. "You sound like an Okie."

"You can take the girl out of the country but you can't take the country out of the girl. So what can I get you?"

"A martini, dry and straight up. Have you seen Taye lately?"

The bartender started mixing the drink. "Yes, he's usually here a little later on in the evening. Sorry to hear about Goldie."

"Thanks." Tony took a sip from the drink the bartender placed in front of him.

"What are you going to do with her, uh, stuff?"

"Sell some, give some away."

"Hey, I can probably help you with that."

Tony just realized what "stuff" he was talking about. He started to explain that he had been talking about Goldie's possessions when Taye entered the bar, holding the arm of a conservative-looking gray-haired, white man, wearing an expensive suit and tie. He looked like he could be a banker, a CEO or a politician.

Taye spoke to a couple dancing seductively on the dance floor and then approached Tony and the bartender with his friend. "Do you like my new auntie? I found her basket shopping in the tea room."

"Do you really need another sugar daddy?" the bartender asked.

"The more the merrier." Taye turned to Tony. "So is Goldie's resting place all jazzed up?"

"I did what she asked: ashes in the take out carton, jar of gefilte fish, mezuzah by the door."

"How come you didn't put anything in to commemorate her career choice?"

Tony decided to ignore Taye's last question. "Did you do what you were supposed to?"

"Don't be so paranoid. I got rid of some."

"How much did you skim off?"

Taye smiled slyly. "Oh Tony darling, you know me so well. But I know you didn't give me everything, either."

"It's mine to give or take."

"I know, I know. You're the anointed heir to the throne."

Tony pulled Taye away from the others. "Where's the rest of the stuff and where's the money?"

"I need it for business purposes."

"What do you mean you need it for business purposes? What business?"

"Did you want everything to stop? Goldie's business was doing really well. We can keep it going."

Taye was right but Tony had given it a great deal of thought and had made up his mind. "I don't want to."

"What? Don't be a fool! You know all her contacts. I know where to get it. You're coming into the money. Hell, you've been in charge anyway. At least you have been for the last few months."

"I want to be done with this."

"I've still got enough to keep things going until her house sells. Then we can really go to town. My new Grimm's fairy here has a fishwife with more money than she needs. If I keep him happy, he'll keep her happy and she can keep us happy. We can be one big happy family."

"No Taye. I've made up my mind."

Taye's face tightened and his eyes blazed. "Then give me the book!"

"What book?"

"Her ledger."

"Lay off, Taye. It's over. I tell you what, keep the stuff you have and leave me alone."

Taye looked at a young, blonde pretty-boy wearing very tight jeans and a pink tank top standing at the bar and nodded at him surreptitiously. He was one of the couple Taye had talked to on the dance floor. "You prick!" Taye sneered at Tony and went back to his date.

Tony watched as the young man at the bar approached him. "Hey, is it hot in here or is it just you?" the man said seductively.

Tony smiled at him and decided to flirt back. It had been a long time. They exited the bar and walked toward Tony's car.

Just as they were about to get in, a muscular, brawny bear-type man called from down the street. "Where do you think you're going, Brad?" He was the other member of the dancing duo.

"Stu!" Brad looked away.

"Who's this?" Tony asked Brad but he didn't answer.

"Are you trolling my queen?" Stu poked Tony.

"Does he belong to you?" Tony asked Brad who still kept his eyes averted and remained silent.

"Damn right he belongs to me."

"Hey man, he came on to me. I didn't know."

Stu punched Tony who fell to the ground. Stu continued kicking and stomping on him while Tony curled into a ball, knowing full well he didn't have a chance if he tried to fight back. Brad watched and did nothing. When it was obvious to Stu that Tony was unconscious, he looked through Tony's pockets and found his wallet. He emptied it and continued looking but didn't find anything else of consequence so he and Brad walked away.

They went into the bar and found Taye. "What did you find?" Taye asked.

"Just money and cards."

"Nothing else?"

"Nope."

"Shit! How much money?"

"Just a few bucks."

Taye knew they were lying but he didn't care. He wasn't after money. He wanted the good stuff and the ledger. He doubted Tony had the ledger on him so he had broken into Tony's car while Stu was beating him up. But, of course, he came out empty-handed "Just keep the money for payment, but give me the cards."

Stu gave him Tony's credit cards. "Got anything else to add to the payment?"

"No. I'll be in touch." Taye turned back to his date and took him on the dance floor. The older man looked totally out of place and couldn't dance for beans, but he was having a good time.

Tony opened his eyes inside the ambulance. "You've been hurt. We're taking you to the hospital. Do you remember what happened?"

He tasted blood and it spilled out of his mouth when he opened it to speak. The EMT wiped it off his chin. "No."

"You were found on the street. You were beaten."

Then Tony did remember. What a fool he had been. It was those two guys. It was all a set up. Luckily he didn't have much money on him and he had left the stuff in his car. Shit. His car would be towed. He didn't care about the impound fee, but he was afraid it would be searched. Who could he trust? No one. Goldie had been the only one.

The ambulance arrived at the hospital and Tony closed his eyes, trying to block out all the excitement and commotion. They took him into the ER where he was prodded and questioned. The doctor decided to keep him in the hospital so he was brought to a room. Finally he could rest. They gave him a shot to help him sleep and before he could worry too much about the appointments he wasn't going to keep and the money this was all going to cost, he fell fast asleep.

20

JED OPENED THE COLUMBARIUM AT NINE SHARP AND STARTED HIS ROUNDS. He went to Goldie's apartment first and sang "Summertime" as he polished her door. "This is the only Broadway show tune I know, Goldie. Tony said you like them. Maybe you can find Frank LaRue and ask him to sing you some of your favorites. His buddy, Ray, said he had a great voice and knew every old song that was ever written." He moved to Frank's door and continued singing while he cleaned.

"Your singing has me all ver clempt," Sam called from the first floor.

Jed peered over the railing and saw Sam holding a shopping bag. "Sam, where have you been? It's been a few days."

"I'm not doing so well."

Jed gestured to the shopping bag. "Are those Sadie's tomatoes?"

"These are the last of the good ones. The rest are dreck. Now I'll have to get them at the grocery store."

"Can you come upstairs by yourself?"

"Sure thing." Sam plodded up the stairs. Jed got him a chair and Sam sat down with a sigh." Oy yoy yoy."

"This is Goldie. I wanted to show you something." Jed pointed to the mezuzah. "I wondered why you didn't put one of those next to Sadie's door."

"Mezuzahs are only supposed to be attached to the entranceway of your house or maybe on the doorways of separate rooms."

"Maybe Tony didn't know that." Jed turned to face Goldie's apartment. "Did you hear that Goldie? But it's what you wanted and that's what's important."

"Maybe she wasn't that religious," Sam added.

"Do you think it will matter?" Jed asked.

"To who? To God? To some other Jew? Who cares!"

"I don't know. I just wanted to do the right thing."

"Don't worry, Jed. It's bupkes. We're all full of mishegoss."

"I know bupkes. But mishegoss?"

"Craziness."

186

"And what's mezuzah?"

"Literally? It means doorpost."

"I get it."

"What's to get?"

"That the people will be protected and they are never alone. That everyone matters, whatever they may have done in their past."

"Oy vey. Enough already. My head's spinning."

"Okay." Jed smiled. "Let's go see Sadie." Jed took the shopping bag from Sam and helped him to Sadie's condo where Sam carefully replaced the old tomatoes on the sconces with the ones from the shopping bag. "Maybe we can find her some artificial ones, Sam."

Sam looked horrified. "Artificial tomatoes are schlock! Not for my Sadie!"

"I mean just until her garden tomatoes are ready again next year. I could get some of those wax ones. We could ask Sadie if she'd approve."

"Jed, you are such a luftmensch. She'd never approve."

"Okay, Sam," Jed agreed. "No wax tomatoes for Sadie."

Sam took out his handkerchief and wiped his eyes. "I thank God for you every day, Jed. I don't know what I'd do without you, knowing you're taking care of her."

Jed patted his arm. "Would you like to meet some of the others?"

"Not today. They're expecting me at the deli for pinochle. Another time." He turned and shuffled down the hall. Jed was about to take his arm to walk him out, but he decided against it. Maybe Sam didn't want Jed to see him cry.

Jed watched him go and then opened Chloe's apartment door. He picked up the teddy bear and gave it a hug. "Here's your hug for the day, Chloe. Mom and Dad will be here next week, I think. Don't forget. You look for that rainbow." He put the teddy bear back inside and closed the door. He had others to visit before checking on the outdoor plants and flowers.

Tony woke up when the nurse opened the window shade. "How are you feeling today? You must be hungry. I'll get you a breakfast tray."

Tony didn't answer, but the nurse left without waiting for one. She returned quickly with a tray and set it on the over-the-bed table. "I'm not really hungry," Tony said.

"You need to eat to get strong enough to be discharged. The doctors want to run a few tests, just to make sure, but they don't think any permanent damage has been done." She took his wrist to feel his pulse and put a thermometer in his mouth. After a couple of minutes she took out the thermometer and took his blood pressure. "Any pain now?"

"I wouldn't know. I'm too drugged up to feel any pain."

She smiled. "Well, talk to the doctor when he comes in if you want to alter the dosage. I have to give you what's prescribed."

Tony answered weakly. "I didn't say I minded."

She laughed. "Let me help you to the bathroom." She peeled back the covers and helped Tony out of bed. He got a flashback of Goldie's last days. That jolted him out of his stupor.

"I can walk myself." The nurse let go of his arm and Tony walked unsteadily into the bathroom.

"I'm going to fix up your bed while you're in there so call me if you need me."

Tony came out of the bathroom and got back into bed. "I think I'll sleep some more."

"The doctor should be here later this morning. Do you know where the call button is if you need anything?"

Tony had spent plenty of time in hospitals with all his sick and dying friends. He knew the routine well. "Yes. Thanks." He closed his eyes and fell back asleep.

He woke up a couple of hours later when the door to his room opened and Taye walked in. "Jesus, what happened to you?" Taye asked with no real trace of empathy or surprise.

"I don't know, Taye. You tell me."

"What are you talking about?"

"You knew that guy had a boyfriend, didn't you."

"Now Tony, honey, would I let you go off with a pretty thing already spoken for?"

"Yes. I think you would."

"How did you know I was here, anyway?" Tony asked.

"The club was all abuzz about it when the ambulance came."

"What do you want Taye?" Tony was annoyed and exasperated.

"We still have some business to attend to."

"I told you I'm not interested."

"Now we don't want to let this mishap get in the way."

"We have no more business together. What part of that don't you understand?"

"Fine. Then just give me the book."

Tony turned his head and looked out the window. "No."

"Why do you care if you're not going to use it anyway?" Taye asked.

"Just leave me alone and get out."

Taye stood indignantly and shouted, "You haven't seen the end of this! This is just a taste!" He stormed out of the room.

Tony stared out the window for a while and then decided maybe he was hungry after all. He took the top off the tray and saw a bowl of cold oatmeal, a plate of soggy toast and a glass of warm orange juice. He made a face, but ate the food anyway.

He thought about Taye's threat. He definitely had it in him to cause more trouble and injury. Maybe he should just give him the ledger and be done with it. But Goldie would not have wanted Taye to have it. If anyone was going to continue the business, it had to be him. And he was adamant about the decision he had made. He and Goldie had been incredibly lucky; forty years and they had never been caught. There was no need to tempt fate. Just then the doctor walked in.

"Hello, Tony. My name is Doctor Morris." Tony ignored him and continued to eat. He found it extremely arrogant that doctors always addressed you by your first name, but called themselves by their last name. "How are you feeling?"

"A little groggy and disoriented," Tony mumbled.

"To be expected. We want to take a CT scan to make sure there hasn't been any internal damage or a concussion. You were beaten pretty badly, but I think you'll be fine after a few weeks. I'd like to keep you here for a couple of days just to watch and make sure. The orderly will be here right away to take you down for the scan. Any questions?"

Tony thought about what the nurse had said about asking the doctors to reduce the dosage. Nah. He might as well be groggy if he was going to be stuck in the hospital for a couple of days. "No."

"Okay then. I'll be in tomorrow with the results." Doctor Morris left and the orderly arrived with a wheelchair within minutes. He helped Tony into the chair and off they went.

When the CT scan was over, the orderly wheeled Tony past an atrium on their way back to his room. "Is that for patients or visitors?" Tony asked.

"Both." He pushed Tony back to his room where he helped Tony back into bed. As soon as he left though, Tony got up and walked toward the atrium. He had to take it slow, but he wasn't too dizzy anymore and he was quite bored with lying in bed. Even terrible television shows sounded good to him.

There were a few other people in the atrium. A middle-aged couple sat on the couch, whispering. The woman was in a bathrobe and the man wore a suit. An elderly man wearing hospital garb sat alone in a chair reading. And then there was Rose, sitting about six feet from the television, watching it intently. She wore her Giants' jacket but instead of her Giants' cap, she had a bandage wrapped around her head.

Tony took the chair next to her. It took him a minute to focus on the screen. He wasn't used to sitting so close. A rerun of *Seinfeld* was on. Rose looked bewildered but absorbed. Tony settled back to watch the show. He'd always enjoyed *Seinfeld*, but he wondered whether an elderly Chinese woman would get the jokes. When the show was over not only hadn't she laughed, she hadn't smiled once. Then the music started for the next show and it turned out to be another *Seinfeld*.

"Do you want to watch something else?" Tony asked.

"No. Giants game not until tonight."

"There are other shows we can watch."

"I like this one. It funny."

"You think it's funny?" Tony asked.

"Yes. I hear you laugh too."

"I do think it's funny, but I didn't think you did."

"I laugh quietly."

"So you get the jokes?"

"Why you talk so much? Show start now."

193

"Sorry." Tony sat back to watch the show but he couldn't relax. He kept jiggling his leg and fiddling with the ties to his robe.

"Why you such Nervous Nellie?"

"Excuse me?"

"You so jittery. Make me nervous too."

"Sorry. It's just a habit." He tried to stop his leg from moving and he let go of the ties.

They watched together silently, but soon his leg started bouncing and Rose let out an annoyed sigh and glared at him. "Why you not find something to do if you so fidgety?"

"Like what?"

"How I know. Get a hobby."

"A hobby?" Tony asked.

"Something make you feel good. Something you like to do."

"I don't know what that would be."

"Everyone need a hobby. Maybe you like baseball?"

"Not particularly."

"Too bad. That good hobby."

"So you like these television sitcoms?"

"I like old ones best."

"Yeah, the old ones were good."

"My favorite *I Love Lucy*. You ever watch it?"

"Sure. Everyone over the age of fifty has watched it many times. It was a classic."

"That Lucy make me laugh so hard."

Tony's leg stopped jiggling. The relentless tension in his shoulders eased and the tight lines in his face relaxed into a smile. "Me too."

They watched together silently until the end of the show. Rose picked up the remote. "Maybe another show on." She flicked through the stations and found a *Golden Girls*. "You like this one?"

"Sure." Tony lost himself in the antics of four retired, sixty-something women living together in Miami Beach. Goldie had been the same age and he wondered how Goldie would have done in that situation. Could she have become a Blanche or Rose or Dorothy or Sophie instead of the pot-dealing agoraphobic hippie she had chosen to be? He looked at the elderly Chinese woman sitting next to him. How diametrically opposed this woman was to the *Golden Girls* or to Goldie! "My name is Tony." He smiled at her and put out his hand.

"Rose." She didn't shake his hand. She just nodded without taking her eyes off the television.

"What other shows do you like?" he asked.

"Lots. I have tapes of real old ones like *Father Knows Best* and *Ozzie and Harriet*. On TV I watch *Frasier* and *Friends*, any I find."

195

Tony laughed. "Quite an assortment."

"What funny about it?" Rose scowled at him.

"I don't know. I just wouldn't expect someone like you to enjoy those shows."

"What you mean someone like me!" She was pissed.

Tony felt terrible. Why did he say that? "I'm sorry." He tried to smooth it over. "I guess I put my foot in my mouth on that one."

Rose shot him a quizzical look. "You talk crazy. Your foot not in your mouth."

"It's just a figure of speech. You know, when you say the wrong thing and embarrass yourself. I think it's wonderful that you have these hobbies. Watching baseball games and old situation comedies."

"I not just watch baseball game on TV. I go to all Giant home game."

"Really?"

"I keep score."

"You'll have to teach me. I don't know that much about baseball."

"You no play when kid?"

"Nope. I wasn't really that interested in sports. I liked to draw and daydream."

"Daydream?"

"I'd sit and let my mind wander. I grew up in Ohio and I just dreamt about getting out of there. I imagined myself in exotic places."

"So you draw pictures? Then that your hobby."

"Not really. I haven't drawn anything for many years."

"Never too late."

Tony changed the subject. "So what are you in for?"

"In for?"

"It's just a joke. What's wrong? Why are you in the hospital?"

"I got hit in head by ball at Giants game."

Tony laughed so hard that tears flowed down his cheeks. "You're kidding?"

"Why I kid you. That what happened. Not funny."

"I'm sorry. I just never heard of anything like that. I mean what are the odds?"

Rose shook her head and glowered. "I not think it so funny."

"I'm really sorry. I don't mean to make fun." He tried to suppress his giggles.

"What wrong with you?"

"I was beaten up by a couple of hoodlums trying to find drugs and a valuable book of people's names and contact information."

"That sound pretty funny to me too."

Tony smiled. "You're right. We're quite a pair."

21

JED WAS OUTSIDE WEEDING HIS FRESHLY PLANTED FLOWERBEDS WHEN A CAR DROVE UP. Eric got out and Jed went over to greet him. "Heather isn't coming today?"

"She's having a very hard time, Jed. She lies in bed all day and weeps. I can't get her to come. But I think it would be good for her to come, don't you? It might help her accept it."

"People grieve in their own way. Maybe for her it's easier not to come."

Eric shrugged his shoulders. "I guess. For me, it's better to see her niche, I mean apartment. I have to move forward. I have to get to acceptance." He smiled half-heartedly. "I've read Elizabeth Kubler-Ross's book, *On Death and Dying* more than once."

"I'm not sure we ever truly move on but we can at least try and go forward. It's especially hard for you, losing a child so young." Jed glanced away and took a deep breath. "But we do have to accept it. We are still on this planet for better or worse, so we might as well live the best life we can."

"You're a wise man, Jed."

Jed shook his head. "Not really. I've just had a lot of experience. I've had no choice but to figure it out."

Eric took a Teddy Bear out of the back seat. "I'm sorry, Jed."

"Sorry?"

"For all your losses."

Jed was very moved by Eric's statement. It was hard to believe that a father could care so much about someone else's losses when his daughter's death was so recent. It had taken Jed many years of anger and sorrow and brooding to reach the point in his grief when he could be compassionate toward others. As they walked toward Chloe's apartment together Jed wanted to ask why he was replacing the teddy bear. He decided to wait for Eric to share that information if he wanted. He stood to the side as Eric opened the niche door and replaced the old bear with the new one.

"Mommy has been holding onto Baby Bear because she could still smell you on him. But she wanted me to put him in here with you now. She knows he was your favorite. She still has your blankie and one day she will be able to let that go too. For now, though, I hope you understand that she needs to keep it." Eric let the tears flow and Jed tiptoed away.

Jed went back outside to continue his gardening. Eric came out several minutes later, wiping his eyes and holding the old Teddy Bear. "Please give Heather my regards," Jed said.

"I will." Eric started to get in his car but stopped and walked back to Jed. "This bear is brand new. It was the last one we ever bought for Chloe. I think she would rather see it have a new home. Do you know anyone who might like to have it?"

"Yes. I think I do. Thank you."

Eric nodded and drove off. Jed took the bear into the office. He looked for something to wrap it in to keep it clean. He found some tissue paper and wrapped the bear carefully and placed it on top of the desk. Then he went back outside to weed.

He dug faster and faster to keep the memories from spinning out of control. But it wasn't working. Chloe brought too many of them back. He pictured all those children on the ground, next to their parents after the massacre. Luckily he was interrupted before his mind moved on to the next memory, the most painful one. That was the one he had actually frozen out of his psyche.

It was Frank's friend, Ray. He was tap-dancing down the walk, wearing his signature striped jacket and straw hat. "Top of the morning to you, Jed."

"Hello Ray. I was hoping you'd come by soon. There's something I want to ask you."

"Fire away."

"Goldie's apartment is right next to Frank's and since they both like Broadway tunes I thought I'd like to sing to them every day. But the only song I know is 'Summertime'."

"Follow me, young man. I have the perfect tune. I'll sing it to them now." They went up to the second floor and stood in front of Frank and Goldie. Ray cleared his throat and began to sing "Give My Regards to Broadway."

Jed clapped when he was done. "Could you wait a minute while I get a piece of paper? I'd like to write down the words."

"Sure thing. I'll just talk to Frank here for a while."

Jed went to the office and came back with a pad. Ray dictated the words to him and when he was done, they sang it one time through together. Jed had heard the tune before so he picked it up quickly. "This is perfect, Ray. Thanks."

"Happy to do it. Now I just have one more thing to do before I leave." Ray opened the niche and took out the toy horn and blew it once. "Here's looking at you Frank." He replaced it and Jed watched him tap dance down the stairs and out the door. He liked it when Ray came. He had such a cheerful disposition when he visited. Sunny's daughters were like that too. They came to celebrate their father, not to mourn his passing.

He found Sunny's apartment and figured that he would sing "When the Saints go Marching in." He visited a few more people before going back outside, remarking on their cherished treasures and mementoes, and acknowledging each of their individual personalities. This made him feel better. It helped get his head out of the clouds and to stop being what Sam called a luftmensh.

22

TONY STROLLED DOWN THE HALL TO THE ATRIUM THAT NIGHT AND HE FOUND ROSE WATCHING THE GIANTS' GAME, HER EYES GLUED TO THE TELEVISION. A couple of elderly men watched with her, but they were chatting and only half listening. Tony sat down next to her. "Hi Rose."

She was totally absorbed in the game, keeping careful records in her scorebook. She nodded to Tony and said curtly, "Wait 'til commercial."

Tony sat quietly trying not to jiggle his leg. He didn't want to bother her while she was trying to watch the game. If she watched situation comedies so fervently, he thought she would be even more irritated if she were disturbed while watching baseball. Finally the commercial came on. "How are they doing?"

"Who?"

"Your team. The Giants."

"They winning."

"That's good. The doctor says I can go home tomorrow."

"That nice for you."

"How about you? Has the doctor told you when you can leave?"

"They don't say. They still check for problem in my head. They say they see something on picture of my brain."

"Oh dear. I hope it's nothing bad."

"I don't care. I just want to go home."

"I enjoyed watching television with you and talking with you."

The game came back on and a San Francisco player hit the first pitch toward center field. "Look at that! That ball have eyes!" Rose shouted gleefully.

"Huh?"

"It mean it a good hit. Up middle. Pitcher can't get it. It out of shortstop reach."

Tony smiled at her. "Can you teach me about the game?"

"You bet." Tony moved his chair closer to her and looked over her shoulder at her scorebook. She explained the scoring and what was going on in the field. Tony paid close attention, not because he was that interested, but he really liked Rose and wanted to understand her better. She was quite a character. They stayed there together until the game was over and Rose stood to leave. "I tired. I go to bed."

Tony stood too. "I'll walk you to your room." They left the atrium together and walked down the hall. "I enjoyed meeting you, Rose. And thanks for teaching me about baseball."

"Maybe you start watching too. For a hobby." Rose turned into her room abruptly.

"Bye, Rose," he called to her as she shut the door to her room.

The doctor released Tony early in the morning. He had some bruises and aches and pains, but nothing serious or life threatening. He was expected to recover fully. He walked by Rose's room and peeked in. She was still asleep so he left without saying goodbye.

When he got outside, he debated about where to go. He hadn't thought about it while he was in the hospital. He needed to get his car but he didn't know where it had been impounded and worried whether the police had searched it. He had also missed his appointments. He should probably stop at Goldie's house first and call the realtor to meet him there. But maybe he needed to see the lawyer first to get the papers. He had to prove to the realtor that he was the heir and that he had the power to sell the house. He wanted to get it on the market as soon as possible. He didn't want to have to pay the taxes and insurance on it.

Then there were all the antiques and art. There was still a lot left over, even after she had given away the ones she wanted certain people to have. They were valuable and they should be appraised, not just sold at an estate sale. He was angry with Goldie for being such a hoarder and an agoraphobic. Now he was the one who had to deal with all the possessions she had felt necessary to accumulate.

When he reached Goldie's house, however, any angry feelings he had toward her transferred to Taye. Her front door had been kicked in and he knew it had to be Taye's doing. Although the boxes had been ripped apart and their contents strewn all over the house, it didn't look like anything valuable had been taken. "Did you really think I'd leave the ledger in these boxes, you asshole!" he yelled.

Now he would have to neaten up before he could call the realtor. He took out his phone and dialed the lawyer and made an appointment for that afternoon. He was the sole trustee and beneficiary. The lawyer had told him that all he had to do was sign some papers. That shouldn't take too long. He had enough time to get the house presentable to show the realtor by tomorrow. He would have it cleared out in a couple of days and it would then be ready to show to the public. Things were moving along. He started cleaning up but he needed to get more boxes. The job started to feel overwhelming. He wasn't one hundred percent over his beating and he tired quickly. He curled up on the rug and fell asleep.

Rose woke up when the doctor entered her room. "Hello Rose. How are you feeling this morning?"

She sat up. "I want to go home."

"I know you do." He pulled up a chair next to her bed.

"I feel better. Why can't I leave hospital?"

"Remember I told you there was something suspicious on your MRI and that I needed to talk to the radiologist and the neurologist? Well, I'm afraid there's a tumor on your brain."

"Sure there tumor on brain. I get hit in head."

"No, this has nothing to do with your getting hit in the head by the ball. It's just lucky that you did. We would not have discovered the tumor if you hadn't had the MRI. Now we need to do a biopsy."

"What you do for that?"

"We'll take a small piece of the tumor and —"

"Surgery?" Rose interrupted.

"Well, yes, a small one for the biopsy. Then we would decide if we would do surgery and/or radiation."

"No surgery. No radiation."

"Well, we can determine all that after the biopsy."

"No biopsy."

"Rose, we can't decide how we should proceed without doing the biopsy."

"I no have biopsy. I just want to go home."

The doctor was getting agitated. "The biopsy is not a big deal. It's just a quick process to get a piece of the tumor."

"I said no. I more than eighty year old. What I need to keep going if I sick. I ready to die."

"Is there anyone I can call? A relative or close friend?"

"No. Just let me go home."

"Are you sure?"

"Yes I sure."

The doctor stood. "I can't release you until I feel you can cope at home on your own. I'd like you to think about this. I'll check in with you later today." He left the room and Rose closed her eyes and leaned back into her pillows. She was steadfast in her position. She didn't need to think about it at all.

She rang for the nurse who was waiting for her when she came out of the bathroom. "Where my breakfast?" she asked the nurse brusquely.

"I'll get it. I didn't want to wake you."

"Well, Doctor not care about waking me. Why should you?"

The nurse started to answer but decided it would be best just to get her breakfast tray. Rose finished eating and went into the atrium to spend her day in front of the television.

Meanwhile Tony spent his day cleaning and napping. He called the police station and found out that the car had been broken into. Actually, that was a relief. It probably meant that whoever vandalized it had taken the stuff. He called his insurance company and they took care of picking up the car and taking it to the repair shop.

He made a quick trip in the middle of it all to sign the papers at the lawyer's and have a sushi lunch. The realtor would be by in the morning. An art/antiques appraiser was coming after that and he had the Goodwill truck coming in the afternoon. One of Goldie's best customers was a contractor who was happy to fix the door for an ounce of her finest grass. Although medical marijuana was now legal in California, nobody had the quality that Goldie had. She was known across the state and beyond for what she could get from the Caribbean. It was no wonder Taye wanted that ledger. Even if the state was leaning toward legalizing it for recreational use, there would always be a market for Goldie's product.

Rose passed the day watching some of the newer comedies. She missed her videos. She was always partial to the ones she had already watched. There was no Giants game until tomorrow. Today was a travel day. They were going on the road for ten days so it was a good time to be stuck in the hospital. She wouldn't be missing any home games at AT&T Park.

23

THE DAYS PASSED QUIETLY FOR JED. He sang to Frank, Goldie, and Sunny and blew Frank's horn. He hugged Chloe's bear and reassured her that Mommy would come soon. He talked to some of the others, paying attention to their artifacts so he could personalize the conversation. When he got to Sadie's, he saw that the tomatoes had gotten soft. That was strange. Sam usually noticed that and would have brought more. Come to think of it, he hadn't seen Sam in a while. Maybe he should buy a couple of tomatoes at the grocery store on his way to work tomorrow to replace the ones on the sconces. He glanced at his watch. It had been a slow day for visitors. It still wasn't closing time. He realized that for the first time in many years his time was not his own. He wasn't free to come and go when he pleased. That was the downside of having a job and responsibilities. He felt trapped. It was not a good feeling. But then the door opened and Monica entered the columbarium.

"Are you that shocked to see me?" She laughed at the astonished expression on his face.

"Yes. I am that shocked." Jed smiled back.

"I had an appointment a few blocks from here so I thought I'd stop in and see how you're doing."

"I'm glad you did."

She looked around the room. "It's gorgeous. What a difference! You've brought this building back to life."

"Thank you," he beamed. "I guess I should also thank you for getting me this job." He gazed at Monica and had some long lost sensations. "I close at five. Would you like to get a drink or some dinner?" As soon as he asked it he felt like a fool. Why in the world would she want to go out with him? Just because she flirted with him in her office? And he didn't even have the proper clothes to go to a restaurant.

"I'd love to."

"Really?"

"Yes. Really."

It wasn't until he exhaled that he realized he'd been holding his breath. "I need to go to the office and take care of a few things."

"Take your time. I'd like to look around." He went back to the office and changed into some khakis and a button down shirt. He kept them there for funerals or memorials. He checked his wallet to make sure he had enough money. He did. He looked down at his clothing to make sure they were clean. They were. He'd ask her where to go. She probably knew restaurants in the neighborhood, and particularly places where they wouldn't mind his attire. He felt like a teenager. This was ridiculous. Or maybe it wasn't. Maybe it had just been such a long time since he had cared about a woman that he'd forgotten what it felt like.

He couldn't find her right away after he got back to the main building. He searched the first floor and then looked up to the second and third floors. He was about to go up the stairs when he spotted her standing in front of a niche on the third floor. He climbed the stairs two at a time. When he approached her he saw her wiping tears off her cheek with a tissue. He looked at the nameplate under the door. "Is that a relative of yours?" he asked softly.

She answered without turning around. "Not anymore."

Jed thought that was a weird answer. Of course the man was dead, but people didn't stop referring to them as family members. He looked inside the niche and saw two pictures. One was of a man with his arm around another man. In the other one the same man had his arm around a woman who resembled a younger Monica. The man wore the same shirt in both of them. There was also a quilt square with the word 'AIDS' embroidered on. He stepped back to let her have that moment with the man, the memory, and perhaps the resentment, if he was correct about the scenario.

"Are you ready?" Monica turned around and asked.

"If you are," Jed answered. "Do you know a place in the neighborhood?"

"I know a nice French bistro near my house and I have my car here. I can drive you home after dinner. I don't live too far."

"You don't need to drive me home."

"I don't mind."

"I like to walk."

Monica drove out the gate and waited for Jed to lock it before he got in her car. "I just live down Stanyan, on the other side of the park."

"I don't know the city very well. The last time I lived here I was pretty young. But isn't that Haight Ashbury?"

"Near it. It's a neighborhood called Cole Valley. It's south of the Haight. I like it because it's close to the park and not far from work. The UCSF medical center is there too." She glanced over at Jed to gauge his reaction. She decided to be upfront from the beginning and not hide her diagnosis. Anyway, he had probably guessed it. He had seen the pillbox in her desk. At least he was still interested in going to dinner. She was quite intrigued by this man. He may have led a rough life, but there was something about him, something special and unique, and she wanted to know him better.

Jed glanced back at her, not sure if she wanted him to ask or just acknowledge that he knew she had to take pills every day. He decided to wait for her to bring it up. "Sounds like a nice neighborhood."

"Yes, it is."

What inane banter this was becoming. He wasn't exactly a polished conversationalist but this was ridiculous. He usually responded rather than initiated, but he truly did want to know more about her. So he decided to ask questions, even if it did go against his grain. "Have you always lived in San Francisco?"

"Not in the city, but the bay area." She was surprised that he asked about her. She thought she would have to be guiding the chitchat. "How about you? You mentioned that you had come from southern California on the bus, but had lived in the South as well?"

"I've lived in a lot of places."

"Like where?"

"Do you really want me to list them?"

"Sure. It would help me get to know you better."

"Oakland, Alaska, Alabama, Chicago, Shelter Cove, Seattle, Venice Beach." He took a breath and gazed at her face that was focused on the road in front of her, trying to decide whether he should continue.

"Is that it?"

"Guyana."

She took her eyes off the road briefly and looked at him. "Guyana? Where is that exactly? I've heard of it but I can't remember where it is."

"South America."

"Wow! When did you live there?"

"As a child."

"Really? Did one of your parents have a job there?"

"Sort of."

"That must have been exciting. Isn't it a jungle?"

"Pretty much."

"How long did you live in Guyana?"

"A few years."

"So what did your parents do?"

"You've heard of Jonestown?"

"Of course." Jed exhaled loudly but said nothing. Monica got the hint. He didn't want to

216

continue this conversation. She decided to share some of her childhood now. "I've traveled a bit, but mostly just around the west coast; no place as exotic as you. I have been to New York and Chicago, but I didn't get to sightsee much in those cities. I was there for job-related workshops."

"Do you like your job?"

"Yes. Very much. Do you?"

"Yes, I do."

She drove up to the door of a restaurant on Cole Street. "Well, here we are, but now I have to find a parking space. That's not an easy task in this city."

"Why do you drive, then?"

"For safety. I have some odd hours sometimes and as you know, my job is in the Tenderloin. It's not a good place for a woman alone at night."

"I suppose that's true."

"There's another reason." She paused for a minute and made a sharp U-turn. "Aha - here's a space." She parked the car skillfully and twisted in her seat to look at him after she turned off the car." I have a medical issue and I have both good days and bad days. Sometimes I get very tired and don't want to have to deal with public transportation. It's comforting to have my car to drive."

"I see." Jed didn't know what else to say so he waited for a cue from her.

It didn't take her long to blurt out, "I've been HIV positive for six years." Jed stayed silent and waited for her to continue. "So far it hasn't turned into full-blown AIDS. I am on experimental medication and so far it seems to be working." She sighed loudly, relieved to have gotten it out in the open.

This was one of those confessions that made Jed uneasy about how to respond. Do you say that you're sorry that someone is HIV positive or that you're glad that it hasn't turned into full-blown AIDs? But then he realized that it didn't need a response. He put his arm on her shoulder and smiled. "There. You said it."

She started to laugh and when Jed joined in, the air cleared and the stiffness between them melted away. "Let's go eat." She opened her door before Jed had a chance to walk around and open it for her.

They walked the three blocks to Zazie's. Jed hadn't eaten in a French restaurant before. He didn't know what a lot of the dishes on the menu contained, but he knew beef, chicken and fish and he wasn't a picky eater. The prices were steep, but he could skip some meals the rest of the week. She ordered a glass of wine so he did too. He laughed to himself when he realized that he paid more for a glass of wine than he usually paid for a full meal.

They laughed often and the time went quickly. Too quickly, as neither of them seemed to want the night to end. After three hours, though, the waiter gave them a pleading look that they couldn't ignore any longer. When they got to Monica's car she asked him again if he wanted a ride.

"No. I truly do like to walk."

It was extremely awkward as she got into her car. "Thank you for dinner, Jed. Next time it's on me."

"That would be nice," he answered. They looked at each other, each waiting for the other one to say something or make a move. "I guess you could help me with directions. I need to get to Eddy Street."

"Easiest would be to walk down Haight to Market."

"I saw Haight Street when we drove by it. Thanks."

They hesitated again and then Monica started her car. "I really enjoyed myself."

"I did too. I'm glad you came by the columbarium."

She drove away and Jed walked home. It might be more appropriate to say he flew.

24

TONY WAS AT THE LAWYER'S OFFICE
FIRST THING IN THE MORNING TO
SIGN THE PAPERS. He brought the signed
copies to Goldie's where he was meeting the
realtor at ten. The house was in quite a state of
disrepair and it was not in an ideal
neighborhood, but this was San Francisco so
the asking price was half a million dollars. The
realtor had done her homework. Even if it sold
immediately, escrow would take awhile so there
would be enough time for Tony to get
everything squared away. The trucks from the
antique dealer and the thrift store had come and
gone by one. The house was empty and the sign
was on the front lawn. There was nothing left
to do but wait.

He left Goldie's house and started
meandering back to his own apartment. He
took his time because he wasn't sure what he
would do when he got there. His mind drifted
to Rose and her incongruous interests and how
she had admonished him for not having a

hobby. He crossed the street and found himself standing in front of Flax Art. "What the hell," he shrugged and went in.

When he got home he opened his bag and spread out all his newly bought items on the kitchen table. There were two sizes of sketchpads, a set of charcoal and a set of graphite pencils, three types of erasers including an electric one, tortillons for shading, a hand held pencil sharpener, and a book entitled *The Complete Book of Drawing*. He opened to the first page of the larger sketchpad and looked through the collection of pencils he had bought. He took out an HB figuring that was a safe one to start with, not too hard and not too soft. He started to doodle and before he knew it, he was drawing smoothly and confidently. It was like riding a bicycle. It all came back to him, even though it had been decades.

After an hour or so of playing around, he decided he wanted to draw something real. He gathered his pad, pencils, and eraser and set off for the columbarium. He hadn't visited Goldie in awhile. He wanted to tell her that things were going along smoothly with her estate and about Taye and his hospital stay. He also wanted to talk about Rose and his newfound hobby. Besides, that building would be a great challenge to draw.

When he got to the columbarium he sat on the bench outside. There was still enough sunlight left. He'd visit Goldie when it started to get dark. He took out his pad and started a rudimentary sketch. He was so focused in his work that he was oblivious to people coming and going. Jed approached him close to five to let him know he'd be closing up shortly.

"Are you drawing the columbarium?" Jed asked.

"Yes. It's such a gorgeous building, I doubt I can do it justice."

"May I see it?"

Tony showed him his picture. "It's not finished."

"It's really good. I didn't know you could draw."

"Neither did I. It's been decades."

"What made you start up again?"

"Rose."

"A flower?"

"No, a little old Chinese lady I met."

"I know Rose. The Giants fan?"

"That's her."

"She's reserved an apartment here."

"Has she? No kidding." Tony stood abruptly. "I'd better hurry. I want to go see Goldie before you close up." Tony put his art supplies away and he and Jed went inside. "Did you know she's in the hospital?"

222

"Who?"

"Rose."

"No, I didn't. What happened?"

Tony shook his head. "You won't believe it. She got hit in the head by a ball at a Giants' game."

"That was Rose? It was all over the news. Is she going to be okay?"

"I think so. She's such a character. I met her in the atrium at the hospital. She was watching all these old reruns of television situation comedies."

"Were you at the hospital to visit Goldie?"

Tony hesitated. He didn't really want to share the story but he knew Jed would never pry. "I was actually in myself. But I'm fine now."

"I'm glad to hear that." As Tony expected, Jed didn't ask any other questions. "I've learned a new song that I sing to Goldie and Frank every day," Jed said as they got to Goldie's apartment.

"What song is that?"

Jed started to sing and Tony soon joined in. Broadway certainly got some rousing regards. Jed left Tony alone with Goldie while he closed up the office.

They walked out together and Jed locked the door to the building and the front gate. "I'm sorry to hear about Rose. I wonder if anyone else has ever gotten hit in the head by a home run ball at a baseball game."

"I don't know. It was hard not to laugh when she told me."

"I can see why. It's pretty funny. It's nice to see you, Tony, and I'm glad you've gone back to drawing."

"I am too. I'll be back tomorrow to work on it some more."

"I'm sure Goldie would enjoy another chorus. Goodnight, Tony."

"Goodnight, Jed." Jed watched Tony stroll out the gate and thought about how much his demeanor had changed. He wasn't as irritable and nervous. Maybe it was his new interest in drawing or the death of Goldie. He had noticed it in others. Sometimes after a loved one dies, it's more of an awakening instead of an ending. Not for Sam and not for Heather and Eric, but maybe for Tony. Jed decided to walk on the beach, but not because he was angry. For once it was because he wanted to appreciate his own feeling of serenity.

Tony thought he'd stop at the hospital and see Rose. He could show her his picture and thank her for reigniting his interest in drawing. He wanted to share with her the coincidence that they both knew Jed and about how they sang to Goldie. It wouldn't surprise him to find out that Rose had Broadway shows as another of her diverse interests.

He found her in the atrium sitting in a wheelchair. Her head was bandaged and she did not look happy. "Hi Rose, remember me?"

"How I forget you so soon. It only be a couple days."

"Why the bandage?"

"Doc talk me into another test," she said vindictively.

Tony didn't know how to respond since she seemed so angry about it. He decided to change the subject. "I took your advice."

"What advice?"

"Getting myself a hobby."

"You learn about baseball?"

Tony laughed. "No. I'll wait for you to teach me that." He opened his pad and showed her his drawing.

"That the columbarium?"

"Yes. I talked to Jed and I told him about your accident. He was very sorry to hear it."

"He good man. You good artist."

"Thanks."

"Can I have picture?"

Tony was surprised. "You want this picture?"

"That what I say."

225

"Uh, okay. But it's not finished yet."

"Okay. You give me when you finish."

Tony turned to the television. "What are you watching?"

"Stupid show. I wasn't here first so couldn't change station to my shows. Have to watch what these people want."

Law and Order was on. "You don't like this show? It's won a lot of Emmys. This show and all its franchises are very popular."

"I like my shows. I not like new ones. Older ones better."

"This show is pretty old too."

"Not old enough."

The doctor entered the atrium and scouted out the room. When he spotted Rose he made a beeline for her wheelchair. "Rose, I need to take you back to your room so we can talk privately."

"We talk here. I don't like the room."

Tony stood. "I can leave if you need privacy."

"No. You sit. Tony can hear what you say."

"If that's what you want," the doctor said. "Hello Tony." They shook hands. "I got the results of the biopsy. I'm afraid the tumor is malignant. I made an appointment with an oncologist for you so you can discuss what the next step will be."

"I told you. No next step. You said I go home tomorrow."

"I rushed the lab to get these results and I've scheduled the appointment for you for tomorrow afternoon. I just want you to stay one more day so you can keep this appointment with the oncologist. I know what you said, but I'd like to give the oncologist a chance to explain all the options."

"No. I want to go home tomorrow. You say I could."

The doctor turned to Tony, his eyes inviting him to step in and try to convince Rose. "Why not wait one more day and just find out what the oncologist has to say?" Tony asked.

"I not gonna change mind. I go home tomorrow. I not interested." She turned to the doctor. "I only agree to biopsy because you say I go home tomorrow."

Tony shrugged his shoulders at the doctor. "I'll get the discharge papers ready, Rose. I'll bring them in tomorrow morning. Maybe you can talk to Tony a little more about it." He left and Rose scrunched her nose in disgust.

"Maybe there's something easy to be done and you can be cured," Tony said.

"No want any of it. No surgery. No radiation. No chemotherapy."

"Did the hit in the head cause the tumor?"

"Doc say it already there. He say just good thing I got hit so they take pictures. I no think it good thing. I not need to know."

"Maybe you should at least ask what will happen if you do nothing. I mean, so you'll know what to expect."

"I no like knowing. I rather just go the way I supposed to." She went back to watching television.

"I'll be right back." Tony caught up with the doctor in the hallway. "Doctor, can I ask you something?"

"Yes?"

"Will she die if she doesn't have surgery or radiation?"

"Yes. Surgery is risky at her age, but it's the only chance for survival."

"Even though she's in her eighties?"

"She's strong and she's in good health otherwise. Who knows? She could possibly live a few more years."

"A few more years of what though?"

"That's for the oncologist to explain. I don't have the answer to that."

"So how long do you think she has?"

"Hard to say. A month? Two? I'd be surprised if she'd last longer than that."

"So what will happen? What will this next month or two look like?"

"She'll have a lot of weakness and fatigue. Her eyesight will keep getting worse and worse until she'll eventually be blind. She'll have dizziness, fainting, confusion . . . it won't be easy."

"Thanks." Tony walked back to the atrium and sat down next to Rose. "I'll pick you up in the morning to take you home."

"No. I take bus."

"I'll be here at eight, early enough so you won't sneak out before I arrive."

Rose didn't answer. Tony took that to mean thanks.

25

TONY ARRIVED AT THE HOSPITAL AT EIGHT, AS HE SAID HE WOULD. Rose sat on her bed, dressed in her Giants' attire. "Hi Rose. Are you ready to go?"

"Nurse say I have to wait for Doc with papers."

"Did you have breakfast?"

She spit into the air. "Bad food here. I go home and eat."

"Can I take you out for breakfast?"

"I have food at home."

"I'd like to."

Rose stared at him intently. "Why you do this?"

"Do what?"

"This."

"What do you mean? Why am I being nice to you?"

"You say it. Not me."

"I like you."

Rose continued staring at him, but didn't say a word. They sat there silently for several minutes until the doctor arrived. "Okay Rose, but I'm discharging you against my better judgment."

Rose took the papers. "What else I have to do?"

"The nurse will explain the discharge instructions." Rose was out the door in a flash while Tony and the doctor looked at each other in astonishment.

Tony ran after her. "Wait up!" He caught up to her at the elevator. "You don't seem sick to me!"

"I not sick. That doctor wrong."

"I don't think–." Tony stopped himself. There was no need to say anything. Rose was not going to listen to anyone. She was like Goldie that way. "My car is parked up the street. Will you at least wait in the lobby for me to get it? It's raining."

She looked at him hard, as if to say "no". Then she shook her head and blinked her eyes several times. She put her hand on Tony's arm to steady herself. She was a little dizzy and seeing double. "Okay." They walked out of the elevator and into the lobby. Rose lowered herself gingerly onto a chair by the door. Tony left her there to get his car.

When he pulled up to the entrance, he expected Rose to see him and come outside. He sat for a minute and glanced through the window. Rose sat straight and wooden on the chair, her eyes staring directly ahead. She seemed oblivious to anything going on around her. Tony realized she was not going to notice him. He wondered if it was because she couldn't see that far. He hadn't known her before, so he couldn't determine whether this was a new condition or something that had been developing for years. He got out of the car and had a few words with the security guard who told him he couldn't leave his car unattended. Tony ignored him and went inside to get Rose. He tried to help her into the passenger seat, but she squirmed away. "I no need your help. I not invalid."

Tony shrugged. "I know. I'm just –" He stopped himself. She wasn't listening. Apparently she wasn't comfortable in his car. She seemed nervous and anxious. He didn't know if it was because she didn't know him well, or that she wasn't used to riding in automobiles.

Tony drove up Portrero Street and decided to get on the 101. He had been stuck in some construction going to the hospital and he thought he could avoid it if he didn't take the city streets. "What you doing?" Rose yelled. "Why you go this way?"

"There's construction. I thought it would be easier."

232

"Not easy on highway. Get off." She was quite agitated.

Tony was already on the onramp. "I'll get off at the next exit."

"Well hurry up!" She held on tightly to the sides of the seat with a stern frown on her face. He got off on the Fourth Street exit and turned onto Third Street. They drove through the heart of downtown to get to Rose's apartment. The traffic was especially bad. It was nine a.m. and everyone was trying to get to work. "What kind of stupid shortcut you think you take going that way?"

"I was just trying to avoid downtown and the traffic from the construction. I had planned to get off –." Tony stopped and shook his head. "It doesn't matter. I probably could have gone up Van Ness. But it would be crowded everywhere now. It's the morning commute time."

"I could be home by now if on bus," Rose grumbled.

Tony decided to change the subject. "Do you need anything before you go home? Groceries? Medicine?"

"I walk to store like always."

"Rose. You just came out of being in the hospital. You might as well take advantage of my car and stock up on things you need. You don't know how you're going to feel for the next few days. Let me take you to the store. There's a Whole Foods a couple of blocks over."

"Whole Foods? That like that health food stuff? No. I go to Chinese market near house and my friend's restaurant on Clement. He give me break."

"Then how about I drive you over to the restaurant and you can stock up on some food."

Rose thought for a minute. "That be okay."

Tony took a left on Geary and drove west through Union Square, dodging tourists laden with shopping bags. They passed through the nondescript area that was a mixture of charming townhomes on Nob Hill and rundown tenements in the Tenderloin. There might be a high-rise expensive chain hotel looming over the street while panhandlers sat in front of it. The commingling of the two worlds, however, was easy with neither the tourists nor the derelicts paying much attention to the disparity.

They sailed through Japantown, past the Peace Pagoda. The traffic became less congested and stayed that way through the tunnel. Before they knew it they were at Arguello Boulevard. Tony took a right and a quick left and it brought them in front of the

234

Chinese restaurant. Although traffic was light, parking was still a problem. "I'll let you out and look for a place to park," Tony said.

"No, you wait. I get food myself." Rose got out of the car before he had a chance to argue. Tony laughed when Rose came out with a bag of take out cartons. He could have had as many as he needed if he'd known Rose a few weeks ago. He had noticed a small grocery store on the corner so when Rose got back in the car, he asked her if she wanted to get anything from there. "Maybe some coca cola and waffles," she replied. She got out of the car again, this time more slowly and cautiously. She spent a few minutes in the store and came out with a 12 pack of coke and two boxes of frozen waffles. Her diet was as interesting as her choice of television programs.

"Are you sure you don't want to stop at a drug store?"

"No. Let's go."

Tony made a few stabs at chitchat, but Rose seemed preoccupied so he left her alone. She directed him through the streets of the Richmond district, through the area that had become another Chinatown. There were blocks and blocks of Asian restaurants and shops topped by two or three stories of dilapidated apartments. It was difficult to find the narrow metal doors that led up to the residences in between the store entrances. Just like Chinatown, outside of many of the shops were tables of trinkets and racks of cheap T-shirts with pictures of the Golden Gate Bridge and Fisherman's Wharf. "I get out here," Rose said suddenly.

Tony stopped the car and searched for a door that might lead upstairs. Cars behind him blew their horns in aggravation. "Where?"

"Red door next to bakery."

Tony found the door and pulled up next to a fire hydrant. He reached into the back seat for his sketchpad and tore off a corner of a piece of paper. He scribbled on it and handed it to Rose. "This is my phone number. Please call me anytime."

"Why I call you?"

"If you need something. Or even just a visitor."

"I no have visitors." She stared at him.

"I'd like to visit you. Will you give me your phone number?"

Rose thought for a moment while Tony sat patiently, poised with his pencil and sketchpad. "I write it." He handed her the pad and paper and she scribbled on it.

Tony questioned whether she would ever call him or if she would answer if he called her. "Let me help you upstairs." He wanted to know her apartment number so he could stop in and check on her. She started to say no but she realized that there were too many packages. She got out of the car with her Chinese food bag and left the coke and waffles for Tony. He put on his hazard lights and chased after her. That little old lady could really move fast.

When she opened the door Tony was taken aback. The apartment was tiny and dwarfed even more by the large console television and the wall of tapes. After setting the sodas and waffles on the miniature Formica dinette table, he walked over to the bookshelves to read some of the titles. The tapes were carefully labeled and alphabetized. "This brings me back to my childhood. I watched all these shows." He took one out and chuckled.

"Make sure you put back in right place."

Tony remembered his car parked at the hydrant and quickly returned the tape. "I'd better get downstairs before I get a ticket. I'll check in with you tomorrow."

"I fine."

Tony didn't answer. He didn't want to get into an argument. But before closing the door behind him he called out, "I'd love to watch some of these shows again." He shut the door before she had a chance to reply.

26

JED WOKE UP THINKING ABOUT MONICA. That was a foreign emotion to him. The last time he'd dreamt of a woman was probably fifteen years ago. That was the last time he'd had anything resembling a steady job and a normal life. It was also the last time he'd loved anyone like that. But that had ended in tragedy and failure, just like all the other relationships he'd had, even those that weren't romantic. Everything he touched and cared about seemed to turn into a catastrophe. And what would happen if Monica's HIV became full-blown AIDS? He got up and showered, trying to wash away the past as well as the future.

He stopped at the deli for coffee and a bagel on his way to work. It was too early for the "gang," but Abe was happy to see him. "I'm worried about Sam," Abe said.

"Has he been coming to the deli?" Jed asked.

"Yeah, pretty much every day, but he's so depressed."

"I know. He cries so hard when he visits Sadie."

"You mean a lot to him, Jed. I hope you know that."

"He's a good man."

"This is a time when you want to have children to comfort you. It's too bad they never had any."

Jed was glad that he chose to put Chloe next to Sadie. But, as it always did, allusions to children brought things up that he didn't want to think about. "How old is Sam?"

"Eighty-eight I think." Abe sighed. "We've known each other for over fifty years. We met right after he moved to San Francisco."

"I wish I'd known Sadie."

"She was quite a wonderful woman. And she really did grow the best tomatoes in the city. She won awards and everything."

"San Francisco is not an easy place to grow tomatoes. It's so cold and foggy."

"She was a magician in the garden."

"I sure could use her now," Jed said. "I'd love to plant a flower and vegetable garden at the columbarium."

"It would be nice to have new life sprouting at that house for the dead," Abe

239

mused. He chuckled. "You could be my supplier."

"You will definitely be my first customer if I ever figure out how to do it."

He was working on the third floor when Carl arrived with a middle-aged woman dressed in expensive office attire. Her face was etched into what looked like a permanent frown. "Jed? You in here?" Carl called.

"I'll be right there." Jed came down the stairs and noticed that Carl's usual jovial demeanor was more worried and formal.

"This is Linda Barclay. She's one of the board members that was unable to attend when the others visited."

Jed shook her hand but his eyes were on Carl, letting him know that he understood who she was.

"I can see what everyone is talking about. You have done a nice job with the building."

"Thank you."

"Where can we go to talk privately?"

"I guess to the office." Jed led her out the back door with Carl following a few steps behind.

It was Jed's first inclination to let Ms. Barclay have the office chair, but then he decided that he should be in the more authoritative position for this conversation. He offered her the side chair and he sat in the higher and larger desk one. Carl stood by the door.

"Mr. Henshaw has told you my concerns, I believe?"

"Yes." Jed figured short answers were best, the same as when questioned by police or attorneys.

"Can you explain yourself?"

"I am wanted for questioning by the Los Angeles Police Department about a murder I did not commit."

"Why would they want to question you?"

"Because I was in the room when she died."

"If you're innocent, why don't you let them question you?"

Jed looked at Carl. Should be answer honestly? Does she know about his past? Does she need to? He was not a criminal. He had nothing to hide. And more than that, he was not a liar. "Because I was a homeless Black man who had a motive. I doubt I would get fair treatment. If you want references from my years in Venice Beach, I will get them for you. If you want me to leave, I will leave. But I will not talk to the Los Angeles Police."

Ms. Barclay hesitated and stared into Jed's eyes. She felt it was wrong to hire a man

241

who was wanted by the police. The board was remiss to rely on Henshaw's word. And now her son-in-law expected her to turn him in. She also had her position and reputation to think of. Jed had done much of the hard work already. The place looked better than it ever had. They could find someone to keep it clean. But, she liked him. She liked his honesty and candor. "Get me those references and we'll go from there." She stood and motioned to Carl. "You can let the board know that we are waiting for references before making any further decisions. Let's go." She walked out. Carl watched Jed's reaction to see if it was positive before he said anything. He couldn't tell.

"I'll stop by later and we can talk," Carl said with less conviction in his voice than he had hoped for at the end of this conversation.

Jed sat motionless after they left. He didn't know how he felt or what he wanted to do. It wasn't that he couldn't get the references. He knew Finn and Luis would give him glowing ones. But it meant contacting them both, bringing back everything he had left there.

He thought about the title of Finn's book: *Those Who Forget the Past are Condemned to Repeat It* and how he had never quite come to terms with whether or not he believed that. He wondered if Finn ever truly had. He hadn't told Finn where he was going when he left. He didn't want to put him in a position to have to lie to the police if they questioned him. Now he was sorry he had offered to get the references. Maybe leaving was his only alternative.

And then he thought of Monica again. Could he let down his guard again and open himself up to her? He had done it with Finn and look what happened. It seemed always to end in disaster when he did. His chest burned, his face tightened and his stomach churned. He needed to walk but he couldn't leave the columbarium. Yes he could. He had the keys. He could just mail the keys back to Carl.

He took his jacket and walked out the door of the office, locking it behind him. When he got inside the main building he made the rounds. He tooted Frank's horn and sang to him and Goldie. He hugged Chloe's teddy bear and checked on Sadie's tomatoes. They were now totally rotten: dreck, as Sam would call them. He was really worried now. It had obviously been quite a while since Sam was there. There was nothing he could do about the tomatoes now. He looked at Rose's empty apartment and wondered how she would want it decorated. He had to get outside. He checked that it was empty of visitors before locking the door to the main building.

When he got to Geary he turned left toward the beach. He had thought about

243

turning right and going to Glide Church instead, but he didn't want Monica to see him like this. He promised himself, though, that if he did leave, he would say goodbye. He had never left the people he cared about without saying goodbye and that was one promise he would always keep.

He walked about three blocks and stopped abruptly. There would be visitors and they would find it closed. He thought of Sam, trudging all that way just to change Sadie's tomatoes. And what if Heather finally got up the courage to come visit Chloe and then couldn't get in to see her. And Ray had to come such a long distance from his daughter's house whenever he called on Frank. He turned around and went back. He would do this the right way. He would call Carl and let him know ahead of time. That way someone could be there tomorrow to let people in.

When he got back, Monica was sitting in her car parked outside the gate. Seeing her really lifted his spirits. She got out to greet him and her smile was so genuine that without thinking twice, he hugged her. And then, before he knew it, their lips met. Another car drove up and they pulled apart. "I brought some lunch. Have you eaten?" she asked.

He couldn't believe how calm he felt. All the anger and fear had left his body and he felt protected and protective. "No, I haven't. And I'm starved." He unlocked the gate and the door and they walked inside. Jed pulled a couple of chairs up to a side table and they ate the sandwiches without talking, but with eyes locked.

After they finished eating, Monica said, "I can't stay too long. I have to get back to work. But I missed you."

Jed was in a quandary. He couldn't bring himself to tell her what was going on. As glad as he had been to see her, he was also sorry. He didn't know what he wanted to do about telling her or about the whole predicament. "Can we have dinner tonight?" He finally said with the hope that by then he would figure out what to do.

"Absolutely. I'll be here as soon as I can after five."

"Let's meet somewhere." He didn't want her to see him leave the keys behind if that was his decision.

"I'd be happy to pick you up."

"Let's just meet at Zazie's at six."

"I know I can't change your mind. You like to walk."

"Yes, I do." He pecked her on the cheek. He didn't want any of the visitors to see him kiss her on the lips.

She shook her head and teased him. "I don't think anyone cares if you kiss me."

"I just feel funny about it in here."

She laughed. "In here? Of all places? Do you think people are watching from inside their niches?" She grinned at him and left.

He spent the rest of the afternoon doing busy work and fretting. By the time five o'clock rolled around, he was no closer to a decision than he had been at noon. He locked up and kept the keys, and started walking toward the restaurant.

He got there before six and waited outside. He was always afraid that he would get kicked out of places for the way he looked. He thought they would be more welcoming if he entered with Monica. When she drove up she motioned for him to get in the car. He opened the door and saw a bag of groceries in the back seat. "I thought it would be nice if I cooked dinner for us instead. I hope that's okay with you."

It was okay with him, but he was also nervous and frightened. What expectations would she have at her apartment? He stood frozen at the open passenger door. Her face went from cheerful anticipation to worried embarrassment. He didn't want to hurt her, but he was confused and panicked. "I guess so." Why did he say that? It probably made her feel even worse. "I mean I'd like that." He got in the car.

Monica drove off, but with a bit of trepidation. They drove in silence. Jed knew he needed to say something but he was at a loss. He felt like anything he said would be misinterpreted. He didn't want to pretend that all was fine when he might be leaving tomorrow for good. The best thing, as usual, would be the truth. "I'm glad we'll be at your house tonight. I have a lot to tell you."

Monica breathed a sigh of relief. At least he wasn't rejecting her. She had made a huge leap of faith with Jed, that he would be understanding and amenable. "I'm glad you feel comfortable talking to me."

"I am comfortable with you. I want you to know that, no matter what happens."

She finally found a parking space and pulled in. She didn't get right out of the car after she took the key out. She turned to Jed and looked at him warily. "Tell me, Jed. What's going on? I thought we had a wonderful time. I thought that you . . ." She stopped speaking to catch the lump in her throat.

"I do like you a lot. I do. I just want you to know some things from my past before we go any further." There. He said what he needed to say. He would let it be her decision about where the relationship would go. And he would trust that whatever she said in the conversation would help him choose his own direction as well. There was nothing hurtful in the truth.

She relaxed and opened her door. "My apartment is up the block." Jed took the bag of groceries out of the back and followed her up the street and into her apartment. He put the bag on the kitchen counter and took her in his arms and kissed her. "That's better," she sighed. She busied herself making dinner while Jed looked around the apartment. It was sparsely decorated with few mementoes and new-looking furniture. He thought it strange for someone who said she'd lived in the Bay area all her life to have so little in her apartment. The walls were bare and there weren't any framed pictures or knick-knacks on any of the tables in the living room. She did have an extensive selection of books and CDs.

"Have you lived in this apartment long?" Jed asked as he entered the kitchen.

"About five years. Is that long?"

"For me, yes."

"Why do you ask?" she wondered.

"No reason. Well, I guess I was just curious why you didn't have a lot of things and why the furniture looks new."

She had been cooking at the stove and she turned around to face him. "Shall we begin?"

"You mean dinner?"

"No, telling each other about our pasts."

"Okay." They stood silently for a minute and then Jed laughed. "Shall we toss a coin to see who goes first?"

"Maybe it would be easier of we just asked each other questions," she replied.

"You start, then, by answering the one I just asked."

"Which question?"

"The one about why your apartment is so sparse."

Monica took a deep breath. "I moved into this apartment when I left my husband after he told me he had AIDS and that he had been sleeping with his best friend."

Jed's eyes grew wide. "His male friend?"

"Yep. And I left everything behind because I didn't want any of it."

"So that must have been his niche at the columbarium that you were standing in front of."

"Yes. He died a couple of years ago."

"And that was your picture inside?"

"Yes."

"It didn't look like you."

"It was taken many years ago. We had been together a long time." She turned back to stirring the pot on the stove. "Now it's your turn. Why did you leave Los Angeles?"

"I was living in Venice at the beach."

"Why would you leave the beach to come here?"

"The police were looking for me. They think I murdered someone but I didn't." She turned around and he watched her face to see her reaction. She didn't wince, or look afraid, or look disapproving. She just looked empathetic and concerned.

"Why do they think it was you?"

"Because I was with her when she died."

"Why can't you tell them that?"

He took her hands in his and looked into her eyes. "She fell and hit her head, but I didn't push her. They will not believe me. I was a Black, unemployed vagrant. And I had a motive."

"Was she your girlfriend?"

"Good God no!"

"So what was your motive?"

He took a deep breath. "She was a nurse when I was a child in Jonestown and she was the one who administered the poison to my mother and my sister and killed them."

Monica's eyes widened. "My God!"

"Most of the Jonestown residents were forced to take the Kool Aid. They did not commit suicide. People don't realize that."

She hugged him tightly, holding on for several minutes. "I'm sorry, Jed," she said in a muffled voice, her mouth still pressed into his shoulder.

He pulled away. "And there was another reason the cops think I killed Antoinette. She was blackmailing my friend, Finn."

"He was a friend from Jonestown?"

"No, he was a friend from Venice. She had been the hospice nurse for his wife."

"Why was she blackmailing him?"

"She saw him give his wife an extra dose of insulin."

"And that killed his wife?"

"Yes. But she was dying and she wanted him to do it."

"So the cops think he had put you up to it?"

"I'm not sure what they think but I didn't want to find out."

"I understand why you left Venice. But how did you end up there to begin with? And why were you homeless?"

"Can we stay on this question for a little longer?"

"I'm sorry. Is there more?"

"Well, sort of. I have a problem, now. This is what I wanted to talk to you about. The rest is just the past; the future is what's important to us."

She smiled broadly and kissed him. "Yes. You're right. Dinner's ready if you want to sit down and eat while we talk."

He took a breath. "Sure." They sat down but neither started to eat. "One of the Neptune Society board members found out that the LA cops were looking for me. I'm afraid what might happen if I stay at the columbarium."

Monica's face turned ashen. "Did she threaten to call them?"

"Not exactly, but I think she would. She asked me to give her some references. She said maybe it would be enough for her. But I think that's bullshit. I don't trust her."

"So . . . you have to leave . . . now?"

He looked down and shrugged. "I don't know."

Monica gazed at Jed with moist eyes. "I don't want you to go."

He looked up at her. "I don't want to go."

"Then we need to find a way for you to stay. You could find a job somewhere else?"

"I like my job. I –." He stopped, not sure whether she would think he was crazy for what he wanted to say next.

Monica looked at him expectantly, but he didn't take the bait. After a couple of minutes of silence, she finally spoke. "Then we need to figure out a way for you to stay there. Maybe I can talk to her. I could tell her that her information is incorrect."

"Why would she listen to you?"

She shrugged her shoulders. "I have friends in high places."

He raised his eyebrows. "Higher than her?"

"Yes. I don't think you understand the power and influence Glide Church has in this city. In a good way, I should add."

Jed had a glimmer of hope. But he needed time to think. He needed to be alone, but he didn't want to leave. "Now it's my turn to ask you a question."

She took a mouthful of food. "Okay."

He followed her lead and took a bite himself before asking the only real question he cared about. "What about your disease?" This was difficult for him. He didn't like asking people anything.

"What about it?" she answered quickly. "I already told you. It's not AIDS . . . yet. I have no significant side effects from the medicine I take."

"That's not what I meant."

"Then what did you mean?" He hoped she would figure it out herself. She did. "Ah. I think I get it now." He smiled and she smiled back. "Condoms and being careful. I know what to do."

"Have you . . . um . . . since you were diagnosed?"

Her smile disappeared and her face took on a serious, contemplative expression. "No. You would be the first."

"That makes it even more special." Jed took her hand and she squeezed it. "I'm not that hungry right now."

"Me neither." They stood and walked hand in hand to the bedroom.

27

TONY AWOKE WITH A START WHEN THE TELEPHONE RANG. He rolled over sleepily, picked up his phone, and glanced at the screen. It was an unfamiliar number. He was going to let it go to voicemail, but then he remembered that he had given Rose his phone number. Maybe that's who was calling. The caller had hung up, though, by the time he answered it. He checked his pockets and found the scrap of paper with Rose's number on it. It was the same. "Damn!" he muttered. He called it back but there was no answer. He jumped out of bed, dressed hurriedly and ran out to his car.

When he arrived at Rose's apartment building, he looked for a buzzer with her name on it. Nothing. He banged on the door. He kept ringing other buzzers until someone finally let him in. He ran up the stairs and when he got to Rose's door, he was truly panicked. "Rose! Rose! It's me. Tony."

She opened the door and he saw true terror in her eyes. "Tony? That you?"

"Yes. It's me. What is it? Can't you see?"

"No. I think I blind now." She felt her way back to the couch, touching the wall and tripping a couple of times.

"The doctor said it would happen but I didn't think so fast," Tony said while he helped her sit.

"Doctor tell you that?"

"Didn't he tell you?"

"He no talk to me about anything," she answered disgustedly.

"That's because you wouldn't let him, Rose."

She snorted. "Hah! That doctor not know everything."

"Whatever. But now something needs to be done. You called me to help so let me help."

"Okay."

"When did it happen? I mean the blindness? Last night? This morning?"

"I dizzy last night so I go to bed early. I wake up and can't see. I remember your number. I dial many times before get right one."

Tony smiled and patted her hand. "Where are the discharge papers from the hospital? I'll call the doctor."

"No! I won't go back there. I manage here."

Tony took a deep breath. He, more than anyone, knew what that meant. "Do you have relatives I can call? Or friends?"

"No. I manage myself. I pay you to buy me food. Okay?"

"I will buy you food, but you will not pay me."

"Yes!" Rose said angrily. "I pay you!"

"I don't want your money. I don't need any money. I have enough."

She pursed her lips and folded her arms as if to say "harrumph" like a spoiled two-year old. "I just get used to this. I find my way around apartment. I just scared to go outside alone."

"I understand. We can arrange things so that it will be easy for you to access what you need." They spent the next couple of hours organizing her apartment. She could still see outlines and shadows, but they both knew that it would not be long before she would be totally blind. "I will come every day."

"No. I be okay."

"It's not a problem. I have nothing else to do." After they finished getting the apartment ready, they each had a frozen waffle. Tony got Rose settled in for a morning of *I Love Lucy* and *My Three Sons*. "I'm going home to take a shower and get my sketchbook. I'll be back in a couple of hours. Shall I pick up something for lunch?"

"No. Maybe we go to columbarium later?"

"You want to go out today? Don't you want to rest? You just got out of the hospital."

"I need to go there soon. Today as good as any."

"Sure. We can go this afternoon." He left and Rose grabbed the remote to turn up the volume. She didn't need to see the shows anyway. She knew them by heart. She would just listen and visualize. But the baseball games were a different story. In the old days she had always listened to them on the radio, but she had gotten used to watching the action. She wondered if she would ever go to AT&T Park again. For one fleeting moment, she felt sad, but she didn't allow herself to dwell there.

Jed spent the morning touching up the ornate trim that adorned the columns inside the building. There were so many recesses and decorative features that the painting task was monumental and never-ending. But because the work was so intricate, it occupied his mind and kept him from thinking too much.

He was up on a ladder, repainting a gold flower that adorned a circular plate, when he heard his name being called. He descended the ladder and looked around. He saw Ida, an elderly woman wearing an elaborately embroidered cowboy shirt. She was standing at the entrance with a nerdy-looking man in his forties. Ida was Joe's wife who came almost every week to visit him. She and Jed had become fast friends. "Hi Ida, I'll be right there."

She hugged him when he got to the entrance. "Jed, I want you to meet Henry, my nephew."

"Nice to meet you." Jed put out his hand.

"I've heard a lot about you from Aunt Ida." Henry shook Jed's hand. "She says you take real good care of Uncle Joe."

"She's told me about you too. You live in Phoenix and work for a software company, isn't that right?"

"Why yes. That's right. I do." He was quite impressed that Jed remembered that.

"Let's go visit Joe." Jed led them upstairs. There was a picture of a man on horseback, a cowboy hat and a belt buckle. The urn was in the shape of a horse's head. "Are you ready Ida?"

Jed and Ida started singing "Happy Trails to You" while Henry grinned and joined in. "Hard to believe this is a place of mourning," Henry said after they finished singing.

"Jed lifts us all up. He doesn't let us feel sad. He sings to Joe even when I'm not here, don't you, Jed?"

Jed pretends to tip a cowboy hat. "Yes ma'am."

"I see what Aunt Ida means. Thank you, Jed. My aunt and uncle raised me after my parents died. I only wish they had been buried here too."

Jed smiled. "You two stay as long as you want and visit with Joe. I need to get back to work." He went back up the ladder.

The rest of the morning was pretty quiet. Not too many visitors showed up. Jed put up his "Be Back in an Hour" sign and went to the deli for a sandwich.

Irving and Milton were at a table reading the newspaper while Abe waited on a customer. "Hi Jed. Be right with you," Abe said. Jed waved to Irving and Milton and stood at the counter.

Irving put his paper down and called out, "Has Sam been out to see you?"

Jed thought for a minute. "You know, he hasn't been by to see Sadie for several days."

"He hasn't been in here either. It's understandable, I guess. He's going through a lot."

"Yes." Jed agreed but detected that the worry in Irving's voice matched his own. "Hey Abe, do you sell tomatoes?"

"I don't sell them but I can give you one. I use them on my sandwiches."

"Could you give me two? For Sadie?"

"Of course. And what'll it be for lunch?"

"I'll have a turkey sandwich with Russian dressing."

"You're turning into a Jewish mother's dream." Abe laughed at his own joke and made the sandwich. "Here or to go?"

"I'd better take it with me."

Abe handed him the sandwich and waved his money away as he placed the tomatoes in the bag. "You know, Jed. I don't need any more money. I'm closing the deli in the next few months and retiring. I've sold the business to a Korean couple. Who knows what they'll turn it into, but there are hardly any Jews left in this part of town anymore." He laughed. "Asians don't seem to have the same affinity for Jewish food as Jews have for Asian food."

"What will you all do? Where will you play cards?" Jed asked.

"We'll go to each other's houses. It'll be fine although the wives won't be too happy about having us under their feet."

Jed smiled and thanked him for the food. "If Sam comes in, tell him I took care of the tomatoes for Sadie."

"I will, and hey, if he comes to the columbarium, would you tell him we've been concerned about him?"

"Sure thing."

Rose was asleep on the couch when Tony got back. She had given him a key before he left so he was able to let himself in. Tony checked the TV Guide on the coffee table to see if there was a Giants' game that afternoon. There was one starting at seven that evening. Rose woke up when he shut off the television.

"What you doing? I listening to that."

"I'm sorry, I thought you were asleep."

"So? I like it on."

Tony had never been that much of a television watcher, but he knew that many people who lived alone kept it on for company. "Okay. Sorry." He turned it back on and Rose sat up. "I just checked and there's a Giants' game on tonight. How about showing me how to keep score?"

"That be good."

"How are your eyes now?"

"Eyes the same. Head hurt though."

"How about some pain medication?"

"No." She took a couple of breaths and then said, "Maybe if get worse."

"Do you still want to go to the columbarium this afternoon?"

"Yes. But not now. In little while." She leaned back into the sofa and closed her eyes. Tony took out his sketchbook and they sat together quietly, Rose resting and Tony drawing, while *Leave it to Beaver* droned on in the background.

Jed ate his lunch outside, not because it was a particularly nice day, but because he was hoping Monica might drive up. They had been uneasy and shy with each other when they woke up. They had dressed awkwardly and barely spoke. They left for their respective jobs with only a peck on the cheek and a hasty goodbye. They hadn't really talked about the next step. Last evening had been spent exploring each other physically rather than mentally. Monica did not show up so when he finished eating he went back inside to paint.

28

ROSE AWOKE AND GOT UP SLOWLY, CAREFULLY FEELING HER WAY TO THE BATHROOM. She left the door open. Tony figured that she had forgotten he was there. He didn't want to embarrass her so he didn't say anything. But Rose apparently did remember and called out, "Tony? You still here?"

"Yes, Rose. I'm in the living room." She didn't seem embarrassed at all.

"Let's go to columbarium now."

Tony got up but didn't make a move for the bathroom. He wanted to help her, but he knew she needed to feel independent. He wasn't going to be able to be there every minute anyway. She might as well learn how to get around alone. "I'll be ready in a minute." He gathered up his art equipment. "Do you want to wait here while I get the car or walk with me to get it?"

"How far?"

"Couple of blocks."

"I come with you." Tony took her arm to help her down the stairs. She didn't resist.

By the time Tony and Rose got to the columbarium it was after four. He helped her out of the car and through the front door. "I'll find Jed to ask him where your niche is."

They didn't have to look far. Jed met them at the door. "Rose! It's so good to see you up and about. Tony told me what happened."

"I dying Jed."

Tony and Jed looked at each other. That kind of candor would have surprised them if it had been anyone other than Rose. "The doctors found a brain tumor," Tony said.

"Is it treatable?" Jed asked.

Tony shrugged. "She wouldn't talk to the oncologist."

Jed usually kept to himself in matters that didn't concern him. But this time he decided to step in with an opinion. "Why not, Rose? Maybe there's something to be done."

"I old and I done. Simple as that. We here to look at niche."

Jed looked at Tony and started up the stairs. "Follow me." Jed had forgotten to pick out an apartment for Rose, but he didn't want her to know that. He remembered that there was a man named Andy who liked the Giants too. He had a baseball card of Barry Bonds mounted on a tiny easel. He turned around at the top of the stairs and saw that Tony was helping Rose up the stairs. "She's dizzy and going blind. The doctor said it would happen. We just didn't think this fast," Tony told him.

Jed nodded. "It's a right at the top of the stairs." He found an empty niche on the same row as Andy, just a couple of doors down. He took a rag out of his back pocket and was wiping it out when Tony and Rose got there. "Here's your apartment, Rose. Your neighbor is a man named Andy. He was a big fan of Barry Bonds."

Rose let out a Bronx cheer, startling both Tony and Jed. They both broke out laughing. "He a conman. He not great slugger like Willie. He need drugs to hit home run."

"Does that mean you want to move your apartment? I can put you somewhere else."

"No. I stay here and set Andy straight." Tony and Jed smiled at each other.

"Have you decided how you want to decorate your apartment?" Jed asked.

"I still got time. I think about it more. I tired. Let's go, Tony. See you later, Jed." Rose started to walk away by herself and Tony scampered after her like a puppy dog, afraid she would fall down the stairs.

Jed cleaned up and put the ladder away. It was close to five and he hadn't heard anything from Carl Henshaw or Linda Barclay.

266

But neither had he heard from Monica. He didn't know why he thought he would, but he sure wished he had. He locked up and started walking slowly toward his hotel. He didn't really want to go back there and spend his evening alone. But he was embarrassed to call Monica. He walked aimlessly and found himself at the deli. Abe was alone. There were no customers and no buddies.

"Hi Jed. Are you back for dinner? I'm closing up soon. I don't stay open late anymore. Not enough business."

"I was actually just stopping in to see if Sam had come by."

"Nope. Haven't seen him."

"Maybe I'll stop by his house and see if he's okay."

"Do you know his address?" Abe asked.

"I have it at the columbarium but I didn't bring it."

"Wait here. I'll write it down for you." Abe went back to his office and came back with a scrap of paper. "It's a pink house with beautiful flowers along the front." Abe sighed. "Maybe they're not so beautiful anymore. Sam wasn't the one with the green thumb."

Jed took the paper and looked at it. "I know the street. Thanks. I'll tell him you and the others were asking about him." Abe nodded to Jed as he left.

Jed decided to bring some food with him. He stopped at the Chinese restaurant and bought some chow mein and won ton soup. He found Sam's house easily. Even in the dark, the flowers were gorgeous. They had kept their bloom even without Sadie's steady hand. She must still be looking out for them. That comforted Jed. It meant she was looking out for Sam, too.

He knocked and rang the bell. No one answered. When he peered into the living room window, he saw the lights on in a bedroom although the living room was dark. He walked around the house to the illuminated room, and tapped lightly on the window. "Sam? Are you in there? It's Jed." There was still no answer. He looked through the slit between the two curtains and saw Sam lying on the floor. "Sam!" He ran around to the back door and tried to open it but it wouldn't budge. He ran back to the front and tried that door again. He picked up a rock and threw it at the living room window. It shattered and Jed climbed in. It didn't even cross his mind that he was a Black man breaking into an elderly White man's house.

When he got to the bedroom he knelt down and picked up Sam's wrist to feel for a pulse. He couldn't find it. He put his finger on Sam's neck but couldn't get a pulse there either.

He leaned down and put his ear next to Sam's mouth but there was no breath. "Oh Sam!" He fell onto the bed and for the first time in so many years that he couldn't count, he let the tears come. He cried for Sam. He cried for Rose. He cried for his mother and sister. He cried for Eric and Heather never being able to see their baby grow up. And he cried for Monica being given a life sentence through no fault of her own. When he stopped, he wiped his eyes and blew his nose and found the phone. He dialed 911 and gave them the address. And then he sat back down on the bed to wait.

Jed didn't know what to do after the ambulance left. He didn't want to leave the house with the broken window, but he needed to tell Abe and Irving. He had no way of getting in touch with them other than at the deli. Then he remembered Abe saying that he closed early now. He decided to spend the night at Sam's and fix the window in the morning. He'd stop at the deli and the hardware store early and ask Willie to deliver a window from the glass store. It was a little weird to be spending the night at Sam's house without Sam, but Jed had certainly slept in weirder circumstances than this.

He went to the living room and opened the Chinese food cartons. He wasn't hungry, but he knew he should eat. He turned on the television but didn't recognize any shows since he hadn't watched television in years. He nibbled on the food, played with the remote and soon turned off the TV and threw out the food. What he really wanted was to see Monica. He thought about going to her house, but he didn't want to leave Sam's house with the broken window. There was nothing to do but go to sleep, if he could. He lay down on the couch.

Interesting how life just tells you what to do when you're in a quandary. You just have to wait and be patient and somehow the answers come. Now he knew he had to stay at the columbarium at least until Sam was put into his condo with Sadie. But then who would keep the tomatoes fresh? He may have to get those wax ones after all. And who knew how long Rose had? He'd need to get hers decorated and she didn't even know what she wanted yet. No matter what happened with Mrs. Barclay, he had to stay for a little while longer, for Sam and for Rose. He wished he knew Monica's phone number so he could call her and tell her. Well, that too would have to wait until morning when he would call her at work. He didn't know if it was the letting go of the tears or the relief at resolving his dilemma, even if it was just a temporary resolution. But he was at peace and he fell fast asleep.

29

THE NEXT MORNING WAS A BUSY
ONE, BUT THAT WAS OKAY. Jed didn't
have time to brood. First he stopped at the deli
to tell Abe about Sam. Abe immediately went to
work planning the memorial and getting Sam's
will. Sam had given Abe and Irving all the
information they needed. Then Jed went to the
hardware store where he bought a half sheet of
plywood to nail over the broken window. The
clerk there actually turned out to be helpful. He
said he would take care of ordering the glass
and having it delivered to Sam's house.

Jed carried the plywood through the
streets to Sam's house. He found tools in the
garage and nailed up the wood. By the time he
got all of this done it was after nine. But he
didn't care that he'd be late opening the
columbarium. Sam was far more important. The
hardware clerk promised him that the glass
would be delivered in the afternoon. Jed figured
he could stop at Sam's after five and get it
repaired before dark. There was still no word

from Carl or Ms. Barclay. Maybe Carl had actually been able to stave her off.

The day went quickly. Irving and Milton came over to talk about the plans for Sam's memorial. Jed remembered that Jews like to have the funerals and bury the dead quickly. Willie stopped in to say he would meet Jed at Sam's house at just after five with the glass. Three new people came in to pick out apartments for loved ones. He showed them around and introduced them to some of the others. He made the rounds singing Broadway tunes to Frank and Goldie and blowing Frank's horn. He sang cowboy songs to Joe and blues to Sunny, and gave Chloe's bear a hug.

It was three o'clock before he knew it and he hadn't contacted Monica yet. The urgency had waned and he decided not to bother her at work. He would stop by her apartment after fixing Sam's window. He should go home first, though, and change into clean clothes. But then he wouldn't arrive at her house until nine. The columbarium was empty at the moment so he got his "Back in an Hour" sign and put it on the door. He went to the thrift store and found a pair of jeans that still had the tags on. He bought them along with a crisply ironed button down shirt. He would shower and change into his new clothes at Sam's after he finished replacing the glass.

Willie was right on time and he even helped Jed put in the window. They were done within half an hour. He took a last look around Sam's house. He enjoyed the pictures and the knick-knacks. They gave him more of an understanding of who Sam was. It also helped him know Sadie a little better. They were people Jed wished he had had in his life much earlier. Good people. Caring people. People like Finn. His view of the world was taking a turn away from the atrocities of Jonestown and living on the streets. He no longer felt isolated, like an outcast. It was odd but being around death seemed to give him more hope and optimism about life.

It didn't take too long to walk to Monica's. Although San Francisco was the fourth largest city in California population-wise, it didn't even make the top twenty-five by land mass. His little world was quite compact and concentric, centered on the columbarium, just a stone's throw from Golden Gate Park and a couple of miles from the ocean. He liked it that way.

He got to Monica's after seven and rang the buzzer. No answer. He had managed to get over his immediate grief over Sam and his agonizing over his past losses because he looked forward to seeing Monica. And now she wasn't home. He turned to leave when the door buzzed. He pushed it open and saw Monica standing there, her eyes bloodshot and red-rimmed. When he took her in his arms, she started to sob. He wanted to ask her what was wrong, but decided to wait. She took his hand and pulled him inside.

Jed didn't know what to do. Should he continue to console her? Or ask her why she was crying? Or just go into his own story of sorrow and anguish? He waited for her to take the lead.

"I'm glad you came, Jed."

"Sam died." He was surprised that he was comfortable enough to speak candidly.

"Oh Jed. I'm sorry. How?"

"I don't know. He hadn't been to see Sadie for a while. Abe at the deli hadn't seen him either so I went to his house last night. I found him on the floor of his bedroom. Maybe they'll do an autopsy. I think he died of a broken heart."

Monica nodded in agreement. "When is the funeral?"

"I'm not sure. Abe and Irving are taking care of everything."

She took his hands in hers and kissed him. "He was an old man who lost the love of his life. He's happier now with Sadie."

"Yes. You're right."

"Will you tell me when the funeral is? I'd like to go."

"You would?"

"I know how much he meant to you. I'd like to pay my respects."

"Okay." He looked into her eyes. "Why were you crying?"

Monica pulled her hands away and clasped them in her lap. "You have enough on your plate. You don't need to hear all my woes."

"I want to."

She sighed and looked away. "I had some bad news today." He waited for her to continue. "From the doctor. He got some of the tests back. My viral load is up."

"Is it AIDS?"

"Not yet. But he wants to change my dosage."

"That's not so bad."

"It could be worse I guess."

"Why the tears then?"

She took a minute to answer. "Because I'm falling for you hard and I'm afraid for the future. I want this to work."

"You want what to work? The medicine?"

She smiled. "Yes, of course. But what I meant was I want us to work."

Jed looked away. What did she mean? He hadn't thought beyond the present. She's thinking about a future together? Her face turned red. He thought he should say something encouraging, but he was confused. He liked being with her but he wasn't accustomed to thinking about the future. The easier, more comfortable thing to do would be to do what he usually did - run.

"I'm sorry, Jed. I shouldn't have laid all this on you. Especially now with Sam's death."

He put his arm around her to reassure her, but his mind was miles away. She knew it, but let him be and just snuggled into the warmth and safety of his body.

They made love that night and awoke more relaxed with each other than the last time. He left early so he could stop at his room before going to work. He hadn't been there in three days. When he entered the hotel the front desk clerk called out to him. "I thought something happened to you. I almost called that number you gave me in L.A."

"I didn't know I had to inform you where I was and when I'd be back."

"Don't have to get huffy."

Jed was angry. He certainly didn't want the clerk to call Finn who would then worry about him. He got to his room and went right in the shower. He used to go for days without bathing in Venice. Why did he feel such a strong need for one? He hoped it wasn't a subconscious reaction to sleeping with Monica, needing to wash the virus off him. Maybe it was just a desire to be clean. He had a job and was greeting the public instead of hiding in the kitchen of Luis' restaurant washing dishes. He had thought he knew what he wanted to do, but now he wasn't clear on what path he should take. He would at least be there through Sam's funeral and then he would decide.

30

TONY HAD SET THE ALARM FOR SIX
THIRTY SO HE COULD GET TO ROSE'S
EARLY. When he left to go home the previous
evening he had noticed that her equilibrium was
more compromised. She held onto the walls for
both balance and navigation. He was reluctant
to leave and asked if he should spend the night.
But she was adamant. She was fine without him.
But he knew better. He was angry with himself
for leaving. He should have been more
insistent.

He jumped out of bed and grabbed a
duffle bag. He would pack for a few days. He
threw some extra clothes and his art supplies
inside. He also took a couple of towels off the
shelf and packed them. He doubted Rose would
have extra towels for guests.

He picked up some waffles and coke, in
case she had run out. He also stopped at a cafe
and got a couple of scones and coffees. He
bought them for himself but he got two of
everything on the off chance that Rose would

change her diet. When he got to her apartment, he found her asleep on the couch. She must have been there all night. She was still dressed in the clothes she had on yesterday. He placed the bags of food on the coffee table and shook her shoulders gently. "Rose? It's Tony. Are you hungry?"

"What time is it?"

"About nine in the morning."

She sat up abruptly. "Morning? I sleep here all night?"

"I guess you did. Let me help you to the bathroom."

"No!" she said sharply. Rose was not Goldie. She was not as casual in her social interactions.

"I'll help you to the door. I won't go in with you," he said as he took her arm. She started to pull away, but stopped when he tightened his grip and she finally let him walk with her. He looked through the VHS tapes while Rose was in the bathroom, but he was at the door when she opened it. He helped her back to the couch and took an *I Love Lucy* tape out of the bookcase. "Mind if we watch the 'Stomping Grapes' episode? I always liked that one."

Rose smiled. "That one so funny." He put the tape in the VCR and turned on the television. Rose fumbled for the remote on the coffee table, knocking the scones onto the floor. Tony grabbed the coffees before they also tumbled and gave her the remote. It took her several minutes to find the correct buttons but finally Lucy came on the screen.

"I bought some coffee and scones," Tony said as he helped her settle back into the sofa. "I got you some waffles and coke too if you'd rather have that."

"I take the coffee. You put in cream and sugar?"

"Of course. I figured that's how you'd like it."

"You smart man," she said with just the slightest hint of a smile. He gave her the coffee. "What's a scone? I never have that."

"A scone is kind of a muffin. I got one blueberry and one raisin."

"I try raisin."

He took the scone out of the bag and set it in her other hand. She took a bite. He watched her face as she pinched her lips and furrowed her brow. He finally asked, "Do you like it?"

She shrugged her shoulders. "I guess." Tony took the coffee and set it on the table in front of her and she ate her scone, each bite with more gusto.

"It looks like you do like it."

"It okay." She reached around the table for her coffee. Tony was nervous that she would knock it over. She still had a lot to learn about being a blind person.

"How about I put the coffee in a mug?" A heavy mug would be harder for her to topple.

"I no have mug. Just cup. I use this paper one."

Tony shrugged. It really didn't matter if she knocked it over. He'd clean it up. Big deal. He relaxed into simply eating, drinking, watching and laughing at the antics of Lucy and Ethel.

They finished breakfast by the end of the second episode, the one where Lucy and Ethel were in the candy factory trying to keep up with the conveyer belt. Rose fell back asleep and Tony took out his sketchbook. He could get into this life of quiet and solitude. It had been very different caring for Goldie. There were always people coming and going, either buying or selling or sometimes just visiting. Goldie had always been the life of the party before she got too sick to care.

He glimpsed at Rose and wondered how long she would last. People were more in control of their destinies than they thought. All his friends who had died of AIDS seemed to go quickly after they made the decision that it was time. It had been that way with Goldie too.

After she lost the will to live, it was just a few weeks before she died. Rose made it clear in the hospital that she was ready. Maybe that's why the symptoms of dizziness and blindness came so soon. He hoped that was true. He would have liked to know Rose better and for longer, but he was a compassionate man and he didn't want her to suffer. He closed his eyes and took a nap himself.

Rose called him out of his slumber. "Pregame show starting soon. I need my scorebook."

Tony sat up, trying to comprehend. "Oh, that's right, the Giants game. Where's the scorebook?"

"Not on table?" She shoved things around reaching for it.

"I don't see it."

Rose panicked. She had trouble catching her breath. "They not give me in hospital? It still in bleachers?"

"Maybe it's in the bag of your things they sent home from the hospital." Tony looked around the apartment and finally found the bag in the corner. He looked through it and retrieved the scorebook. "It's here."

Rose sighed with relief. Tony thought it was cool that the EMTs had the foresight to keep it with her when they took her away in the ambulance. "Get pencil and open book. I teach you what to write." Tony got the pencil and the scorebook and he and Rose spent the next half hour going over every mark in the book and what they meant. "Now you turn on game and write starting lineups."

Tony did as he was told and they spent the day with the Giants and the New York Mets, taking time during commercials to toast some waffles and grab some cokes from the refrigerator. Never in a million years did Tony expect to be spending a day like this, but he loved every minute of it.

31

JED STOPPED AT THE DELI ON HIS WAY TO WORK. Abe told him that Sam had wanted a small, quiet memorial like Sadie's had been. It was set for the next morning at ten. Irving would bring the ashes and Jed said he would have the condo ready. Abe wouldn't let him pay for his bagel and coffee and Jed didn't mind since his funds were getting low. He needed his pay, but he was also afraid that Carl's appearance might bring bad news. He used Abe's phone to call Tony because he thought that he and Rose might want to come to Sam's funeral. Tony got him up to speed on Rose's condition and said they would both be there.

He also called Monica to tell her the date and time. She sounded reserved but he attributed that to her being at work. She said she would be there too. He was glad he'd finally had the foresight to get their phone numbers.

He wondered how many people would come to Sam's memorial. Since he didn't have children and he had never spoken of any family members, Jed figured it would be a very small group. He was glad Tony, Rose and Monica would be there to beef up the numbers.

The workday was pretty uneventful. He set up chairs, cleaned the condo, and put fresh tomatoes on the sconces. He made his rounds, singing and hugging bears and blowing horns, but his heart wasn't in it. This was a different feeling for him. He was used to reacting to things with rage, not with sadness. He had made it through the last forty years burying that emotion. But he didn't feel angry that Sam died. People are supposed to die when they reach Sam's age. And it was what he wanted, to be with his beloved Sadie.

Just as he was getting ready to lock up, the door opened and Carl entered with Ms. Barclay. Jed stiffened and his heart started pounding. They hadn't seen him yet and he thought about pretending he had to leave in a hurry and put them off. He could tell them to come back tomorrow afternoon, after Sam's memorial, and then he could be long gone. Carl found him, however, and put an envelope in his hand. "Here Jed. Your pay." Jed wondered if he did that as a clue.

"Do you have those references Jed?" Ms. Barclay asked as she approached.

"Not yet." That wasn't a lie.

"Do you know when you'll have them?" she groaned.

"Soon." He knew that short answers were always the best policy. Carl stared at him and shook his head ever so slightly. Jed took that to mean he had not been successful in convincing Ms. Barclay to let things be. "I'm just locking up."

"I don't think you should be opening and closing the columbarium until we have done a more formal hiring process."

Carl chimed in angrily. "There is no one else to do it so we should be thankful he's here!"

"You can do it," she added. "He can still work here but you can oversee him."

"This is not my job, Linda. I cannot be here all day."

"Well maybe I need to then."

Jed froze. Well, that was the answer he needed. There would be no way he would work here with her. He handed her the keys. "Fine. There's a memorial tomorrow at ten. I'll see you here at nine," he said, knowing full well that he would be gone after Sam's funeral.

"Don't be a fool, Linda!" Carl blurted out. Jed and Ms. Barclay were both shocked at Carl's outburst. "I don't need this crap either! I looked for months to find someone to get this place back into shape. I found you the perfect person who has done an exemplary job. Jed is as trustworthy as they come and for you to treat him like this is unacceptable. The rest of the board is fine with him and if you need to be so much in control, then good luck. You'll need it dealing with the rest of the board on this." Carl stomped away and just before he opened the door to leave, Ms. Barclay shouted after him," Stop, Carl. Come back. Let's discuss this."

She turned to Jed and handed him back the keys. "We can wait until the references come through."

Jed looked at Carl who stood frozen at the door, his back still facing them. "I need to go home and cool off," Carl said before bolting out the door.

Jed turned abruptly and walked away without saying a word, leaving Ms. Barclay standing by herself. He went upstairs so he could watch her. She needed to leave, obviously, before he could, but he certainly wasn't going to stand around with her. He needed desperately to walk. Even the breathing wasn't working. He paced the circumference of the second floor, his eyes on Ms. Barclay. She stood motionless and stone-faced, not happy about being challenged. His patience was starting to run out and he was getting agitated. She'd better leave. Finally she did.

Jed kept up the deep breathing as he locked the doors and then the gate. He made an abrupt left turn, away from home and from Monica's, and toward the ocean.

He walked for hours but instead of pushing aside his thoughts, he let them percolate. He thought about Monica and what she was going through. He'd had to face a lot of deaths, but never his own. He couldn't imagine what that must be like. He thought about Sam and how death for him had been welcome and sought after. He wondered if he'd ever feel that way. He thought about Finn and how he'd have to live with what he'd done. He had aided in killing his own wife, even if it was at her request and it was getting her out of her misery. But worse was thinking about Chloe and how Heather and Eric had to face the death of their child. That's when he started yelling and crying. That's when it all became too much. Luckily he was on the beach by then and it was dark and cold and no one else was crazy enough to be there.

32

JED HAD SET THE ALARM BEFORE HE FELL INTO A DEEP BUT UNRESTFUL SLUMBER. He had gotten home very late and he wanted to make sure everything was ready for Sam's memorial. He planned to talk to Monica afterwards and tell her what he had decided to do. He would not run away from San Francisco, but he would leave the job. He was convinced that Linda Barclay was even more upset by Carl's outburst and would dig her heels in even further. He would call Carl and tell him and ask him where he should bring the keys. He felt relieved. At least he had reached some kind of resolution.

On his way to the columbarium in the morning he bought a coffee and breakfast burrito at a Mexican restaurant. It made him think of all the burritos he used to share with Mother. Luis always gave them leftovers after his dishwashing shift. It was interesting how much his diet had changed in his move from southern California to northern California.

There was a pizzeria on the Venice Beach boardwalk that gave out food to the homeless. There was also usually a church or school group that came periodically with bag lunches. The bags were filled with hard-boiled eggs, bologna sandwiches, an apple, a bag of chips, and maybe a cookie. Now he was frequenting Chinese restaurants, Jewish delis, and French bistros.

The main vestibule was polished and sparkling when the guests started to arrive. Abe, Milton and Irving got there early to help, but Jed had already put out the chairs and set up the table for the guest book. They wore yarmulkes and asked Jed if he wanted to wear one. He thought Sam might like that so he did. They had also brought a scrapbook they had made with pictures of the group of men and their wives throughout the fifty or so years they had known each other.

Jed greeted Tony and Rose. He was shocked at how quickly she was deteriorating. She was barely able to walk. There were more elderly men and women than he had expected. Monica came just as Irving stood to welcome everyone and ask for stories they wanted to share. It was not a religious ceremony. There was no rabbi, but Irving said some prayers in Hebrew. There were many stories, both heartwarming and funny. It may not have had the liveliness and joyousness of Sunny's, but it was not a sad memorial. Jed enjoyed hearing more about Sam's life.

At the end, Irving asked Jed if he wanted to say a few words. Jed had never spoken before a large group in his life. He wanted to shake his head no, but felt compelled to say at least a couple of words. His legs shook when he stood with all eyes on him. But the faces were friendly and welcoming and he could hear Sam's voice calling him a luftmensch - a dreamer. "Sam showed me how to cope and how to hope." He looked into Monica's eyes. "But more than that he showed me how to love." He then scanned the crowd until he found Abe, Milton and Irving. He smiled at them when he added, "He was my haimisher mensch." There wasn't a dry eye in the house, but the sound was a mixture of both laughter and weeping.

When the service was over, the group went upstairs to the condo where Jed placed Sam's ashes next to Sadie. It was noon by the time people started to leave. Rose and Tony came over to say goodbye. "That was a wonderful service. What you said was beautiful," Tony told him. "And I even know what a haimisher mensch is. Goldie spoke Yiddish often."

"Yeah. Tony tell me what it mean so now I know too. That nice of you to say those things about Sam. He like Giants too. He fan even when they in New York. He tell me that."

"Do you know that famous Abbot and Costello routine, Rose, about Who's on First?" Jed asked.

"Sure. Everyone know that."

"The first time I met him was at his friend's deli, and they did that routine."

"He have nice friends."

Monica had stayed in the background, waiting for Jed to finish, but he called her over. "Monica, I'd like you to meet Tony and Rose."

"Hi Monica," Tony shook her hand. "Nice to meet you."

"Jed's told me about you both. It's a real pleasure," Monica answered. She turned to Rose and took her hand in hers. "Hello Rose. I like the Giants too."

"Good," Rose said. "Then you okay." They all laughed. "You Jed's girlfriend?"

Jed and Monica looked at each other and smiled. "I, um, got him the job here at the columbarium. I work at Glide Church."

"Do you want to see your apartment, Rose?" Jed interjected and then realized what he had said. She couldn't see it. He added quickly, "Have you decided what you want to put in it?"

"I leave that to you and Tony." Jed glanced at Tony who shrugged his shoulders.

"I've been trying to get her to talk about that," Tony said. Jed had a moment of regret. How could he leave before helping Rose decorate her apartment? But he had faith that Tony would do a good job.

Tony and Rose left and Jed was finally alone with Monica. He brought her back to the office where they kissed and hugged for several minutes. "We need to talk." Monica took the words right out of Jed's mouth.

"Yes we do," he agreed. "Do you want to get some lunch?"

"I'd rather talk privately," she replied.

"Are you hungry? We could pick something up and bring it back." Jed was procrastinating. He felt that once he told Monica that he was leaving the columbarium he would have to follow through. Seeing Rose and knowing that her time was coming soon made him all the more ambivalent.

"I'm not hungry," she answered. Jed leaned on the desk and pulled the chair over for Monica to sit. He would let her go first so he waited quietly for her to gather her thoughts. "I thought you'd be over last night. It's difficult because you have no phone. I have no way to get in touch with you."

"I wanted to see you but I couldn't. I'm sorry."

"You couldn't? What do you mean?"

He inhaled deeply. "Sometimes I get so angry that all I can do is walk. I just need to calm myself. I went to the ocean and it was very late by the time I got home."

"Well I needed you." As soon as she said that, she was sorry. But then she thought, what the hell difference does it make. If there was anything positive about thinking you were going to die, it was that you could do and say whatever you wished.

Jed didn't know how to respond so he didn't. He waited for her to continue. But she wanted him to respond so she was quiet also. "I'm sorry." That was all Jed could think to say.

Monica had hoped he would ask her what was wrong. She didn't want to have to blurt it out. But she knew him well enough by now to know that he didn't ask questions. "I need to be in the hospital. They want to assess me for a clinical trial. They say that's my best hope."

Jed took her in his arms. "I should have been there for you last night." It was slowly dawning on him that he had spent his whole life being self-absorbed and selfish. What a fool he had been. And still was. Everyone had reasons to be angry if they let themselves. Others worked out their lives by not giving in to it. Finn didn't, Sam didn't, Rose didn't, and

Monica didn't. They worked through it and moved on.

They held each other for several minutes until Monica pulled away and asked, "What did you want to talk about?"

"It's nothing. It can wait." Jed didn't want to bring up his problems now. "How long will you be in the hospital?"

"Awhile. It's a regimen that keeps me hooked to an IV and they need to monitor me closely. If I respond well, they can let me go home with an IV. But they can't tell me how long I'll be off work. It's very experimental."

"What about side effects?"

"They don't know. But since I'm very healthy other than this nasty virus and fairly young, they think I should respond well."

Jed pulled her toward him and held her tightly. It was becoming clearer to him what direction he should take. He wasn't used to making decisions first and then acting on them. He usually ran away and let things fall into whatever place they did. But he knew some of what he wanted. He not only wanted to be with Monica, but also to take care of her. Until he started working at the columbarium, he had only worried about himself and his cat. He knew that he would not leave Monica now. He pulled away abruptly when he heard a car pull into the parking lot. "I need to see who's here."

"Go ahead. I have to get to the church."

"I'll be at your house after work. We can go out to dinner at Zazie's."

"That would be nice." She kissed him and they both left the office. He walked her to her car and watched her drive away. Then he noticed Linda Barclay getting out of her car.

His face reddened, his temperature rose, his muscles tensed. He did not want to talk to her. He went inside the main building and did a fast, cursory look around to see if there were any visitors. There were none, so he locked the door and walked quickly out of the gate, leaving a shocked and frozen Linda Barclay in the parking lot. He would come back later to lock the gate.

He walked south down Stanyan toward Golden Gate Park. That gave him a few blocks to decide whether he would make a left toward his hotel or a right toward the ocean. He hated that his life was not in his own hands. Damn Linda Barclay. Damn Antoinette Delion. Damn Police Lieutenant Bukowski. Damn Jim Jones.

It took less than ten minutes to get to the park and he had worked himself into such a frenzy that there was no question which way he would turn. He walked past the Conservatory of Flowers and the De Young Museum, but stopped briefly at the Japanese Tea Garden. It was a reminder to breathe slowly and evenly, counting each one as he exhaled. He slowed down his pace to time it with his breaths so that by the time he reached Stow Lake and the other smaller lakes, it was more like a stroll in the park. Soon he was at the windmill and tulip garden and could stop and admire the flowers before getting to the beach.

It was at this point he was reminded that he had not put up a "closed" sign and he had left the gate unlocked. His irresponsibility weighed heavily on him. Maybe he wasn't cut out for this. He didn't like the trapped feeling of having a job where he was in charge. But he felt so guilty leaving people behind who depended on him. That brought him back to that awful place that he had never been able to face. The place so buried that even in his worst moments, hadn't risen to the surface. Until now. All this death surrounding him unearthed the burdens he had always repressed.

He turned back and walked rapidly. He figured he'd be back in time to lock up for the day and call Carl to set up a time to hand over the keys. And then he would take care of Monica. She needed him and she was still alive.

33

IT WAS PAST FIVE WHEN JED GOT BACK TO THE COLUMBARIUM. After locking the gate, he set out for Monica's. He wanted to spend the evening with her sorting things out. He would call Carl from her house.

Monica had just come out of the shower when he rang the bell. She answered the door in her bathrobe. "Were you in bed?" Jed asked.

"No. I just wanted to take a long hot shower. I'll be done in a few minutes." She went back to her bedroom to get dressed while Jed wandered around her apartment. He looked for anything that might resemble a personal artifact. He wanted to learn more about her. There was less on the shelves in her home than there were in several of the niches at the columbarium.

She came out a few minutes later dressed in a low cut black cocktail dress with high heels and understated jewelry. She looked gorgeous. "Monica, you know I don't have any clothes like that."

"It doesn't matter. I wanted to dress up tonight. I'm scared and apprehensive about the weeks ahead and it's just something I need to do. Please don't worry about it. You look fine just the way you are." She kissed him. "Let's go have a wonderful night."

Jed decided not to bring up any of the stuff he had originally wanted to talk to her about. He would give her this night. There would be plenty of time in the hospital to talk. He could even put Carl off another day. He would not let Linda Barclay ruin his and Monica's evening.

They ordered drinks and wine and appetizers and desserts besides their entrees. They ate a lot and drank a lot and laughed a lot. It was close to eleven when they left the restaurant and their waiter was not too pleased. The rest of the night was taken up with sensual exploration and amorous passion. They slept little.

As soon as he arrived home the next morning, he showered and dressed and then hurried back out the door. He stopped at the deli for coffee and a bagel and still got to the columbarium by nine. The gate was ajar. He was sure he had locked it the night before. Then he saw that the lock had been tampered with. He walked up to the front door warily. The first thing he noticed was a trampled flowerbed in

299

front of one of the windows. There was broken glass scattered over the flowers and when he raised his eyes, he saw the hole in the window. "Jesus!" he exclaimed out loud. He unlocked the front door and went inside. The place was a disaster. He finished his exclamation, "H. Christ!"

There were glass shards all over the floor and the contents of the niches were strewn about. Many of the urns or containers were broken so ashes covered much of the debris. Jed froze, barely able to breathe. He wasn't even at the point of rage yet. He was too devastated. The glass could be replaced; even the memorabilia and keepsakes were just things. But the ashes!

He stood there for ten minutes or so before he could pull himself together enough to check out the damage. A cursory look around showed that most of the niches had their front doors smashed. It seemed to be random as to which ones had their interiors destroyed, at least on the first floor. He went to see Sam and Sadie. The tomatoes were smashed but nothing seemed to be done to the inside. Chloe's, however, was a different story. The teddy bear was ripped and the stuffing removed. The heart-shaped urn was in pieces and the ashes were all over the inside of the niche. That was the moment that brought Jed to tears and anger.

He rushed to the closet and got a whiskbroom and paper bag and immediately went to work sweeping the ashes into the bag, cursing loudly as he did. He set the bag of ashes inside Chloe's niche and went to check on Goldie and Frank. His wasn't too bad. The door was smashed and it was kind of a mess, but hers was a disaster. Her ashes were out of the carton and swimming in the gefilte fish broth that was smeared all over the inside. There was anti-Semitic graffiti on the walls of her niche and the mezuzah had been ripped off the wall. Sunny's and Joe's were about the same as Frank's.

He finally pulled his thoughts together enough to realize that the police should be called and that he shouldn't touch anything. He wondered if Linda Barclay would go so far as to accuse him of doing it! He couldn't be the one to talk to the police, though. He would call Carl. He ran to the deli to use Abe's phone.

After making the call he hurried back to wait for Carl. The board would have to be notified but Carl agreed to meet him there by himself first. Jed walked around and around the rotunda, floor by floor, while he waited. He wanted to start cleaning up, but he knew he shouldn't touch the evidence. All his hard work destroyed by a couple of Nazi skinhead thugs! That's who he figured had done it since they seemed to have targeted Goldie. Maybe they were clients who blamed her for something, or maybe they were some other drug dealers. The pacing helped calm him down. He had started his rounds of the three stories in a state of rage that he hadn't felt in a long time. He stomped and yelled for quite awhile before he was able to calm himself enough to face Carl who arrived about half an hour after the phone call.

"Oh my God! This is terrible!" Carl cried out when he entered. "Jed? Where are you?"

Jed came down the stairs. "I think it was Goldie who was targeted."

Carl looked puzzled. "Goldie?"

"Come on up. I'll show you." Jed went back upstairs and Carl followed. "See this?" He pointed to the graffiti.

"Why would they target her?"

Jed didn't know how to answer. He didn't want to disclose her career choice and he certainly didn't want to get Tony into any trouble. But he did want to help in the investigation and find the culprits. "I don't know," he said after a couple of minutes of brooding.

"I've got to call the police." Carl took out his cellphone and dialed 911.

"You know I can't talk to them."

Carl held up his finger as if to say, "just a minute" while he spoke into the phone. He hung up and took the keys that Jed was holding out to him. "Yes. I know. Lay low for a while but please, stick around until this all blows over. I need you now more than ever."

Jed exhaled loudly. "I'll stay in San Francisco."

"How can I get a hold of you? Trust me, Jed. I will not share the information. Not with the board or the police."

"I do trust you." Jed tried to think what to do. "You can get a hold of me through Monica. I promise I'll call you later with her number."

"You'd better go. The police will be here momentarily."

Jed rushed out and turned left toward the ocean. He needed to walk. He thought he should call Tony, but he didn't want to go back to the deli. He'd call him later.

It took him a little more than an hour to get to the ocean and then he walked north to Point Lobos. He followed the coastal trails past the Presidio and the Legion of Honor and turned down Clement. He kept up his fast pace, barely stopping to notice the scenery. He decided to cut through Golden Gate Park so he wouldn't have to pass the columbarium. He meandered through the park and the streets of

303

the Sunset district before reaching Monica's. There was a note on the door in an envelope addressed to him. It said that she had checked into the hospital.

He found Monica sleeping and hooked up to an IV. He sat and waited for her to wake up. He breathed rhythmically and slowly while he watched her sleep. A nurse came in after a few minutes. "She may sleep for quite awhile. Her body is just getting used to the medicine. Why don't you go down to the cafeteria and get something to eat."

"Okay. Thanks." Jed realized he hadn't eaten all day and was starved.

He found the cafeteria after a few false steps moving through the maze-like series of hallways that all hospitals seem to have. He gobbled down a withered piece of meat on a hamburger bun and a pile of soggy French fries. He was sipping a cup of coffee and nibbling on a cookie when a young couple sat down at the table next to him. They looked exhausted and spent, their clothes disheveled and their eyes glazed and rimmed red either from weariness or crying or both. He noticed them picking at their food and finally the man spoke. "Well at least there's finally some good news."

"I guess," the woman answered listlessly. "But we still won't know the long term effects."

"I know, but we can take her home soon. Then we'll be able to be with her all day every day."

She squeezed his hand and lay her head down on the table. "I'm so tired."

"Your body hasn't had time to get over the birth yet. And you've been spending all day in the hospital since then."

Jed sat upright and swallowed the last of his coffee. He took his dishes to the tub in the corner of the room and went back to check on Monica. She was still sleeping. He asked at the nurse's station for directions to the wing of the hospital where the newborns were. He found the picture window where you could see the bassinets with all the healthy babies. Their family members cooed at them through the glass. He meandered around the hall, past private and semi-private rooms filled with joyous parents and grandparents. He finally found the room he was looking for. There was a sign that said no admittance without permission. He went to the nurse's station. "I'd like to volunteer."

"Have you gone through the proper channels?"

"I don't know what I have to do."

"Well, what is it you want to volunteer doing?"

"I want to rock the babies, the ones who need someone."

The nurse smiled. "We could sure use some help but you have to go to the volunteer office and fill out the paperwork. I'm afraid they won't open again until tomorrow morning, though."

"I'll sign up in the morning but can I help now?"

The nurse looked into Jed's eyes and saw what everyone else saw in them: pure kindness and pure integrity. "I can show you the room." She beckoned him to follow her.

It was a large, brightly lit room with several bassinets and a ton of noisy machines, beeping and dinging. Some of the babies were tiny enough to fit in your hand. Some of them were screaming, in obvious pain, while others were barely breathing. Hospital personnel scurried around checking machines. Jed couldn't tell who was a doctor or a nurse or a therapist of some kind. In one corner of the room were a couple of rocking chairs and a lamp. It was quiet and homey looking, but no one was sitting there. Jed made a beeline for the screaming babies and bent over their bassinets, speaking to them in a soothing voice. A staff member, who could have been a doctor, a nurse, or a therapist of some kind, approached him. "Is that baby yours?"

"No. I just want to volunteer to rock them."

"Oh that would be wonderful!" she said. She unhooked the screaming baby from the machine and handed him to Jed. The nurse who had brought him in started to speak, but then she noticed how quickly the baby quieted in Jed's arms. He went to a rocking chair and sat down gently. The baby and Jed rocked silently while the hospital staff went back to what they were doing.

34

MONICA WAS AWAKE AND EATING A
BLAND, LIQUID DINNER WHEN JED
ENTERED HER HOSPITAL ROOM. "Got
any beef wellington on you? I'm starved and
this is all they'll let me have."

Jed kissed the top of her head and
pulled the chair up to her bedside. "Can't be
worse than what they call a hamburger in the
cafeteria." He sat down and smiled at her.

"You look so . . . um . . . serene, Jed.
Did something happen?"

"A lot happened, but I want to savor it
for a minute."

"I will happily watch you savor." She
slurped her broth and spooned the Jell-O into
her mouth.

Jed sat quietly watching her eat. "How
do you feel?"

"Just tired. They don't want me to eat
solid food until they're sure I don't get
nauseous from the medication."

"How long do you have to wait?"

"I think tomorrow morning. And how are you?" She leaned back into the pillows.

"The columbarium was vandalized."

Monica's eyes widened and her mouth dropped open. "You're kidding."

"It's terrible, but it made my decision for me."

Monica looked at him quizzically. "How so?"

"I can't be around while the police are investigating."

"How bad is it?"

"Pretty bad. They broke the glass doors and threw the urns and everything else around. They even emptied out the ashes."

"But won't they need you to fix it back up?"

He shrugged his shoulders. "I don't know what they're going to do." He just remembered he had told Carl he would give him Monica's number. "Can I borrow your phone?"

"It's on the table." Jed picked it up and stared at it. Monica laughed. "You don't have a clue how to use it do you?"

"I had finally figured out those flip phones but no, I haven't used one of these smartphones. I've seen people touch the screen, I think."

"Hand it to me. I'll give you a lesson." She showed him how to use it. He called Carl and waited for an answer. "His phone will show the phone number so if he doesn't answer and you leave a message, he'll be able to see what my number is."

"No kidding. I guess I have a lot to learn." He shook his head. "Carl, this is Jed. You can reach me at the number that shows up." He hung up after leaving the message and put the phone back on the table. He let it go quickly, as if it was hot or contaminated.

Monica laughed again. "I think you're going to have to get used to the fact that this is a high-tech world now."

"I guess."

"So what are you going to do now?"

"I'm going to come here."

"Here? The hospital? You're going to sit with me all day every day? You'll go crazy. It's enough that I have to do it. Anyway, it's a great opportunity for me to catch up on my paperwork while I'm stuck in this bed."

"I won't bother you. I'll spend time in the neonatal ward too."

"You will?"

"I just came from there. Rocking the babies born to drug addicts or —" he stopped himself.

"Or AIDS mothers? You can say it, you know."

"Okay. They scream and need to be rocked. I did it at this woman's house in Venice."

"That's really sweet," Monica said softly.

"I do it for me, too," he answered just as softly.

Monica touched his hand and he squeezed it. "I can see that." They sat quietly for a few minutes until Monica broke the silence. "Are you ever going to tell me your whole story?"

Jed looked hard at her. He wanted to tell her everything. He wanted to tell her all about Jonestown and his escape and his tumultuous teenage years and his wanderings since then. He wanted to share it all, just as he had with Finn. But it was so hard to bring it all up again. But then he had a thought. "I'll bring you Finn's book tomorrow. You can read it. I'm the one he's talking about. He tried to disguise my identity some, but you'll see through it. After you read it, I'll tell you the rest of my story."

"Fair enough."

Jed stood. "It's getting late. I'll be back in the morning." He kissed her and left.

It was raining. He wondered what Carl had done about the broken window and whether the rain was getting inside. He also wondered if the police were keeping a constant presence there. It wasn't his responsibility anymore, he told himself, but he didn't believe that for a second. Sam and Chloe, Goldie and Frank, Sunny and Joe: he felt responsible for them all.

His temperature started to rise again. That damn Linda Barclay was ruining everything! Just as Antoinette had done to him and then to Finn! Holding him hostage! He stomped through the puddles as he walked through the Tenderloin to his hotel, splattering everything and everyone in his way. By the time he got to his room, he had worked himself back into a frenzied state, and all the rocking had been for naught. He found the copy of Finn's book and stared at the cover, *Those Who Forget the Past are Condemned to Repeat It*. He opened it to the first page, intending to leaf through it quickly, but found himself rereading the whole book. It took him most of the night.

He jumped off the bed when he saw the time. Then he remembered that he didn't have to be anywhere. He took a long shower, took his time getting dressed, and fretted for a minute about how he was going to pay for the room now that he was back to having no income. He kind of wanted to walk by the columbarium and see what was happening there, but knew he shouldn't. He picked up a coffee and an Egg McMuffin (his breakfast options were going to have to change now) and sauntered over to the hospital.

And then he was faced with another decision. What was he going to do about signing up in the volunteer office? Last night may have been just a lucky break, letting him rock the babies. The staff on today may not be so accommodating. But he was reluctant to fill out paperwork and possibly have to get fingerprinted in the volunteer office. He certainly didn't want to open that can of worms again. He decided to take his chances. He walked past the volunteer office door and headed to Monica's room.

Monica was on the phone in animated conversation. She seemed quite fine, no side effects from the medication. He waited for her to finish. "What a crock!" she exclaimed when she got off.

"What's wrong?"

"Oh just bureaucratic crap at the office with my sick leave."

"I brought this for you." He handed her Finn's book.

She picked it up and looked at the title. "An apt title."

"Maybe so. I'm not sure. Sometimes I wonder."

"Wonder what?"

"Whether it's best to forget the past."

"I don't think you really can, Jed. Learning to embrace the past seems to me the only thing you can do."

"I don't know anymore," he said.

She opened the book to the first page. "So what are you going to do while I read this?"

"Go see the babies."

She smiled and shook her head. "You are an enigma, Jedidiah Gibbons. Oh, I almost forgot. Carl Henshaw called."

"What did he say?"

"Just to tell you he called. He said to call him when you have a chance."

"Doesn't sound like there's much news then."

"It made the television news, though. I saw it this morning."

"What did it say?"

"They mentioned you, but not by name. Just that there had been a caretaker who had fixed it all up and that made the vandalism even sadder." Jed stiffened. Monica saw his face redden and his lips purse tightly. "They didn't say your name, Jed. They interviewed Mr. Henshaw. He wouldn't tell them, although I'm sure he was asked."

"Yeah but what happens if they interview Linda Barclay?"

314

"Why would they? Please don't worry."

Jed stood. "I'll be back later."

He got to the neonatal unit and tried to walk straight in, but was stopped. "Can I help you?" one of the nurses asked.

Jed decided to play cool, like he had already gone through the volunteering process. "I was here last night to rock the babies. I'll be able to come every day for a while. Is there any baby in particular that needs rocking? I hear a couple of them crying."

"I didn't see any papers from the office."

"I don't know about that. Is there anyone here from last night? They can vouch for me."

"No." Jed looked into her eyes and once again, his honorable, compassionate nature shone through. "Well, okay. I'll call the volunteer office," she said.

Uh oh. Jed thought fast. "Why don't you just call one of the doctors or nurses that was here last night?"

She looked at Jed and her stern face softened into a half-smile. "Come on. I'll show you which baby needs to be rocked first." He followed her through the swinging doors.

He took the first baby she handed him. He was very comfortable holding her, even as tiny as she was. The baby stopped crying and snuggled into his arms. "Wow. You do have a magic touch," the nurse commented.

Jed smiled and took the baby to the corner of the room with the rocking chairs. "Hello precious one," he cooed at her as he settled into the chair. He closed his eyes and started to rock. The effect was fast and absolute, for both of them.

After an hour or so, he placed the baby back in her crib and motioned to one of the staff members that he should hook her back up to the machines. He found the first nurse he had talked to and asked her who he should do next. She followed him back in and unhooked another baby from a machine. Jed spent the rest of the morning going through the cribs. He finished about one o'clock and headed back to Monica's room.

Her bed was empty and the book was on her table with a bookmark sticking out of it. He opened the book to see where she had stopped reading, but then she was wheeled back into the room.

35

THE COLUMBARIUM WAS LIKE A THREE-RING CIRCUS. Policemen tried to keep out the crowds of mourners who were angry and upset while the detectives were inside trying to dust for fingerprints. The yellow police tape was not doing its job. The Neptune Society had sent emails and letters to all the owners of the niches and they had come out en masse. They were trying to find out what had happened and what was going to happen.

The board members had arrived after a long, arduous meeting and Carl greeted them. "Where's Jed?" one of them asked.

Carl stared at Linda Barclay and answered, "Ask Linda." The other board members all turned toward her.

Linda shot Carl a piercing look. "Does it matter anymore? The insurance company has informed us that our coverage is not enough to pay for all the damage. We just spent three hours meeting and still haven't figured out how we are going to afford the repairs. Anyway, I'm not so sure that he didn't have something to do with this, considering his background."

"What?!" The rest of the board members yelled at her, angrily.

Linda took on a defensive stance but before she could speak, they were interrupted by a commotion at the door. A furious and frantic crowd led by Tony and Ray had broken through the barricade and rushed inside calling Jed's name. Carl went over to the group. "Jed's not here."

"Where is he?" Tony demanded.

"I don't know," Carl answered.

"When are you going to get this place cleaned up?" someone else asked.

"I don't know that either. First we have to see what the insurance company will pay."

"Where's Jed? He'll fix it. He'll take care of everything," another crowd member said.

"He's not here." Carl was nervous. He didn't want to face the barrage of questions and demands that were coming at him.

"Where is he?" the crowd asked in unison.

"As I said, I don't know." He turned toward Linda and the board members. Linda took the opportunity to walk away and have a conversation with the detectives.

One of the detectives approached Carl. "Mr. Henshaw? Can I speak to you alone?"

They walked away from the group. "Yes, what is it?"

"I need to talk to the caretaker, a Jed Gibbons. Ms. Barclay says you have his number."

Carl didn't want to give it to him, but he couldn't obstruct the investigation either. "I don't have his number on me," he lied. "Give me your card and I'll call you with it."

The detective gave Carl his card. "I'd appreciate it if you would do that as soon as possible."

The policemen who had been guarding the door rushed over to the crowd. "You need to wait outside. You can't be in here!" One of the cops gently nudged some of them, but they ignored him.

Tony pulled Carl aside. "Does Jed know what happened?"

"Yes."

"I can't believe he's not here then. That's not like him."

"I'm sure he wants to be here. It's not exactly his choice."

Tony looked at him warily. "Did something happen to him?"

"No. I'm sorry. I can't discuss this. We're trying to work it out."

"Do you have a phone number for him?"

"Yes. But I cannot give it to you. I'm sure, if you know Jed, you understand that."

"Yes, I do." Tony nodded his head. "Could you do this for me then?" He looked through his pocket and found a scrap of paper and wrote on it. "Would you call Jed and ask him to call me?"

"I will." Carl took the paper.

"You know, these people here are not going to stand for their loved ones' ashes strewn all over the floor."

"I know. The board is working to get things done as quickly as possible."

Tony shrugged and went back to the group. "I'll try to get a hold of Jed and find out what we can do. Let's meet back here tomorrow at noon."

The crowd grumbled but acquiesced. "We need to see the damage to the niches," Ray said to one of the policemen. The detectives signaled to the policemen that they were finished.

"Okay, but just for a few minutes," the policeman answered. The group scattered to check out the apartments of their loved ones.

Tony was determined to find Jed. He racked his brain trying to remember if Jed had ever told him where he lived. He knew it was some SRO hotel downtown, but there were many of those. He thought of going down to the tenderloin and checking with each one. Then he remembered that Monica worked at Glide Church. He drove over there and finally found a parking space. By the time he got inside, it was late afternoon.

He asked an office clerk if Monica was there. She informed him that she was out on medical leave and then escorted him to Monica's temporary replacement.

"I'm sorry, I don't know if I can help you. Monica is in the hospital."

"You don't have any records for Jed?" Tony asked.

"Most people who come in here don't have an address or a phone. There's nothing I can do. I'm sorry."

Tony was about to leave when he had an idea. "Do you know what hospital Monica is in?"

"I'm not sure I can disclose that."

"She's a friend of mine. It would sure save me a lot of time. You know I can find out by just calling all the hospitals."

"I believe she's at UCSF Medical Center."

"Thanks."

Jed had spent the day rocking the babies. Monica had gone through a bunch of tests so she was out of her room most of the day. She was exhausted when Jed came to visit.

"Why don't you just go home. You need the rest and I'm not going to be very good company."

"Okay. I'll be back bright and early." He kissed her and left.

Monica was eating dinner and watching mindless television when Tony entered her room.

"Hi Monica. My name is Tony. I'm a friend of Jed's. I met you at Sam's funeral."

Monica smiled weakly. "I remember."

"I'm sorry to bother you. I thought you might know where he lives. I need to talk to him."

"He's at the Windsor on Eddy."

"Thank you so much. I didn't know you were ill. I hope you're okay."

"I'm under treatment. Thanks."

"Is there anything you need? I could get it for you before I go."

"I'm fine. Thank you Tony. That's very kind of you."

Tony smiled and went out to his car. He drove over to Eddy and found the Windsor Hotel. It was dinnertime and rush hour. People were either leaving work or eating before going to a show. As he walked past a Chinese restaurant on his way to the hotel, he realized he hadn't eaten all day. He went inside and bought some chow mein for both Jed and himself, chuckling about how appropriate that was.

The clerk at the front desk didn't seem to care about giving him Jed's room number. Hotels like this were not bedrocks of security. And the sleeping couch potatoes certainly didn't care. He knocked on Jed's door.

Jed had gotten out of the shower and was lying on his bed when he heard the knock. Who could that be? He opened the door a crack and then swung it open when he saw Tony. "Well what do you know."

"I brought dinner. Have you eaten?"

Jed pulled the cover up on the bed so they'd have somewhere to sit. "I can always eat again." Tony pulled out the cardboard boxes and two pairs of chopsticks. They laughed about how fitting it was for them to be eating chow mein out of take-out cartons.

Jed took a bite and then put down his chopsticks. "How did you find me?"

"I remembered that Monica worked at Glide Church. I went there and they told me that she was in the hospital. I went there and she gave me the name of the hotel. I hope you don't mind."

"No. It's okay. So you've been gone all day. How's Rose managing without you?"

Tony put down his chopsticks and folded his hands in his lap. He looked into Jed's eyes. "She died."

"So fast? I thought she had more time. I'm sorry, Tony."

"You know Rose. When she makes up her mind to do something she doesn't waste any time, even dying."

"Yep. She was one determined lady." Jed shook his head. "What a character."

"I'd say feisty would be the best word to describe her."

"What are you going to do? You heard what happened at the columbarium I assume."

"Yes. I was with a whole bunch of people there today. We were looking for you. The Neptune Society says they don't know what they are going to do about the damage."

"Who says? Carl?"

"I guess. The Neptune Society board members were all there too. The guy I talked to — Carl? — wouldn't tell me anything when I asked where you were and why you weren't there."

"It's a long story. But what are you going to do about Rose? Where are her ashes now?"

"I have to get them. They're at the crematorium." Tony shrugged his shoulders. "I'm going to put them in the cookie jar I had

324

bought for them. It's in the shape of a baseball."

"Perfect!" Jed exclaimed.

"I had been working on a mural for the background of the apartment. I had drawn all her favorite television characters."

"What a great idea."

"It's too bad that she never got to see it," Tony said wistfully. "Are you going to come back to fix up the columbarium again?"

"I don't think so, Tony."

"Why not?"

"I just can't go back."

"I don't get it. I thought you liked working there."

"I do. Let's just say I'm having a problem with one of the board members."

"That's hard to believe with all you've done for them." Tony took another mouthful. "So what are you going to do?"

"I don't know yet."

"Then come back. We'll figure out a way to get around that board member."

"I don't know how."

"Then what can we do?"

Jed felt those seeds of anger starting to spread through his veins. He didn't want to think about Linda Barclay. He took a few breaths. "You'll be the first to know if I figure it out. Do you mind if I use your phone?" Jed asked.

"Not at all." Tony handed it to him.

Jed dialed a number. "Monica? It's Jed."

Tony stood. "Do you mind if I use your bathroom?" Jed nodded and pointed to a closed door.

"Did Carl call? Yes, Tony's here now. Okay. I'll call him with Tony's phone. Sleep well. See you tomorrow." He hung up and dialed Carl's number. "This is Jed. I thought they would. Thank you for letting me know. Just a minute." Jed rummaged in his pocket got a pencil and scrap of paper. "Okay, give me his number." Jed wrote. "You're sure she won't be there? Okay. I'll see you at eight." He hung up just as Tony came out of the bathroom and gave him back his phone.

"Some of the others are meeting me at the columbarium tomorrow at noon. Can I tell them I saw you? Everyone is asking about you."

"Sure. Say hello to them all and just tell them I'm fine. Who's been there?"

"Ray, a guy named Eric, a woman who's husband is Joe, two sisters who's dad's name is Sunny, and a few others."

"What are you meeting for?"

"We're angry and we want to find out what the Neptune Society is going to do. The police don't seem to have any idea who did it."

326

Jed contemplated telling Tony what he thought. Maybe if he did, Tony could help the investigation without implicating himself. "Maybe they were targeting a particular individual," Jed finally said.

"Why do you think so?"

"Did you see Goldie's apartment?"

"So you think she was the one?" Tony had not shared everything about Taye and the circumstances that had led to Tony's hospitalization. He knew, though, that Jed had figured it out after those thugs had done the first vandalizing.

"What do you think?" Jed asked.

"I think you're probably right. That asshole Taye wants her ledger with all the names and numbers of her contacts."

"Why would he think you had put it in her niche?"

"Because he already had his goons look everywhere else and that includes my apartment."

"It would be hard to hide it in there."

"He probably thinks I've transferred the information into another format or something."

"Maybe you wrote them on a piece of gefilte fish?" They had a good laugh.

"I should probably go now. Will you please call me tomorrow?" He handed Jed a piece of paper with his phone number.

"I will, Tony. Thanks for dinner and the company."

Tony hugged him and left. Jed lay on his bed and closed his eyes, but he doubted he would sleep.

36

CARL WAS IN THE PARKING LOT
WAITING FOR HIM WHEN JED
ARRIVED AT THE COLUMBARIUM THE
NEXT MORNING. "Thanks for coming, Jed.
Let's go inside." The policeman at the door let
them in.

"Why are the police still here?" Jed
asked.

"They haven't fixed the broken window
yet so they stayed all night. Did you call the
detective?"

"Not yet." Jed followed Carl inside. It
looked exactly the same as it had when Jed
found the devastation. "Do you mind if I go
upstairs for a minute?"

"I can wait." Carl took out his phone
and dialed a number while Jed went to pay Sam,
Sadie and Chloe a visit. He sang a couple of
bars to Frank and Goldie and stopped by Rose's
empty apartment. Carl hung up when Jed
approached and nodded in understanding. "I
met with the board yesterday afternoon. They

voted Linda off the board. They want me to ask you to come back."

Jed was shocked. "They can do that?"

"Yes. Does it surprise you that she isn't well liked by the other board members?" Carl smiled.

Jed actually did think it might happen, but not this quickly. He had hoped he could skate along for a while before having to make a decision. "I appreciate what you and the board are doing, Carl, but just because she's off the board, I can't be assured she won't talk to the LAPD. She might even do it in retaliation. And what about this detective? He might run my name through the system and it's going to show that the LAPD is looking for me."

"That's true. But that could be the case anywhere you go and anything you do, for the rest of your life. We will do everything we can to ward off the LAPD." Jed didn't answer, unsure what to say or how he felt. He just nodded. "Jed, you can't keep running forever," Carl continued. "You might be found or you might not."

"I'm not sure what I want to do, Carl."

"The president of the board, John Simpson, is planning to talk to Linda and he feels he can persuade her to leave you alone."

"How can he do that?"

"He claims to have something he can hold over her."

"That's interesting," Jed laughed.

"I didn't ask what, but John was quite convinced." Carl couldn't help but smile too.

"I hear the insurance company may not pay for the repairs," Jed said.

Carl sighed. "I'm afraid that's true. The board will know more about the insurance later today. You can at least get started. We'll just see what happens."

"Why won't the insurance company pay?"

"I can't talk about that yet."

"What will happen if they don't pay?"

"They'll have to close down and people will have to move their loved ones to another columbarium or bring them home, I suppose."

Jed shook his head. "That's terrible!"

"I know. The board hasn't yet decided what they will do in that case." He dangled the keys in front of Jed. "What do you say?"

Jed stared hard at Carl before speaking. "Can I have the morning to think about it?"

"Sure. I'll be here all morning. Golden Gate Glass is coming to fix the window. The police have more important things to do than guarding doors."

Jed got serious. "I think guarding the columbarium is very important. I'll be back to

331

let you know what I've decided." Jed started to leave but abruptly turned around. "Thanks Carl. I appreciate your confidence in me."

"I'm hardly the only one. Oh, by the way, someone asked me to give you this." He handed Jed the paper with Tony's name and number.

Jed looked at it and grinned. "Thanks."

Jed walked straight to the hospital and right up to the neonatal ward. He wanted to be clearer about how he felt before talking to Monica. He rocked for an hour before going to Monica's room.

He kissed her and woke her up. "The San Francisco police want to talk to me about the vandalism."

"That makes sense. You were the one who found the damage."

"I know. But I don't want to call them."

"You're either going to be found or not, but you can't keep running."

Jed smiled at her comment. That's just what Carl had said and he had told Finn that very thing in Venice. Now he needed to heed his own advice. "Okay. I'll work this afternoon and then see what happens with the insurance company. Maybe the decision will be made for me. But I'm still not going to call the detective."

"I think you'll be happy to be back at work."

"Probably. So what has the doctor said about how you're doing?" Jed asked.

"There's nothing to say yet. But I can tell you that I feel well enough to be bored out of my mind."

"Is there anything I can do?"

"You're doing it. Just visit."

"That's hardly an imposition," Jed smiled.

"I do have something I'd like to suggest though," Monica said.

"Suggest? What do you mean?"

"There's no need to pay for a room in a hotel when you could stay at my place."

Jed was taken aback. The thought alarmed him. Live with Monica? That would be more of a commitment than he had ever made in his life. "I don't know."

"Don't worry. I'm not asking you to marry me!" Monica was miffed at his reaction. "I'm not even there, for God's sake. I just thought it was a good idea to save you money."

Jed thought for a minute. "I guess that would be okay."

"Gee, don't do me any favors!"

"I'm sorry. I was just surprised I guess."

"The keys are in my purse." Jed got her purse out of the closet and handed it to her. She took a couple off the ring and gave them to him. "The one with the red ring around it is the door to the building. The one with the blue ring is to the apartment."

He put them in his pocket and sat on the bed. "I am sorry, really. I didn't mean –"

"Don't worry about it," she interrupted.

He kissed her. "I'll be back tonight after I get my stuff from the hotel."

"You have stuff?" She smiled.

"A few things." He smiled back and left.

It was half past eleven when he got to the columbarium. The police were gone and the one broken outside window was replaced. He found Carl sitting in his car in the parking lot, talking on the phone animatedly. Jed got a box from the office. He started filling it with shards of glass that were all over the flowerbeds under the newly replaced window. The expression on Carl's face was sullen and disgusted when he approached Jed. He shook his head and exhaled loudly. "The news is not good from the insurance company."

Jed surprised himself by feeling a sense of relief. He didn't have to make a decision. It was already made. "I'll stay as long as it takes to get things organized for everyone while they make arrangements."

"Take as much time as you need. There's enough money to pay you a salary for a while." Carl handed him the keys. "I'm sorry, truly sorry. For all of us."

Jed nodded, took the keys, and went inside. He didn't want to think about the consequences of this new development so he got to work. First and foremost was to bag and label the ashes. While cleaning up he realized that no one else could have done this properly. No one else knew what had been inside each niche. Many of the urns and memorabilia had been smashed beyond recognition. But he knew everyone's apartment contents and their locations.

At noon the doors opened and a crowd poured in led by Tony and Ray. "Jed!" they all shouted in unison.

After the initial hugs and tears, Tony gathered them into a circle. "Mr. Henshaw said he would be here to talk to us."

Jed went back to the task he had started. He didn't want to let on that he knew what Carl would say. The group socialized, talking among themselves, while they waited for Carl. The door opened and they turned toward it, expecting it to be Carl. It was the detective. "I'm looking for the caretaker, Jed Gibbons. Is he here?"

Tony caught on and answered quickly before anyone else in the crowd could speak. "No. He's not here."

Jed watched the exchange from the second floor, hiding behind a pillar. Carl arrived and the detective turned to talk to him. "I thought you were going to call me with Jed's number?"

"What do you want with Jed?" Ray asked before Carl could answer.

The detective turned back to the crowd. "He's just a person of interest."

"What?!" the crowd shouted in unison.

"You think he did this vandalism?" Eric yelled.

"Are you nuts? He's the one who fixed this place up better than it's ever been," Ray said.

"Jed would never do anything to harm anyone or anything!" Ida said. "You should be ashamed of yourself!"

The rest of the group chimed in with accolades and outrage and easily convinced the detective that he need not look at Jed as the culprit. A grinning Carl stood by quietly.

The detective left and the group fumed noisily among themselves. When Carl approached them, however, there was a stony silence and Carl's demeanor became serious. "I know you are all waiting to hear the outcome of the board's meeting with the insurance company. It is not good." The crowd started yelling. "Please let me finish. This is as hard for me as it is for you."

"I doubt that!" someone shouted from the crowd. "It's not your loved one who is being desecrated!"

"Let him finish," Tony said. They quieted down.

"Our insurance company required us to have a security system in place in order to cover vandalism but we hadn't gotten one installed yet."

There was more yelling. "Have you assessed the loss? Do you know how much it would cost?" Tony asked.

"Not entirely. But the Neptune Society has basically run out of money. Remember, they just paid out quite a lot for all the work Jed has done." The noise level started to rise again. "The board wants me to let you know that they will do everything they can to help you find new places to put your loved ones, if that's what you want to do. They will be in touch with you soon." He ignored the screaming and nasty comments being thrown at him and walked out. He didn't want them to see his own watery eyes.

The commotion continued for several minutes. Some cried openly. Some vowed to sue. Some discussed quietly what they would do with the ashes. Some stood motionless and mute in a state of shock. Tony, however, took the bag he had brought and went upstairs to Rose's apartment. He got to work decorating.

Jed walked over and silently held up one side of the mural so Tony could tack it up to the wall in the back of the niche. "I'm going to give Rose a chance to be in her apartment, even if it's just for a short time," Tony said.

Ray appeared next to them looking around the floor. He found Frank's horn buried under a pile of rubble and wiped it off with his sleeve. He blew it and said morosely, "Here's looking at you, Frank." The three men stood silently. Tony finally spoke to Jed. "How much do you think it would take to fix everything back up?"

"I have no idea. I bought the stuff but I just had the bills sent to Mr. Henshaw. I didn't even look at them first."

Ray shook his head in disgust and went downstairs. Jed went back to work and watched Tony go downstairs and gather the crowd together again. He talked to them but Jed couldn't hear what was being said. The crowd dispersed and Tony returned to putting the finishing touches on Rose's apartment. He stepped back to look at it and Jed came over. "Do you think Rose would have been happy with it?" Tony asked.

The background mural was peppered with the faces of Lucy and Ethel, Ralph and Alice, Ozzie and Harriet, and other television characters. On one side of the niche was Rose's

Giants' cap and on the other was her scorebook. In the middle was a cookie jar in the shape of a baseball. "Absolutely," Jed answered.

Tony picked up his bag and winked at Jed. "See you tomorrow." A puzzled, curious Jed watched him leave.

Monica was asleep when Jed got to her hospital room. He didn't mind as he, too, was exhausted and was happy for the opportunity to rest in the chair by her bed. It didn't last long, though, as her room had become something resembling Grand Central station. Apparently every infectious disease specialist in the San Francisco area was scrutinizing her clinical trial so she was inundated with doctors parading in and out of her room. Just as Jed was about to fall asleep, seven men and women in white coats arrived. Monica opened her eyes and gave Jed a look of reluctant resignation. "It's been like this all day."

"I'll go visit my babies. I'll be back shortly."

He slipped out of the room and headed for his rocking chair. When he returned, the room was empty except for an exhausted Monica. He hadn't eaten all day and it was eight o'clock. He was starving. Monica was glad to see him, however, and he had so much to tell her. He decided to forego his hunger pangs and stay until the nurses came to kick him out. Jed told her the whole story of the vandalism. "How long do you think it will take you to clean up?" she asked when he was finished.

"I just want to get everyone's ashes bagged and labeled and the floors swept. Shall I get your ex's and bring them to your house?"

"No!" Monica replied bitterly. "I'm not responsible for his ashes!"

"There's nothing to repair since they're closing it down. I just have to get things in order so it shouldn't take that long."

"I can call Glide tomorrow and see what jobs they have listed."

"Okay. Thanks. How about you? Any news from all these millions of doctors examining you?"

"Nothing."

"Do have they any idea when you can go home?"

"Not for at least a week. That's all I know. So are you ready to talk?"

"I'm not trying to be evasive, but I'm really tired and hungry. Can we do it another time?"

"How about just telling me what happened with Antoinette. Why are the police after you?"

He took a deep breath and looked into Monica's eyes. "I was in her motel room when

340

she died." Monica narrowed her eyes. "It was not what you think. I went there to talk to her. She fell and hit her head and died and the police found my fingerprints in her room. That's it."

"That's not it, Jed!" Monica was angry. "That tells me nothing. I want to know your whole story, just as I want you to know mine. I've already revealed how I feel about you. If you feel the same way, then I think we should be honest and open with each other."

"You think I'm lying to you?"

"Absolutely not. I just happen to think that's a lame explanation."

"I'm not good at this. I've never opened myself up like this before." He took a deep breath and started to tell his whole story. He didn't think the words would come as easily as they did.

He started with how his baby sister and mother had died in the Jonestown massacre and how he had managed to escape. He told her that he knew his mother would never have taken the Kool Aid voluntarily. She would never have chosen to leave Jed. She had been forced to take the poison. He watched Antoinette murder his sister by pouring the poison down her throat and his mother by plunging a needle into her arm. He tried to erase the feelings of rage and revenge when they reared up. He tried to forget all he had witnessed. But then, Antoinette appeared in his life by chance when she tried to blackmail Finn. And now he was a fugitive. But he never committed any crime, much as he may have wanted to.

He told Monica about Malcolm, a Venice Beach street kid about the same age Jed had been at Jonestown. His mother died too, leaving him all alone. Thanks to Charlie at the homeless shelter, he had found Miss Ruthie who took him in as a foster child. Last Jed knew she was trying to adopt him.

And then there were the poor babies at Miss Ruthie's. They were sick because their mothers had been addicts or HIV positive and they suffered so. He used to go to Miss Ruthie's to rock them because that was sometimes the only thing that soothed them. He and Miss Ruthie would spend hours and hours in those rocking chairs. He loved how it soothed his own soul as well.

He shared with Monica about how Finn had discovered the picture of his mother and him in Jonestown in his backpack. That was how the book idea started. He told her how he had found Mother on the boardwalk and that Finn and his daughter, Kate, had taken care of her when he was on the run.

"Now I can see why they are all so important to you."

Jed looked away, not wanting her to see his quivering lip and moist eyes. "They are all very good people."

Monica softened and took his hand. "I'm sorry. I don't mean to push you. It's just that I want to know all about you. I feel like I might not have much time left." She started to cry.

"Monica!" He hugged her tightly. "I don't mean to ——"

"Please don't say anything Jed! Just hold me and let me cry!" And that's what he did.

37

JED SLEPT WELL AT MONICA'S HOUSE.
He wasn't sure if it was the comfort of her bed
and apartment, the comfort that a decision had
been made, the comfort that rocking the babies
brought, or the comfort of being in love.
Whatever the reason, or a combination of all of
them, the tranquility that loosened his muscles,
traveled through his veins, and settled into his
bones was becoming less foreign. He got up
leisurely, drank a couple of cups of coffee and
spent more time in the shower than the
California drought allowed. He enjoyed being
back on his own time schedule. He had liked
the routine and structure, but it had already
served its purpose in grounding him.

He stopped at the deli on the way to the
columbarium to make sure Abe was aware of
what was going on. He didn't know if the
Neptune Society had notified him or Irving.
There were arrangements to be made for what
to do with Sam and Sadie's ashes. Irving and

Milton were in their usual spots and happy to see him.

"Can you stay for coffee and a bagel?" Abe asked.

"Sure," Jed replied. He could get to work whenever he wanted since it wasn't open to the public. "Have you heard what happened to the columbarium?" he asked them.

"Sure. It's all over the news. But you'll have it fixed up again in no time, won't you?" Irving said.

"That's not what's going to happen, I'm afraid."

"What are you saying?" Abe asked.

"The Neptune Society didn't have a security system so the insurance company won't pay a dime."

"That's bupkes!" Irving shouted.

"It's fercockt!" Milton yelled even louder.

"Fercockt? I don't remember Sam teaching me that word," Jed said.

"Fucked up!" Milton replied.

"I guess Sam didn't want me to use that one."

"So what are we supposed to do with Sam and Sadie?" Irving asked.

"There are other columbariums. Or maybe we should sprinkle them in Sadie's garden," Abe said.

"We'll figure it out, Jed, and let you know what we decide," Irving said.

"Thanks." Jed took a napkin and wrote down Monica's number. "You can reach me here."

"You'll still come visit us won't you?" Abe asked.

"Sure. But aren't you going to retire soon and close the deli?"

"We'll be somewhere playing pinochle. I guarantee you that."

"I'll be there, I promise." Jed gave them all a hug.

He walked up Stanyan and made a right on Anza. As he turned the corner onto Lorraine Court, he saw a crowd gathered at the front gate of the columbarium. "There he is!" someone shouted and the group turned around simultaneously and surrounded him.

"What are you all doing here?" Jed asked. "I don't have everyone's things ready yet for you to move them."

They turned to Tony. Apparently he was the spokesperson. "We won't have to move them. We're here to help."

"I don't need help. It won't take me that long."

"You may have more work to do than you originally thought." Tony took an envelope out of his pocket and handed it to Jed. The

346

addressee was "Neptune Society, Attn: Carl Henshaw."

"What's this?" Jed asked.

"Could you give it to Mr. Henshaw?"

"What's inside?"

"You'll see." Tony winked at Jed.

Carl drove up and got out of his car. He approached the crowd. "You'll all have to disburse. I don't want to have to call the police."

"This is from the group," Jed said as he gave Carl the envelope.

"Is this some kind of petition or something? It's not going to work. There just isn't any money. It's as simple as that."

"I don't know what it is. They just handed it to me. It's sealed and it's addressed to you."

Carl opened the envelope and took out a wad of bills. Then he took out a check and looked at the amount. His eyes almost popped out of his head. He handed the check to Jed and when Jed looked at it, he was also taken aback. He turned to Tony. "This is a lot of money."

"Don't worry," Tony said. "It's clean, honest money. It's from the sale of Goldie's house."

"But don't you need it to live on?" Jed asked.

"No. I don't. You and Rose have taught me a lot about living simply. I'm comfortable. I have everything I need."

"Will that be enough to keep it open?" Ray asked Carl.

"I think so, but I have to bring it to the board."

Everyone turned toward Jed. No one had to say anything. The unspoken question hung in the air like a canopy over the crowd. Jed knew he had to say something. He took a deep breath. "Well, I guess I have a lot of work to do, after all." The crowd cheered and followed him into the main building. Carl got back in his car and took out his phone.

Jed unlocked the building and went to the closet. Most of the others went to their respective loved ones' niches to check out the damage and to see what Jed had already done. Ray, however, watched Jed take out a bucket of dust rags and a ladder and climb the stairs to the top floor. Tony, Eric, Ida, Harmony and Melody moved toward Ray and without a sound, they took out some brooms and rags and started working as well. Jed, meanwhile, was lost in thought and didn't notice right away.

It was the sound of singing voices that jolted Jed out of his daydreaming. He got off the ladder and looked over the bannister to the floors below and saw the busy laborers singing a medley of "Give my Regards to Broadway," "Take me Out to the Ballgame," "When the Saints Go Marching In," "Happy Trails to You," and "Let it Go," the song from Chloe's favorite movie.

They stayed all afternoon, singing and cleaning. At about five they put the cleaning equipment away. Decisions had been made on what new urns and memorabilia were needed to adorn the apartments and condos. Jed took care of Sam and Sadie's. Eric had helped Jed measure the niche doors and said he would drop off the order at the glass shop on his way home. Carl had not been back to give the official "OK" from the board, but no one doubted that the amount Tony had contributed would cover the costs.

Jed had decided to stay as long as it took to get everything back in order. Then he would decide whether he could stay longer. He didn't want to let Linda Barclay run his life. If she wanted to go after him in retaliation for being kicked off the board, he would fight. He thought about calling Finn and asking him if he had heard anything from the lieutenant. Maybe Monica had some insight. By the time he got to the hospital, he was feeling so good that he didn't even feel the need to see the babies for himself. He stopped in anyway, though, because he knew they needed him. He rocked for about an hour and then headed for Monica's room.

His joy and calm spirit was quickly diffused when he opened the door to her room and saw her sitting on the bed, dressed to leave without any tubes coming out of her body. "What's happening?" he asked, surprised but wary.

She looked up at him, defeated and morose. "They stopped the clinical trial."

"Why?"

"I guess a couple of people got gravely ill and one is close to death. They think it may have something to do with the drug combination so they had to pull the plug, literally."

"Oh Monica. I'm sorry." He took her in his arms.

"I just want to go home. I've already been discharged. I was just waiting for you." She took out her cellphone and called for a cab. They stopped at the nurse's station and one of the Nurse's Aides got a wheelchair.

"I know you don't need it but it's hospital rules."

Monica sat down and Jed took her suitcase. They went down to the front entrance of the hospital. The Nurse's Aide chattered incessantly, but neither Monica nor Jed said a word. They got in the cab, still silent.

It didn't take long to get to Monica's. Once she was settled on the living room couch, Jed went out to get some dinner; pizza and beer seemed the easiest. He had thought that Monica's first night home from the hospital would have been a wonderful evening at Zazie's, but neither of them felt particularly cheerful.

Jed told Monica the events of the day while they ate dinner. She tried to be happy for him, but the gloomy mood was pervasive and won out.

After they ate, she went to bed and Jed sat in the dark living room. He wasn't angry or even sad; just resigned. He was sorry that her chance for a cure from this clinical trial was thwarted, but maybe there would be other trials. And it wasn't like it had become full-blown AIDS yet. He tried to be optimistic and vowed to work on bringing Monica along with him. There was still hope even if this particular one hadn't worked out. He was pensive and melancholy, but those were emotions he could handle easily.

38

IT DIDN'T TAKE LONG TO GET THE
COLUMBARIUM BACK TO PRISTINE
SHAPE WITH EVERYONE'S HELP. Linda
Barclay never came by so Jed was able to let go
of most of his fear and apprehension. Monica
also went back to work, although somewhat
reluctantly. She was depressed over the halting
of the clinical trial and it spilled over into her
job. When she wasn't at work she spent all her
time searching the Internet for other possible
treatments. She felt desperate and it affected her
relationship with Jed. But he was feeling so
good about being back to work and being left
alone by Linda Barclay that he was able to
weather her moodiness. He continued rocking
the babies at the hospital and that helped keep
the demons away.

Tony got more into his art and even
started selling some pieces. Although he had
given a sizeable amount to Carl, Goldie's house
had sold for quite a bit (after all, this was San
Francisco). Tony was still able to live

comfortably without resorting to any illegal business practices. He never heard from Taye again. Jed had originally encouraged him to tell the police that they thought Taye was behind the vandalism, but they agreed that there was no need to stir things up at this point.

Jed had gotten into a routine that worked well for him. He was happy living with Monica. He liked taking care of her and in her present state of mind, she didn't mind relinquishing her independence. He stopped at the deli almost every morning for breakfast until one morning Abe told him the news. He was retiring and closing the deli the following week. Jed knew it was coming, but it was still upsetting. Abe promised that he would keep in touch and let him know where "the fellas" would be hanging out so he could join them. Jed stopped at the hospital three or four times a week after work to rock the babies. Then he spent his evenings like every other family in Middle America. After dinner he watched television or read while Monica googled and web-surfed. She wasn't feeling any worse and her tests hadn't shown any more changes. She was so absorbed in her search for a cure, that she stopped asking Jed questions. That suited him just fine.

Tony stopped by the columbarium often and he and Jed became close friends.

What the babies did for Jed, drawing and painting had done for Tony. He was calm and all his nervousness and irritation had dissipated. They spoke of Rose and Sam and death, in general, but they never delved into their pasts. They both had things they wanted to hide, or at least ignore. One day, though, their conversation turned personal.

"How is your girlfriend doing?"

"Monica?"

"Isn't she your girlfriend?"

"Yes. She is." Jed thought for a minute and decided to speak freely about her illness. He knew that the Gay community in San Francisco had lots of experience dealing with AIDS. "She's HIV positive."

Tony put his hand on Jed's shoulder. "I am too."

"You are? You certainly don't seem ill."

"I know. I've been positive for thirty years. It used to be very rare to be positive and it not turn into the AIDS virus. It's still uncommon, but there's been a lot of research into new medications that seem to be working."

Jed was visibly relieved. "That's good to know. I'll tell her."

Jed had become quite adept at controlling his emotions until one day when Heather came to see Chloe. She didn't come

354

often. Eric came every couple of weeks but Heather rarely came with him. This was the first time she came by herself and Jed knew it was a huge step for her. She had lost a lot of weight and she had not been a heavy woman to begin with. Her face was so full of lines and so drawn that she looked decades older than her thirty-plus years.

Jed was on the top floor doing some touch-up painting on the medallions that adorned the columns. He noticed her holding onto the railing as if she would collapse at any moment. He got off his ladder and went down to the floor she was on. He didn't want to intrude if she didn't want him to, but he wanted to make himself available if she needed some support. He pretended to check on the tomatoes in front of Sadie and Sam's condo, even though he had already replaced them earlier that day.

"Hello Heather," he said.

She turned and looked at him. The last time he saw such vacant, sad eyes was his mother's the day she was murdered. "Hello Jed." She hiccupped which Jed knew was really catching a sob in her throat. He squeezed her arm and started to walk away when she called out to him. "Jed! Could you stand next to me?"

"Of course." He walked back over and she collapsed into his arms.

"I can't do this. I'm trying so hard, but I can't. I'm on so many different medications and none of them are working."

"You know, everyone grieves in their own way. Maybe you don't need to visit Chloe. She knows you love and miss her. You don't have to come here to show her that."

"I must. I don't think anyone can get past losing a child without reaching some form of acceptance. Coming here is the only way. Seeing her ashes, seeing her sweet teddy bear. It is necessary. You can't know what it's like, Jed. You are a kind, compassionate, empathetic, wonderful person and you help everyone who comes here so much. And I'm sure you have personally dealt with the deaths of loved ones. But there is nothing, absolutely nothing, that compares with losing your child." She wailed and sobbed and Jed held her silently, glad that she was so beside herself that she didn't notice the tears falling down his own cheeks. They stood like that for several minutes. Heather finally pulled away. "Eric was right. I have to come alone and do this. And I have to come often until I can try to rebuild my life."

"You know I will be here for you when you come. Shall we sing Chloe's favorite song?"

Heather started to sing and Jed joined in, but she started to sob and they stopped singing. "I hope soon I can do this without

356

needing you, but thank you, Jed. Thank you for just being you." She turned abruptly and walked away before Jed had a chance to respond.

Jed was numb and speechless as he watched Heather dash away. After he heard the front door of the columbarium close, he turned toward Chloe's niche and opened the door. He took out the teddy bear, hugged it and let his shoulders shudder and the tears flow. Thankfully, no one else came in for the few minutes he stood there. He knew what he had to do. He had come so far, faced so much of his past, allowed himself to open up to the future. But there was another very important thing that had to happen before he could truly heal.

He finished his work that day in a dream state. No more thinking was necessary. He would talk to Monica that night and make the arrangements. He wondered if Tony would be interested in working for him while he was away. He wouldn't have to do any cleaning or painting. He would just have to be there to keep it open. He cleaned the paintbrushes and put the ladder away and took one more walk around the rotunda on each floor. He did that every night just to make sure he hadn't forgotten anything. He sang a few bars of the appropriate songs as he passed everyone's apartments. Ray had taught him a new one for Sam and Sadie,

"Oh you Beautiful Doll." Jed could just imagine the twinkle in Sam's eyes singing that to Sadie.

He locked up the office and was about to lock the gate when Irving drove up. He yelled to Jed, "Wait! I have to talk to you!"

Jed walked over to the car and put his head through the open window. "Hi Irving. Is everything okay?"

"I have some news for you."

"About the deli? Is Abe okay?"

"Abe's fine. The deli is sold but that's not the news."

"What is it then?"

Irving handed him a piece of paper. "Read it for yourself."

Jed's eyes popped as he read the words. "What?!"

"Sam loved you like the son he never had."

"But leaving me his house?"

"A lot of childless people don't know what to do with their estates. Should he have left it to a nephew he hardly knew? You were a godsend to him when he needed one. Anyway, you need to go to this lawyer's office and sign some papers. Call him in the morning. It shouldn't take very long. Congratulations, Jed. I can't think of anyone more deserving." Irving got back in his car and drove away.

Jed locked the gate and set off for Monica's to give her the news. He'd stop by the hospital tomorrow and let them know he'd be gone for several days.

Monica wasn't home from work yet so Jed showered and dressed in his idea of nice clothes. He had decided as he walked home that they should go out to dinner. He was sitting on the sofa when she opened the door. She was surprised to see him there.

"Aren't you going to visit the babies tonight?"

"Not tonight. I thought we'd go out to dinner. I have a bit of news. Are you up for it?"

"Is it good news? I'm not up for hearing bad news."

"Yes."

"Okay. Give me a few minutes to freshen up."

"You look beautiful just the way you are." She smiled and went into the bedroom. "Can I use your phone?" Jed called to her.

"In my purse," she called back from the bathroom. "But when are you going to get your own? It would be really nice to be able to get a hold of you during the day."

"Soon," he answered. "Tomorrow." He was anxious to call Tony and ask whether he could take over for him for a few days, but he didn't want to tell Tony the news without telling

359

Monica first. He called the bus station instead and wrote down the schedule. He would see if he could get an appointment with Sam's attorney the day after he got back. It would take a little more than a week to get there and back again. He was sure it could wait.

Monica came out looking dazzling. "Are we going to Zazie's?"

"Wherever you want."

"It's kind of our place, isn't it?"

"I suppose you could say that," Jed laughed.

They had to wait a few minutes for a table, but when they were finally seated and had a couple of full wine glasses in front of them, Jed pulled out the paper and gave it to her. He didn't say a word. Her eyes popped even larger than his had. She looked at him with her mouth wide open. "Sam's house must be worth at least a million dollars! Do you realize that?"

"I'm not sure I would sell it. Maybe we could live there."

She fell back into her seat. "Wow!"

"I have to call the lawyer to sign some papers. I'm a little anxious because I could be found pretty easily that way, I assume."

"Like we said, you can't keep running forever," Monica answered.

He smiled remembering Finn and the title of his book. Both he and Monica knew that he had a hard time following that advice. But now, he was going to try. Now he would take that last trip and take care of that last piece that he had refused to confront.

"Have you spoken to the lawyer yet?"

"No. Irving just gave this to me a couple of hours ago. I'll call in the morning. But I'm sure I can wait to sign the papers for a week or so. I have something else I have to do first. And it means I have to go away for several days."

Monica was puzzled. "Where? To Venice to talk to the LAPD?"

"No. There's something else more important that I haven't told you about yet. Something I never talked about to anyone, not even Finn."

Monica opened her mouth to speak, but then wisely shut it again. She could see how Jed was struggling, trying to find the words and the fortitude to tell her. She took a breath and finally said, "You don't have to explain where you're going or why."

He looked deeply into her eyes and took her hand. "Yes. I do. I've buried this secret for too many years."

"Okay, Jed. It's up to you."

The conversation became more somber and neither of them ate much of their dinner. By the time they got home, they were both emotionally exhausted and they went straight to bed.

Jed got up early so he could use Monica's phone to make the arrangements for his trip. He bought himself a prepaid cell phone and made an appointment with Sam's attorney. He called Tony and Carl and they were both fine with the arrangement. Tony would meet him at the columbarium later for Jed to show him the ropes and to get the keys. He knew most of the songs and routines already and they practiced together just to be sure. He promised Jed that he would keep an eye on the tomatoes as well.

Jed wasn't leaving until eleven at night, so Monica would see him before he left. They would try to have the dinner they didn't eat the previous night, although Jed was perfectly happy to just bring home some take-out. She went to work reluctantly, wanting desperately to go with him, but this was a trip he needed to take by himself. He had to make peace with this part of his past.

This time they ate their dinner and shared a bottle of wine. They got back to Monica's early enough to make love and for Jed to pack all his meager possessions into his backpack. He only needed one change of clothes, he figured. He would be on a bus for two and a half days in each direction. He would just change clothes one time when he got there. There was plenty of room in the backpack for the last item. The bus got in at nine thirty in the morning and the return bus left about twelve hours later at nine fifty that night. He didn't need a lot of time to do what he needed to do.

39

THE SUN ROSE AS THE BUS PULLED
INTO THE BIRMINGHAM, ALABAMA
TERMINAL. The next one he needed to take
wasn't leaving for a couple of hours. He didn't
mind, though, since he was starving. He saw a
24-hour diner right next door to the terminal.
Monica had given him food for the trip, but he
had ended up sharing most of it with his seat
partner, an elderly man with little money. The
man was going to his daughter's to live out the
rest of his days. Hearing the man's story was
just what he needed to pass the time. It was like
he had never left the columbarium.

He enjoyed his breakfast of grits,
sausage, biscuits and gravy, but he was glad it
was not his daily diet. He wasn't exactly a
California cuisine gourmet and he certainly
hadn't become a crunchy granola, gluten-free
vegan hipster, but he had come a long way from
being a good old, southern boy glutton. It had
been more than twenty years since he'd been in
Alabama and he had never liked it. He didn't

like the heat and humidity or the racist, gun-loving mentality.

He read the newspaper with his second and third cups of coffee while waiting for the first outbound bus of the morning. It was about a two-hour ride to Selma and then he had about an hour's walk from the bus station. He read the words in the newspaper, but his mind was elsewhere. He couldn't have told you any news of the day.

He thought about Finn and Mother. He had transferred buses in Los Angeles, and would again on the way home. There was a two-hour layover and he thought about calling Finn. Maybe he could come to the bus station with Mother. He had wanted to share all that had happened to him since he had fled Venice. But he didn't want to put Finn in a position of having to lie if the police ever questioned him. He wanted Finn to be able to say truthfully that he didn't know the whereabouts of Mr. Jedidiah Gibbons. Maybe after he settled into Sam's house, he would call him. By then, with his name on a deed, the police would have other ways of finding him. He hoped they would have already closed the case, calling it the accident that it was.

He thought about Jonestown and tried to get past the horror and look at the positive things he had brought away from that experience. He had learned empathy, perseverance, self-reliance, communality, and to eschew materialism. He had learned to survive in the most desperate environmental conditions. Those had all been invaluable lessons. And now he was allowing himself to experience love again. He was opening himself up to being hurt and to those painful feelings of loss and abandonment. But he was confident that he could cope with them. Sam and Rose and Tony and Ray and Eric and Heather and all the rest of them had given him that. He looked at the clock, paid his bill and went back to the terminal. It was almost time to get on the bus to Selma.

He hadn't slept much on the last leg from Dallas to Birmingham. He tried to use his backpack as a pillow. The bus wasn't crowded at all, so he could sit by himself. But sleep didn't come. He would have to wait until the return trip. He wouldn't have this anticipation pulsing through his body then. He hoped it would be relief instead.

It was a slow ride through the Alabama countryside, a far cry from the urban chaos of San Francisco. He missed the unhurried pace of rural living in some ways, but he could never live here again. Coming back here was the hardest thing he'd ever done. He needed to do it, but he also needed to leave it behind, just as he had finally done with Jonestown.

It was in the nineties and muggy in Selma. The walk would be arduous for a man who had spent the last several years living by the ocean. He bought a couple of quarts of water. They would be heavy to carry but he would need them. Unless a lot had changed since the last time he was here, there would not be much in the way of retail stores on the walk. He had to force himself to start this trek. Deep down he would have rather turned around and gotten back on the bus to Birmingham.

The environs looked pretty much the same. Things in the rural south don't change very quickly, if at all. One would certainly never use the word "gentrification" in this neck of the woods.

There was no gate and the property was overgrown with weeds, but there was no garbage. It was nothing like what he had encountered that first day at the columbarium. He was surprised at how he remembered precisely where it was. Some things never leave your memory. Anyway, the place wasn't that big. He would have stumbled on it eventually, even if he had forgotten its exact location. He walked slowly and deliberately. His feet seemed to know where to go.

There it was:
Genevieve Gibbons
Born October 12, 1988
Died August 15, 1992
Loving and much loved Daughter

Jed sat down next to the tombstone and opened his backpack. He took out the two pictures he had always kept with him and placed them side-by-side on the ground. He gazed at them for several minutes. Then he took Chloe's old teddy bear out of the backpack, the one Eric had given him. He unwrapped it and set it down on the grave. He reached in his pocket and took out the necklace that had been draped over his mother's picture. He picked up the teddy bear and put the locket around its neck. He hugged it, kissed it and laid it gently on the grave.

40

JED GOT TO THE BIRMINGHAM BUS
STATION WITH ABOUT AN HOUR TO
SPARE. He went to the men's room to wash up
and shave. Then he changed into his other set
of clothes. He had become quite adept at
cleaning up in public restrooms since he'd had
years of practice.

He went to the diner next door and ate
a hearty southern meal of fried chicken, biscuits,
and greens fried in bacon grease. He asked for a
couple of pieces of sweet potato pie to go. It
might be the last time he would eat that kind of
food, which was probably not a bad thing for a
guy in his fifties. He hoped it would last him
until he got to Oklahoma City where he could
get something else to eat. Albuquerque would
be the next stop and that was about eight hours
from Oklahoma City. Then it would be another
twelve hours or so until Los Angeles where
there was a two-hour layover. He could get
another large meal there. The terminal was in

downtown L.A. and the area had become so gentrified that you could find high-end bistros as well as the usual greasy spoons next to bus stations.

He slept most of the way to Oklahoma City and in fact, he didn't get off the bus until Albuquerque. He bought a burrito and thought about Mother. She had loved the ones from Luis' restaurant. He missed her. It would be about seven thirty at night when he got to Los Angeles and he had two hours there. He decided he would definitely call Finn and see if he wanted to meet him for dinner near the bus station. That's what friends do. They keep in touch. And maybe Finn could bring Mother with him. He called Monica first. He had called her at every stop along the way. That's what boyfriends do. They keep in touch.

After hanging up with Monica he dialed Finn's number. He wasn't sure what he'd say. Would he tell him he lived in San Francisco now? He didn't want to put Finn in a position where he'd have to lie to the police. But at this point, he might be found anyway so what difference did it make. He would just leave it up to Finn.

"Hello?" Finn growled. Jed smiled. He was still a curmudgeon.

"Hello, Finn."

"Jed? Is that you? Where the hell are you? Are you here in Venice?"

"Actually I'm in Albuquerque."

"Albuquerque? You live there now?"

"No. I live in San Francisco."

"No shit. Kate's moved up north too. She's teaching in some town north of San Francisco. What the hell are you doing in Albuquerque?"

"On my way home. Long story. Lots to tell you. The bus will be in Los Angeles about seven and then it doesn't leave for San Francisco until about nine. Would you like to meet me for dinner near the bus terminal?"

"You bet Jed! I look forward to it."

"One more thing, Finn. Could you bring Mother?"

"Of course! She wouldn't let me leave her behind!"

"I'll see you then, Finn." Jed hung up and grinned as he walked back to the bus.

The bus pulled into Los Angeles about half an hour early. Jed figured he'd wait by the information booth but he didn't have to. Finn was already standing at the gate waiting for him, his arms wrapped tightly around Mother. After hugs and kisses and a surreptitious wipe of the eyes with their sleeves, the trio took off for a coffee shop down the block.

They snuck Mother in by hiding her in Jed's backpack. Once they ordered their food and the waitress left the table, Jed took Mother out and put her on the seat next to him. He would just cover her up with the backpack when their food arrived. Jed did most of the talking, a true reversal of roles for him. But Finn was a writer and therefore a good interviewer and listener. And for once, Jed had a life he was happy to share.

After Jed finished it was Finn's turn. He told Jed that Kate had sold her house so he was living in an apartment. He was contemplating moving back to New York, but promised Jed that he would come up north to visit both him and Kate. And Jed took Kate's number so they could try to get together as well. He thought Monica and Kate would like each other a lot, both of them do-gooder activists.

Jed looked at his watch and realized he had better get back to the bus terminal. He cleared his throat. He had one more thing to ask Finn. "Has that lieutenant been pestering you about me?"

"You mean you didn't know?" Finn was truly surprised.

"Know what?"

"They closed the case. They determined Antoinette died from a fall. You're in the clear. I can't believe they didn't tell you."

Jed laughed. "No, they didn't tell me because I've been hiding from them."

Finn joined in laughing. "Why are we laughing exactly?"

"Suffice it to say that my life would have been very different if I'd known."

"Well, all turned out for the best so who cares?" Finn added.

They walked back to the bus terminal and hugged goodbye. Jed kissed Mother on the scruff of her neck and handed her back to Finn. "It was wonderful seeing you both," Jed said.

"Do you want Mother back?" Jed stared at him. The thought hadn't even occurred to him. "You have a house now and a job and a woman," Finn continued. "What's that song about two cats in the yard?"

Jed wondered if Sam had ever had a cat in the yard. "But what about you? You're alone now."

"I'll probably be moving back to New York anyway."

Jed smiled at Finn and took Mother. She crawled up his arm onto his shoulders and curled herself around his neck. "Thanks for taking care of her." Jed walked up the stairs onto the bus with Mother in his arms. The driver didn't protest. He nodded and smiled. Jed just had a way with people.

Emily Gallo's next novel, *Kate and Ruby* will be published in 2016. An excerpt follows:

It wasn't a large apartment building, but it wasn't one of those beautiful Victorians either. It was a rather nondescript building with eight buzzers inside the doorway: four stories with two apartments on each floor, she guessed. She saw the buzzer for Martin's apartment and pushed it. No one answered her ring for a couple of minutes. Just as she was about to press it again, the front door to the building opened and an attractive, muscular fiftyish man stood in front of her, smiling. He wore tight jeans and a white T-shirt with a red awareness ribbon and the words 'San Francisco AIDS Foundation' written across his chest. He reached out his hand and said, "You must be Kate. I'm Peter. We spoke on the phone."

Kate shook his hand tentatively, a little taken aback by the words on his shirt. "Yes. Hi. Is that how Martin died?" She nodded towards his chest.

"Yes. He'd been HIV positive for years, but hadn't contracted full-blown AIDS until three years ago, just after his longtime partner died then. It was almost as if Martin waited so that he could take care of John first."

Kate smiled. "That wouldn't surprise me. He was always such a caretaker."

"He was an exceptional man and a extraordinary friend. Come on up. I couldn't remember where the buzzer was in the apartment to ring you in." She followed him up the stairs to the third floor. The door to the apartment was ajar and as Peter pushed it open, she could see an elderly black woman dressed in a housedress, sitting on a chair in the living room. Kate stopped short and gasped when she saw the woman. "Ruby, Kate's here," Peter said as he walked into the room.

Ruby sat motionless, staring out the window. She didn't move her gaze or speak, but nodded ever so slightly in response. Kate didn't acknowledge the nod or Peter's comment; she just walked into the room, glancing around guardedly. The apartment was small and its furnishings were sparse but stylish. It was a far cry from their hippie days with bookshelves of cement blocks and planks and a mattress on the floor. She was curious to know what Martin had ended up doing career-wise, but once she saw that Ruby was there, she just wanted to exit as quickly as possible. Anyway, her car was illegally parked and the last thing she needed was a ticket or a tow. "Where's the box?"

"Oh, it's in the bedroom." She followed Peter into the bedroom. There were piles of boxes, all neatly stacked and labeled. The only pieces of furniture were a bed and a dresser.

Peter lifted a box off a pile with "KATE" written in neat block letters.

"You did all this packing of his stuff?" she asked.

"Oh no. Martin did all this the last couple of months, until he couldn't stand for any length of time. The apartment looked pretty much like this the last few weeks. The only difference was Martin was lying in the bed."

Kate smiled again, remembering what a neat freak he had been. They were a good couple in that respect. She too had a penchant for organization and cleanliness. "So he had boxes for all the people in his life?"

"No. Most of the stuff is going to thrift stores. There are just a couple of other boxes going to specific people."

Kate cleared her throat. "What about Ruby? Won't she take anything?"

Peter sighed. "Martin and Ruby were estranged after he came out. They hadn't spoken in forty years. I called her when he was dying and they were able to have a phone conversation before he passed away. She just arrived yesterday by bus from Mississippi."

"So she didn't see him before he died?"

"Nope."

"Why did she come then?"

"To get the things he had left her and maybe to assuage some guilt. Anyway, Martin had sent her a ticket before he died."

"Too bad she didn't get here in time, I suppose," Kate said, but she didn't sound particularly sorry about it.

Peter smiled. "I can see there's no love lost between you and Ruby."

"You got that right. She and Martin fought terribly when he married me, you know. I guess being gay is even worse than marrying a honky!" Kate said derisively. "Hah! She probably thinks it was my fault; that I turned him into a homosexual."

Peter put his arm around Kate's shoulders. "I think it's very sad, though, that a mother and son don't speak for their whole adult lives."

Kate looked into Pater's eyes and thought of her own relationship with her father. Her mother had died when she was a baby and it had obviously left a huge hole in her heart that her father's love had never been able to fill. She took a deep breath and let it out with a barely audible sigh. "Yes. I suppose it is." She bent down and lifted the box.

"Let me help you bring it to your car."

"No. I'm fine. It's not too heavy. I can manage it." She walked back in the living room. This time Ruby looked into her eyes. Kate decided to take the high road. "Nice seeing you again, Ruby." No matter how much she tried to soften her voice and color it with sweetness, those words sounded extremely sarcastic.

Ruby's answer was a harrumph. Peter opened the door to let her out. "I'll go down with you. Is your car parked nearby?"

"Yes, just a few houses down." Peter and Kate left with a stone-faced Ruby staring at them. She took a handkerchief out of her pocket and wiped away the lone tear that rolled down her cheek.

A retired teacher, Emily Gallo was born and raised in Manhattan. She lives with her husband, David and Schiller Hound, Gracie on 2 1/2 acres in northern California and 750 square feet on the beach in southern California.

Made in United States
Orlando, FL
14 August 2022

21025095R00232